Death in Show

**Center Point
Large Print**

Also by Judi McCoy
and available from Center Point Large Print:

Dog Walker Mysteries
Heir of the Dog
Hounding the Pavement

Death in Show

A DOG WALKER MYSTERY

JUDI McCOY

CENTER POINT PUBLISHING
THORNDIKE, MAINE

This Center Point Large Print edition
is published in the year 2010 by arrangement with
NAL Signet, a member of Penguin Group (USA) Inc.

Copyright © 2010 by Judi McCoy.

The text of this Large Print edition is unabridged.
In other aspects, this book may vary
from the original edition.
Printed in the United States of America
on permanent paper.
Set in 16-point Times New Roman type.

ISBN: 978-1-60285-863-3

Library of Congress Cataloging-in-Publication Data

McCoy, Judi.
    Death in show : a dog walker mystery / Judi McCoy. — Center point large print ed.
        p. cm.
    ISBN 978-1-60285-863-3 (lib. bdg. : alk. paper)
    1. Dog walking—Fiction. 2. Dog shows—Fiction. 3. Large type books. I. Title.
    PS3613.C385D43 2010
    813'.6—dc22

                                                                    2010018950

Acknowledgments

A huge thank-you to Jessie Esposita, my lady in blue who recently left the NYPD. Jessie, thanks for keeping me honest. To my readers, please don't blame Jessie when I stretch proper police procedure to construct my books. She tries to rein me in, but like I keep telling her, I am writing fiction.

Lawyer Jokes

Thanks to Brian Ritzler for the lawyer jokc in chapter eight.

Thanks to Melodie Stickrath for the lawyer joke at the end of chapter thirteen.

Thanks to Mary Ann Angros for the lawyer joke at the end of chapter sixteen.

Thanks to Elsie Hogarth for the lawyer joke in chapter eighteen.

Chapter 1

Ellie pulled the lapels of her black wool blazer close as she crossed West End Avenue and headed for the Javits Convention Center. This was the best place for a dog lover to be on a cold November day, she told herself as she passed people leading canines of all shapes and sizes into the center. Though she'd sat in the viewing area of the Westminster Kennel Club show many times, this was her first visit to the Mid-Atlantic Canine Challenge.

And she was attending as a special guest, which allowed her backstage access for the most exciting part of the competition. Flora Steinman, the owner of Lulu, a Havanese Ellie walked twice a day, had requested she be here to offer moral support for both her and her dog. In fact, since the petite pooch had come to Ellie's home to share a playdate with her own dog, Rudy, she put Lulu on a par with Mr. T, her best friend's Jack Russell, and considered the Havanese a full-fledged member of her family.

She entered the crowded conference center and headed for the jammed escalator with a full heart. She was more than happy to spend today and tomorrow at the second most prestigious of all dog shows. If Lulu won the MACC, she would be well on her way to Westminster in

February. And even if she only got as far as Best in Breed or Best in Group, she would still be in a good position to take the big prize at Madison Square Garden.

Juggling her schedule had been daunting. Since Ellie had lost Hilary Blankenship as her assistant a couple of months ago, she had hired and fired several others. But just last week she'd found someone who might actually work out—a Columbia University student named Joy. The girl's usual chore was simple: Walk five dogs in Paws in Motion's farthest north building for the next two days. But because of Ellie's commitment here, Joy now had to walk thirty dogs, some twice a day, in four different buildings. Definitely not an easy task.

It had been even more difficult explaining the rearranged schedule to her charges. Canines thrived on routine and weren't happy when their regular walk time changed. She'd promised special treats for the rest of the week if they agreed to the time adjustment, which they did, and she told herself again that her dogs were worth every extra penny.

Continuing her upward ride on the escalator, she recalled the information Flora had given her on the ins and outs of the dog show world. First and foremost, competition was fierce and beset by politics. Over the course of a competitive year, judges came to know each handler as well as the owners and their dogs, which brought friendship and a canine's reputation to every event. Right now, the gossips predicted that tiny furball Lulu would handily take Best in Breed and go on to win Best in Group, but anything could happen to change that belief.

Ellie still wasn't sure of the reason the Havanese had amassed so many championships, but it was clear that Flora had taken an unusual route on the road to Lulu's success. Many canines were owned by multimember partnerships and the dogs lived with their handlers. Even the professor, Ellie's first client, had sent Buddy to his handler several weeks prior to a major outing in order to ensure that the pair would appear as a single unit at the competition.

Instead, Lulu spent her life with Flora, who brought the dog to each conformation showing in which she was entered two days ahead of time. Arnie Harris then worked with Lulu long enough for them to compete as a synchronized team. The unusual practice made getting here expensive and arduous for a woman in her seventies, but Flora had been adamant. Lulu would live with no one but her until forty-eight hours before a show.

Ellie still wasn't sure if the Havanese owed her success to continuous coddling or to her stellar pedigree, but it didn't matter. Lulu had amassed enough points to be allowed entry here, and since today was one of the little dog's biggest appearances, she couldn't say no when Flora asked her, Lulu's secondary caregiver, to share the momentous experience.

She was determined to give Flora and Lulu the support they needed, and she looked upon her attendance more like a mini-vacation, with the right to be near some of the most well-known and prestigious purebreds in the country.

After stepping off the escalator, Ellie flashed her pass at the guard and received directions to the backstage area where the contestants waited for their event. It was there the dogs in the morning rounds were made ready to compete. Inside the packed holding zone, filled with owners, groomers, handlers, hundreds of canines, show sponsors, and a variety of news reporters, she realized it was the most exhilarating place she'd ever been that had to do with her favorite four-legged friends.

Sidling past Malteses, Chihuahuas, Yorkies, and dozens of other miniature breeds, she took note of one oddity. The area was filled with the racket of human chatter, snipping scissors, and busy blow dryers, but not a single sound came from the canines. At the very least, she'd expected to hear some of their excitement, but nothing penetrated her brain. These had to be the most focused hounds in the world.

Ellie almost sighed in ecstasy. She'd never been this close to so much pooch perfection.

Rudy was a pound puppy, which was fine with her, but she'd never spoken to a professional judge or handler, and she was looking forward to doing both.

Fighting her way through the crowd, she kept her tote bag under her arm and her eyes peeled for a sign that marked the holding area for the Havaneses. After several minutes of swimming through a mass of bodies, she decided this event was a pickpocket's dream. People had to walk sideways to get through the throng, brushing against each other like lovers sharing a group dance. If Lulu won today, Ellie planned to tuck her keys in an inside pocket and stuff cash in her bra for tomorrow's more important competition, instead of carrying her jumbo bag.

Rising on tiptoe, she saw Flora speaking to a man she thought might be Arnie, and she headed in their direction.

"My darling girl, you made it," said the older woman when Ellie reached her. Dressed in a lilac suit and matching pumps, Mrs. Steinman wore a double strand of pearls that Ellie guessed had cost more than her yearly income.

"I wouldn't have missed this for the world."

"Good, good. And here's someone you should meet." Flora smiled at her companion, a tall, burly man of about fifty wearing navy blue Armani. "This is Edward Nelson. He used to be Lulu's handler."

Used to be? Ellie held out her hand and she and Edward shook. "Hello. It's nice to meet you."

"Same here. Flora tells me we have something in common," Edward said in a deep voice thick with a New York accent. "I walk dogs, too, some in the very building where Lulu, Flora, and I live."

Flora had fired Mr. Nelson, and he lived in the Beaumont? She raised a brow at Lulu. Ensconced on a pillow, the snobby Havanese pointed her muzzle in the air.

"Don't look at me," the Havanese announced. *"Firing him was Flora's idea, but he always wore too much aftershave, so I approved. He made me sneeze up a storm."*

Ellie waggled her fingers at Lulu and returned her gaze to the handler. She'd never seen Edward Nelson before, and she'd thought she knew every dog walker on the Upper East Side. "In the Beaumont? I can't believe we haven't met before now."

"Oh, but I've seen you and your charges marching up and down the avenue like a marine platoon. Natter speaks very highly of you," he said, mentioning the Beaumont's doorman. "As does Flora."

She filed the information away, planning to bend Natter's ear about the handler/dog walker as soon as she saw him again. "We should compare notes sometime."

"Sounds good," said Edward, glancing over his shoulder. "Now if you'll excuse me, I have to find my boy." A grin that seemed more of a smirk graced his ruddy face. "Flora, nothing against you and Lulu, but I look forward to bringing Fidel to the winner's circle today. No hard feelings, I hope."

"Of course not," Flora chimed as the man shouldered his way through the mob.

"Fidel?" Ellie asked, quirking her lips.

"The other Havanese I told you about, the one that gives Lulu so much competition," said the older woman. "If Edward hadn't found a dog in the toy group to handle today, I would have paid him a compensation fee for taking Lulu away. I only hired Arnie a few months ago, you see, and most handlers are booked well in advance for a show as prestigious as this one. I wasn't sure Edward would find another client in this group in such a short amount of time, but he managed, though it did surprise me that he found a second Havanese."

"Hey, Mrs. Steinman." A young man dressed in a navy suit and matching tie called as he pushed his way through the crowd. When he neared, Ellie saw that he was accompanied by a twenty-something man wearing the same type of suit and tie in dark brown. The first man, short and stocky, with a pleasant expression, spoke. "Jim Hiller." He took Mrs. Steinman's hand and shook it lightly. "We met at that open show in Connecticut last spring. Are you still using Edward Nelson to handle your prize bitch?"

"Why, no," Flora answered, not offering Arnie's name or Ellie's. She turned her gaze to the other man. "And who is this fine fellow?"

"My pal Josh. I've been telling him about Lulu ever since she won Winner's Bitch at that competition. We heard a rumor about Edward being out of the picture and hoped you'd ask one of us to show her today. I sent you several e-mails, but you never answered them, so I called and left a few phone messages. Guess I should have known you weren't interested when you didn't respond."

"I'm afraid I'm a total novice on a computer, and I'll have to speak to my housekeeper about those phone messages."

"Yeah, well, I still want you to know how much I admire your bitch. I don't have a dog in the toy group and . . ."

Ellie ignored the rest of their conversation, thinking instead of the terminology dog people used. She had a difficult time referring to female dogs as bitches, though it wasn't a slur but proper canine classification. Still, this kid's pushy attitude was hard to swallow. She'd been told that handlers had a lot of confidence, but as far as she was concerned, his comments were just short of rude.

Flora didn't seem a bit flustered and spoke politely to the young men. They left a moment later, and she gave a loud harrumph. "Sorry I didn't introduce you, but those boys are brazen upstarts, too eager to push the pros out of the way. Inexperienced handlers looking to break into the big time often campaign for new customers, but not in such an unprofessional manner."

Then the older woman's eyes sparkled, and she nodded toward the crowd. "I think Arnie has arrived, and he's stopped to greet Edward. That means he'll be here any moment." She touched her head of silver hair. "How do I look?"

"Like you own the place," Ellie assured her.

Flora stopped fussing. "I hope the two of you get along."

Ellie peered through the crowd. Mrs. Steinman had to have radar or X-ray vision, because it was easy to spot Edward's tall figure but almost impossible to see who he was talking to. Then a short, dapper man, somewhere between Edward's age and Flora's, wearing an impeccable gray suit and matching tie, plowed through the human traffic jam, stopped in front of them, and grasped both of the woman's hands.

"Flora, my dear. Ready to celebrate Miss Lulu's big moment?"

"I'm all atwitter, Arnie," answered Flora, a blush gracing her papery cheeks. "At the very least, my little girl deserves to win Best in Breed, and I'm hoping you'll make that happen."

"I deserve Best in Breed no matter who the handler is," rang a voice in Ellie's ear.

She turned to Lulu, who watched from her pillowed throne, and sidled backward. "I wouldn't be so cocky if I were you. Fidel and the other seven Havaneses here have each won major competitions. They have the right to Best in Breed just as much as you do."

"Ha! I've beaten every one of them already. Any judge with a brain will see that I'm the most typey of my breed."

"Only time will tell, missy." Ellie noted that Flora Steinman and Arnie were involved in a discussion, so she asked Lulu the big question. "Besides too much aftershave, why did your mistress fire Edward Nelson?"

"You mean you can't tell?"

"Afraid not," she said, still staring at the senior couple.

"Ellie, Ellie, Ellie. Rudy is right. You are a babe in the woods when it comes to male/female relationships."

When Lulu's explanation sank in, Ellie blinked. "You mean Flora and Arnie are—are—"

"Not yet, but she hopes they will be. The moment she met Arnie it was bye-bye Edward."

"Wow," Ellie muttered. "Who would have thunk it." Her attention returned to Flora and

Arnie, who were now grinning at her as if they had heard both sides of her conversation with the Havanese.

"I assume this is the young woman you've been telling me about, my dear," Arnie said to Flora as he reached to shake Ellie's hand. "You're Ellie Engleman, right? Flora's done nothing but sing your praises from the moment she and I met."

"Mrs. Steinman is a very kind lady," said Ellie. "It's nice meeting you, too."

"I see Flora was right about your ability to communicate with canines. It appeared that you and Lulu were holding quite a discussion a few seconds ago."

"I know it's eccentric, but chatting with my charges is a habit I've developed over the course of my dog-walking career," she confessed.

"Good for you," said Arnie. "You can never tell how much a dog understands, and Lulu is bright. I'll bet she's aware of everything you say to her."

You don't know the half of it, Ellie almost blurted, but she knew her unusual ability was unexplainable, even to the most fanatical dog lover. "Please forgive me if I stare like a Chihuahua milling with a pack of St. Bernards, but this is my first time behind the scenes at any kind of canine competition. I'm still trying to absorb it all."

"You'll get the hang of things soon enough.

Once that little lady is in the ring, everything will come together like gin and vermouth, a fine cocktail and a fine win for our perfect Havanese."

"Uh, okay," she agreed, not certain that the analogy fit.

A buzzer sounded and the mob grew quiet. "Attention group twenty-seven. All Havaneses and their handlers, please report to ring number one."

Ellie checked her watch. "Oh my gosh. It's almost time for the magic moment. We'd better get out there."

"I am so nervous," said Flora, stepping in front of Lulu with a brush raised.

"Now, Flora, that's my job." Arnie eased the grooming tool from her hand and stuffed it in his pocket, then gazed at Lulu. "How's my pretty baby today? Ready to knock the judge's socks off?"

Lulu answered him with a sneeze, and Flora giggled. "Isn't she something, acting as if this is an everyday occurrence instead of the biggest moment in her competitive career?"

Since Ellie was privy to Lulu's bossy outbursts and sometimes snotty innuendos, she said nothing. They would never believe her if she told them she knew exactly what the Havanese was thinking. Instead, she made an honest observation. "There are only nine dogs in her breed. I'd say she has a good shot at winning."

"Remember what I told you about the breed. Because they're one of the newest recognized by the American Kennel Club, there are only about thirty breeders in this country. Hence the small number," offered Flora. "We've already met each of the competitors at other venues, and we've come in first several times. At each competition, Fidel has been the one who challenged my girl the most."

"Enough talk, ladies. It's time we got in line. We're next on the judging block." Arnie slipped an armband, covered with a variety of statistics and the number nine on it, over his jacket sleeve and moved it to his upper arm. Then he picked up Lulu and walked through the teeming mass with Flora and Ellie following.

At the edge of the competition floor, the two women held hands as the nine pairs lined up in number order. It was then that Ellie saw one of the handlers pull a treat from his pocket and put it in his mouth. A moment later, he removed it and fed it to his dog.

She wrinkled her nose. She'd tried Rudy's gourmet biscuits from Bread and Bones, and they were tasty, but the gummy-looking blob of brown that guy had just stuck in his mouth resembled cooked liver. Yech!

"I've seen some handlers putting dog treats in their mouths at the shows I've watched on television, and I know it's called 'baiting' but why, exactly, do they do it?" she asked Flora.

"Baiting is used to keep a dog's attention on

the handler and encourage them to get into the proper 'stack' position. Many canines are more well behaved in the ring if it's done, while others simply like the fact that their handler thinks enough of them to share a treat."

Arnie, who was the last handler in line, stood just a few feet away. When he heard their conversation, he took a step nearer, reached into his pocket, and pulled out a plastic bag holding blobs that looked very much like the one the other handler had used. "Ellie, here. You have a dog." He handed her a brown lump. "Try giving him one of these, and see how he reacts. I make them in my own kitchen . . . a special recipe and all that. If your boy likes it, I'll give you instructions on how to prepare them."

Ellie pulled a tissue from her bag and held it out so Arnie could set the sticky blob inside. No way was she going to let that mess touch her hands. After wrapping the tissue, she tucked it in the side pocket of her blazer. She had no idea if her fuzzy buddy would enjoy the gummy bit of goo, but champions did and Rudy was a champion to her. He deserved the best.

"Though I always carry treats for the dogs I handle, I've never used this technique in a competition with Lulu before, but she and I have practiced for the past two days and she's taken to it quite well. It should help with her presentation today," Arnie added.

"Contestants in group twenty-seven, prepare to head into the ring," the announcer called.

The handler cocked an eyebrow and gave a cheeky grin, then stood at attention and followed Edward and Fidel, the number eight pair, onto the floor.

Flora squeezed Ellie's fingers hard. "This is so exciting. If Lulu wins, I'll collapse with sheer happiness. I don't know how I'll get through the Best in Group and Best in Show events."

Admiring the older woman's confidence, Ellie said, "Hang on to me, and whatever you do, don't faint. You'd probably never hit the ground in this mob."

Craning her neck, she checked out the competition area. The convention floor was divided into four rings, with each section holding a specific breed of dog, spectators who were probably owners, MACC stewards, and a judge. Since the Havaneses were a small group, they stayed directly in front of Flora and Ellie. It was obvious that the judge, a middle-aged woman with a stern expression, planned to make quick work of these tiny canines.

"We're in luck. Alleyne Dickens is judging," Flora whispered. "The last time she and Lulu met, she awarded my girl Winner's Bitch in the toy group."

It amazed Ellie how much there was to learn about dog competitions. Understanding the correct terminology was almost like absorbing a new language. "I realize you've been to hundreds of shows, but how did you get comfortable with all the terms? My head is spinning, and I've only just begun to get in the swing of things. Seems to me they should hand out dictionaries so the audience can figure out what's going on."

"Why, Ellie, don't tell me you have aspirations of becoming a handler."

"Who, me? Uh-uh. Besides, since I walk twenty-five dogs a day, I'm already a handler of sorts. But it's nothing like coercing them into giving their best in front of a judge." With some of her charges, it was all she could do to have them walk in an orderly manner with the pack. And the grousing they did was enough to send her screaming. "I admire the professionals, but I doubt I could be one. It's enough that I spoil my brood rotten and let them get away with more than I should."

"That's the reason I fired Bibi and hired you, well before they caught the girl working with that despicable dognapper. You're very sweet with your canines, and all pets deserve a little TLC. A real handler takes no nonsense, which is the reason I don't want my baby living with one. Besides, once the animals get used to the ring, they find their rhythm and act just as they should. With some of them, it's almost instinctual."

Instinctual? She couldn't imagine her

yorkiepoo having the competitive instincts to perform in a show ring. Not that it mattered, because Rudy was perfect for her in every way. "I still don't think I could do a proper job."

"Nonsense. You're intelligent, and I bet you're a quick study. Besides, I've always thought you had some sort of special rapport with the dogs you walk. I sensed it from the first day I saw you herding them up Fifth Avenue, if you want the truth."

Ellie and her charges did have a "special rapport," but if she told Mrs. Steinman what it was, the woman would laugh out loud, call her crazy, and probably fire her. "That's a very nice thing to say. I do try to bond with them. It usually works, but not always."

"Which only proves that dogs are just like people. They hit it off with some, merely accept others, and simply ignore the ones they don't like." She glanced in the ring and gave Ellie's fingers another squeeze. "Fidel and Edward are at the table. Let's see how they do."

Edward Nelson stood on one side of the platform while the judge stood at center stage with Fidel. The judge ran her hands head to tail over his black furry body as if checking his bone structure, then looked in his mouth. After that, she put her hands under the rear of his belly to make certain, Ellie imagined, that all his "important" parts were in good order. Finally, Ms.

Dickens gazed into Fidel's eyes and the pooch gazed back, as if he knew exactly what she was doing and why.

When finished, the judge nodded at Edward and said, "Up and back, if you please, then return to the line."

Placing one hand under Fidel's neck and the other under his tail, Edward picked up the dog and set him carefully on the floor. Fidel stood in the stack position, something an experienced canine knows how to do without encouragement, and the crowd cheered. Ellie had to admit that, Fidel, with such an outgoing personality, was quite a showman. Edward and his charge paced to the end of the oval and back again, then returned to their place in line while Alleyne Dickens observed them with a glint in her eyes.

"Oh, dear," said Flora. "I can tell by Alleyne's interested expression that Fidel made quite an impression. That doesn't bode well for Lulu."

Ellie gave the older woman's shoulders a hug. "Don't be discouraged. Lulu has a unique personality, too. Judge Dickens will recognize that and treat her accordingly."

"I can't watch," Flora muttered, putting her hands over her eyes when Arnie and Lulu made their move. "I think I might be ill."

"You have to watch," Ellie said. "Lulu will do her best, and it would be a shame for you to miss her big moment." Lulu was a grade A ham. No way would she waste her opportunity to shine. "Just keep your eyes open and remember to breathe."

Alleyne Dickens inspected Lulu as she had the other canines. When she told Arnie to take his dog "up and back" he pulled the brush from his pocket and gave his charge's coat a quick groom while Lulu raised her head like a movie star. The display got the crowd laughing, and Arnie lifted his dog and set her on the ground. There the Havanese pranced in a circle, giving the spectators a reason to applaud.

Hearing the applause, Lulu did something none of the other competitors had done. She executed a quick back flip. The throng roared in approval, and Arnie grinned. Reaching into his pocket, he pulled out one of his "special" treats, stuck it in his mouth, and started their parade around the ring.

But he didn't make it more than a few steps before he began to totter as if in the throes of a dizzy spell. Then he held his hand over his chest and gasped for breath. He never offered the treat to Lulu. Instead, his muscles seemed to collapse and he fell to the floor in a heap.

Chapter 2

Sam Ryder closed his cell phone and glanced at his partner. "Hey, Fugazzo, we're needed at the Javits Convention Center. You ready to roll?"

Vince raised a brow. "Isn't that the place you

said Ellie would be today, participating in some kind of dog show?" He grinned. "Could be your favorite girl is in trouble again."

Sam winced internally. Trouble was Ellie's middle name, but Vince had no business jumping to conclusions. According to the newspapers, thousands of dog lovers would visit the convention center for the next two days, viewing or competing in one or another of the prestigious events. The way he understood it, Ellie was supposed to accompany some senior citizen whose dog she walked a couple of times a day, but that didn't mean she had anything to do with the department official's call.

"She's there giving a client moral support, but I doubt she's involved in whatever happened."

"Uh-huh," said Vince, shrugging into his parka.

Sam didn't bother with a coat. He never seemed to need one unless it was below freezing. Besides, it was only November and the Weather Channel had promised the sun would be out today, keeping the temperature at a pleasant and steady fifty degrees.

"What's that supposed to mean?" he asked Vince as they left Midtown South and headed for the parking lot.

"Just uh-huh," his partner muttered while they crossed the street. "Kind of like 'be prepared.' "

They climbed into Vince's car and he started

the engine. "Look, smart-ass," Sam said, giving his partner a friendly verbal jab. "Ellie promised to stay out of trouble after her run-in with Veridot's brother, and I believe she meant it. She's just been in the wrong place—"

"At the wrong time, or so you keep telling me. Well, cross your fingers and hope she spoke the truth, or you will again be the butt of department jokes crafted by all the jerks who love to rub you the wrong way."

Sam had to admit Vince wasn't far off the mark. Ellie didn't have to look for trouble; trouble found her. Since he'd met her and she'd helped him solve the Albright case, other officers had taken to making cracks about his needing a woman to do his job. Though the second incident, a homeless man's murder, hadn't been on his docket, he'd put himself on the line in a dozen ways just to keep Ellie safe, then ended up rescuing her from a ransom gone wrong.

They'd been dating steadily for a couple of months now, and he recalled some of the stories she'd related about her dog-walking business. The mutts she cared for kept her hopping, some running away while on their walks, a couple making messes in their owner's apartment foyer, even one who bit a passerby, which it did, according to Ellie, because it was provoked.

To compound her "trouble," she was on her third or fourth assistant since her first one had moved, and each new helper had been more unreliable than the last. Ellie was a soft touch who believed in giving every nutcase who answered her Help Wanted ad a chance, even if they were on their fifth job in three weeks or had been picked up for fighting in public. Hell, she'd even hired a guy who'd lost his license for reckless driving—three times.

So far, this new girl—Joy or Joyce, he wasn't sure of the name—seemed on the up-and-up, but she'd only been on board a week. There was still a chance she might be anything from a druggie to an ax murderer, and Ellie would never know it until the roof caved in.

"The sergeant just said someone called about a possible death. The EMTs are on their way and we need to take a look," Sam said as Vince turned onto Eleventh Avenue a few minutes later. "How could Ellie be involved in a death when she won't even swat a fly? Besides, it's a dog *show,* not a dog *fight.*"

"I don't know, pal," said Vince, a smile in his voice. "I hear those dog people are killer competitors. Wouldn't surprise me if there was some kind of altercation over a bad judging decision and one of them decided to take matters into their own hands. You know, like 'My Poodle can beat your Poodle any day, fella.' "

Sam shook his head. "I don't know how Natalie puts up with you. And whatever brain freeze you're suffering from, I sure as hell hope it isn't hereditary. Angela deserves better."

At the mention of his eight-month-old daughter, Vince grinned for real. "Did I tell you? My little girl said daddy yesterday morning, clear as a bell, and she looked straight at me when she said it. What do you think of that?"

"I think she has a Class A idiot for a father," Sam answered in a sincere tone.

They pulled up to the convention center, and he took note of the ambulance and flotilla of squad cars parked in front of the building. The two men left Vince's car with its blue roof light flashing and walked to the main door, where they were met by a security guard and a patrolman.

"We got the call," said Sam. "What happened?"

"All we know is someone's in distress," the patrolman answered. "There are guards at every entrance, and they're not letting anyone in or out, just to be on the safe side."

"Then it may not be a homicide?" Fugazzo asked.

"Beats me," the patrolman said. "You're the guys with the shields."

Sam headed inside with Vince on his heels. "Jesus, this place is packed," Vince said, taking in the hundreds of people milling in the lobby. Walking freely was next to impossible with a crowd of complaining humans filling the area. "Reminds me of the Knicks emptying out after a play-off game."

If Ellie were here, he'd never find her, thought Sam as they made their way to the escalators, where they met another security guard and patrolman.

"Go up one level and follow the row of guards posted at each entry point until you get the high sign," the officer told them. "They'll make sure you find the body."

"Are we the first to respond?" asked Sam.

"That's right, so it looks like you boys are in charge."

He muffled a groan. Too bad he and Vince had been on the ball or they could have been the second-string detectives instead of the ones on lead. From the way Vince frowned, he had to be thinking the same thing.

"Just one victim, right?" his partner asked.

"Far as we know," the guard answered.

"Would the elevator be any faster?" Sam questioned the security guard.

"Probably, but you'd have to play salmon swimming upstream to get to it. Don't know if you want to do that."

Vince shrugged. "The escalators are right here, and they're moving along. I say we just go up."

Three minutes later they were in the hallway leading to the main floor. After they followed a row of patrolmen and security guards, a cop named Murphy waved them over.

"Fastest way to the competition area is this corridor. Take the stairs straight ahead and go down to the floor," Murphy advised. "Rumor has it the EMTs didn't have much to do when they arrived. Just a routine go-over, with no luck."

The detectives entered the arena to the disgruntled sounds of a thousand complaining humans. Sam had to admit securing a mob of this size was a job better suited to the National Guard than the NYPD, but it had to be done until they could check out the scene and get a handle on the cause of death. And depending on the condition of the body, that might be tricky.

Unhappy comments followed them as they made their way to the circle of people surrounding a suited body lying on the floor. Sam spotted a patrolman he'd worked with on another case, and he and Vince pushed their way toward him. "Hey, Bartell, what's up?"

"One of the dog handlers dropped while he was taking a mutt around the ring. From the way I hear it, folks think he had a heart attack."

Great. All this ruckus for a natural cause of death. They shouldered through the ring of people surrounding the body and stood beside an EMT. Sam had to ask, even though he could read the layout. "Is he gone?"

"By the time we got here, it was too late," said the medic.

"TOD?"

"We estimated the time of death at ten thirty-three."

Sam jotted the info in his spiral notebook, then said to Vince, "How about doing a survey of the area while I take care of things here?" When Vince left, he said to the medic, "Any idea who he is and what did him in?"

"Name's Arnie Harris, and from the description of his death that was provided by the participants here on the floor, I'd say heart attack, but that's just a guess. Especially since we found this when we tried to clear his airway." The EMT held out a brown glob of . . . caramel?

"What the hell is that?" asked Sam.

"Dog food." The man grimaced. "Seems a couple of these guys actually slip the stuff into their own mouth before passing it to their charge. The victim did so, and directly after that he fell to the mat."

"Who gave you that information?"

"Some woman who runs the show. You might want to bag it for evidence, though I can't imagine anyone dying from ingesting a dog treat."

"If it was stuck in the airway—"

"Not stuck, just sitting on his tongue," the medic said, correcting him.

Sam accepted a plastic bag from one of the men handling the crime scene kit. "And this is common practice?"

"That's what the lady said."

After sealing the bag, he stuffed it in his side pocket and made a mental note to ask Ellie if that was true. A year ago he wouldn't have believed the med tech's explanation, but since he'd started dating a dog walker, he'd learned that canine lovers did a lot of crazy things. He'd seen her feed her own dog ice cream right from her spoon, then take a slurp herself, and ditto a bite off her fork. Swiveling around to locate Vince, he came face-to-face with a frowning woman built like a Mack truck.

"Are you the officer in charge?" she demanded.

A man who appeared as anxious as the woman hurried to her side. "I'm Sidney Huff, general manager of the show. How long is it going to take to clear this up?"

"We have to wait for the medical examiner," Sam responded. "Until we know whether or not this was a homicide, no one can leave the premises."

"No one?" asked the woman.

"No one," he repeated.

Just then Vince joined the group. "It's pretty much like the EMT said. The deceased was taking a dog around the ring when he put something in his mouth, then grabbed his throat and dropped to the floor."

Sam nodded. At least people were in agreement there.

"Looks like the security guards did a fairly good job of corralling the crowd," Vince continued, "but they have no idea how many people slipped out before security realized they had a situation on their hands. It's going to be hell questioning this mob. I say we make an announcement, ask those who were on the show ring floor to come down and stand where they were when he went down. Then we get names and addresses and let everyone in the stands go."

"Go? They can't go," said Mr. Huff. "We have a show to put on. We've been filming this event—"

"Filming?" asked Sam, glad to hear a piece of good news. "You mean you have a recording of what happened?"

"Of course. We plan to air Best in Group this evening and Best in Show tomorrow night. Since we never know when a TV station will want to play a portion of the event in a news segment, or run it at a later date, we film it in its entirety," said Huff. "There are several video cameras spaced around the center that should have caught the competition ring from all angles."

Sam gave Vince a nod. "Call TARU and tell them to send a couple of men to watch the tapes. That should give us an overview of who was on the floor, people's placement around the body, that sort of thing. Then go to the announcer's booth and give the evacuation order over the loudspeaker."

Vince left and Sam faced the officials. "We still have to wait until the ME gets here to decide our next move, and that could take a while. That means the competition is finished for today."

"Finished?" The Mack truck's jowls colored red. "It can't be finished. We're paying for this convention center by the day and we have a two-day contract with a strict schedule to follow. Canceling will force us to add a third day to the competition, which we cannot afford—"

"Look, Ms. . . . ?"

"Mrs. Bernice Pomeroy. I'm the current president of mack."

Sam swallowed a smile. She had to be pulling his leg. "Mack what?"

"M-A-C-C. The Mid-Atlantic Canine Challenge. We hold the event every year during the second week of November, and it's run on a rigid schedule. If we stop the competition now, we'll be forced to add another day, and that will put a financial burden on our organization, not to mention the scheduled television coverage."

Before Sam could answer, there was a tap on his shoulder. "Dr. Bridges. About time you got here," he said to the attractive middle-aged woman when he turned around.

The medical examiner smiled. "Looks like an interesting situation, Detective. Anything you can tell me?"

When Sam nodded toward the victim, the

EMTs stepped back to allow the ME near the body. "The guy is Arnie Harris, a dog handler who was working the ring. Witnesses said it looked like a heart attack, but I'm not so sure. Mr. Harris put this in his mouth right before it happened." He dug the plastic bag from his jacket pocket and handed it to her. "It's some kind of canine edible."

Dr. Bridges opened the bag and smelled the contents, then sealed the bag and handed it to an assistant. Squatting, she gave the victim a cursory inspection and stood. "Okay, have the Crime Scene Unit take photos and do the workup. We'll call it suspicious for now and I'll get back to you."

Ellie stood next to Flora, who was cradling Lulu as one would an infant. She'd been on tiptoe trying to sort out what had happened when she saw Sam enter the show ring. Just her luck. There were more than a hundred homicide detectives in New York City, and he had received the call. If he stayed true to form, he would somehow find a way to blame her for this . . . this . . . incident. But he couldn't. Not really. She was an innocent bystander, merely in the wrong place at the wrong—

Oh, heck, she'd used that inane excuse through two murders already. She had to come up with another line or he'd laugh his ass off, then read her the riot act, deem this strike three, and confine her to her apartment for the rest of her life.

"Can you see what's going on?" asked Flora, who stood about seven inches shorter than Ellie's five-foot-eight height.

She raised herself up again and saw Sam speaking to an EMT. Then he talked to a man and woman she assumed were in charge of the competition. That was when she decided Arnie was dead. Glancing at Flora, she gave the woman a hug. Should Flora be told the truth now or later? And would hearing it from someone official make it better or worse?

Heaving a sigh, Ellie decided that now was best and she should be the one to inform the woman, not some stranger. "It doesn't look good, Flora," she began.

"I know you've been involved in this type of thing before, which frightens me."

"What do you mean 'this type of thing'?"

"People who've . . . who are . . . you know."

Flora meant dead, which told Ellie she was ready to handle the bad news. "I'm afraid you're right. From the actions of the officers and the EMTs, I'm fairly certain Arnie is gone."

Flora shuddered in her arms, almost sagging to the floor, and Ellie grabbed her. Searching the sidelines for an empty chair, she guided the senior citizen to a seat and helped her into it. "Wait here while I try to find out what's happening. And don't move, or I'll lose you in this crowd."

She hooked the strap of her tote bag over her shoulder and headed in Sam's direction. Since Arnie was Flora's employee and she was here with Flora, she figured she had a right to know the details. But that didn't mean she'd get any information out of the good detective. In fact, when he was in investigation mode, he usually refused to tell her a thing.

As she neared the body, a voice rang out over the loudspeaker. "Ladies and gentlemen, please pay attention to this important announcement. The authorities ask that everyone who was on the floor at the time of the incident return to their same position, and those of you who were in the stands come up and take your seats."

Dozens of people made their way down from the viewing area while others moved in the opposite direction. The security guards quickly formed a barrier around the ring's perimeter after the crowd was in place.

"Thank you for reacting so promptly," came the disembodied voice a few minutes later. "Those of you in the stands may leave the building in an orderly and calm manner after speaking with a security guard. The rest of you, please stay where you are."

That sent everyone on the floor into panic mode.

"Why are they keeping us here?"

"Oh, God, I bet we have to talk to the police."

"I didn't even see what happened. How can I help?"

"My dog has to get to the straw box."

The straw box was a three-sided, breakaway lumber stall with a straw-covered floor. The dogs used the contraption as an outhouse, and Ellie could only imagine the disasters that might occur if the animals who'd been competing when Arnie died weren't allowed in the box. Show dogs were trained to hold their business, but some of the larger groups had been competing for a while. With all the excitement, accidents were sure to follow.

She again focused on the cops standing near Arnie, and Sam met her gaze. Frowning, he spoke to a patrolman, then walked her way. "Please don't tell me you were on the floor when the victim went down," he said when he reached her.

"As a matter of fact, the victim is the handler working for the woman whose dog I walk." She furrowed her brow. "Arnie's dead, isn't he?"

Sam rolled his eyes. "It figures."

"Don't be such a pain. I asked if Mr. Harris was dead."

"I'd say that's none of your business, but I know I'd just be blowing hot air," Sam said in a cryptic tone. "Besides, you'll have the answer after the ME's boys cart him off when forensics and the lab guys are finished photographing the area and accumulating evidence."

"What will that do to the show?"

"Hell if I know, nor do I care. Right now, we have to question everyone who was down here."

"But that might take—"

"Hours? Probably. But RTCC will run the names when we're through. That will help eliminate all but the suspicious."

"RTCC?" asked Ellie. She'd been involved in two of these situations before and had yet to hear those initials.

"Real Time Crime Center. It's their job to—"

Before Sam could finish the explanation, a tall, good-looking man of about forty approached, his features marred with worry. "I'm Steven Kincaid, the convention center manager. Detective Fugazzo said you would need a place to question everyone who was on the floor at the time of the incident, so I took the liberty of clearing a few conference rooms and had them rearranged with individual tables and chairs. Will they do for the interviews?"

Sam scanned the crowd of several hundred. "I guess they'll have to. Line these people up and head them in the right direction. And while that's going on, we'll need the tapes that filmed the event. All of them."

The manager nodded. "I'll get right on it."

Ellie opened her mouth to speak, and Sam held up a hand. "Don't say a word. Just get the woman you're here with and follow me."

Flora, Lulu, and Ellie sat on the visitor side of a large desk in a well-appointed office. Mr. Kincaid had been kind enough to give Sam the use of his private space, and Sam had escorted them inside and ordered both women to stay put. He'd be back for their "interview" in a couple of minutes.

Ellie knew better. This wasn't going to be a friendly discussion or a talk in the same vein as what Flora might give to a reporter after Lulu won Best in Breed. It would be a full-blown interrogation, very much like the ones she'd had before, once with Sam and once with a jerk of a detective named Art Gruning. Neither episode had been pleasant or—

"The detective who escorted us here seemed very nice," announced Flora, breaking into Ellie's musings. "And so good-looking, with that blond hair and those lovely brown eyes." She swiveled in her chair and gave her first smile since the competition had ended. "The way he spoke made me think he knew you. Am I right?"

Ellie heaved a sigh. She was a terrible liar, so there was no point in fibbing. Flora Steinman knew her well enough to read right through a "no" answer and figure things out for herself.

"Detective Ryder was the officer in charge of Professor Albright's death."

"Ah, I see." Flora's smile broadened. "I got the impression there might be something of a personal nature going on between the two of you."

"I—we—we're dating—sort of," Ellie confessed. She would own up to that much but nothing more, especially because she and Sam had slept together only one time, months ago. Since getting back together after their estrangement, their so-called dates had been interrupted several times by the NYPD and a few times more by Sam's mother. When they'd actually had a quiet evening together, something else happened to keep them out of the sack. She'd gotten cold feet.

"Dating? How nice for you," Flora continued with a twinkle in her dark brown eyes.

"Rudy doesn't think so," Lulu interrupted from the comfort of her owner's lap. *"In fact, he complains about the guy every chance he gets. Calls him Detective Doofus, sometimes worse."*

"Sam is not a doofus," Ellie muttered, then realized Flora was staring. "I mean, Sam is a good man."

"I should think so, but I doubt he's needed here. Everyone liked Arnie. It's one of the reasons Lulu and I left Edward. There'd be no reason anyone would hurt him or want him dead."

Ellie suddenly realized how Flora must be feeling. If what Lulu told her was true, Mrs. Steinman had probably lost her last chance at happiness with a man. "I apologize for not saying this earlier, but I'm so sorry for your loss."

Flora shrugged her narrow shoulders, then brushed a stray tear from her cheek. "I should have known it wouldn't work out, even though Arnie was in the best of health for a man in his late sixties. Life is fleeting. I see now it was a foolish dream to think we'd be together for long."

"Not foolish, and it never hurts to dream," Ellie told her. "But I wonder—now that Arnie's gone, what are you going to do about Lulu? Will you go back to using Edward as her handler?"

Flora stared at her as if Ellie had grown a third eye in the middle of her forehead. "Goodness sakes, no. First of all, a handler can't show two dogs in the same breed, and Edward is already committed to Fidel. Then there's Edward himself."

Ellie vowed to ask Flora about that last comment when things settled down. She hadn't exactly warmed to the man, but he seemed nice enough, even though Lulu complained about his heavy-handed use of aftershave. "So what will you do? Pull Lulu from the competition?"

"Not on your life," yipped Lulu.

"Absolutely not," Flora replied at the same time. "I realize there are handlers waiting in the wings—those two guys who approached you before the competition, for example. Will you contact one of them?"

"Besides those two, Felicity Apgar spoke to me about the position while I was waiting for you. She's pestered me about the job several times before, and I barely know the others, so I have no idea if I can trust them."

"Then you said yes to Felicity? That's good. It means you and Lulu are all set."

Flora's eyes twinkled again. "Of course I am, but not with Ms. Apgar. And let me tell you, she wasn't happy when I turned her down."

"You turned her down? Why?"

"Because I already have someone in mind. Someone I know who will do an excellent job. After they've had a bit of practice, that is."

Fast work, Flora, Ellie thought. "Really? That's great. I'm sure I don't know the person, but you must or you'd never trust them with your baby." She gave the Havanese's ears a rub. "So who is it?"

"You mean you haven't figured it out yet?"

"Ah, no. Since I've only met Arnie and Edward, how could I guess the identity of a new handler?"

"Sometimes you are so dense," Lulu stated with a bark.

"Why, it's you, of course," said Flora. "There isn't another person I would trust with my girl."

Chapter 3

Ellie opened and closed her mouth, then swallowed a gasp of air. "Me? Oh, no. I couldn't. I don't know a thing about the job. I'm inept, a klutz. I'd trip over my own feet."

Flora patted Ellie's hand, then held tight to her fingers. "Nonsense. You observed everything that went on before and during the competition. I could tell from your comments you understand exactly what's entailed in becoming a professional handler. You already walk Lulu, and she loves you."

"I wouldn't go that far," Lulu gruffed.

"But—but—the judges don't know me. I'd have no credibility," she said, hoping to squelch the ridiculous notion. "I'd only hinder Lulu's chances of winning."

"Hold on! Let's think this through," yipped the Havanese.

"You're being silly," Flora continued. "Yes, politics are involved in this type of thing, but all Lulu has to do is perform tomorrow exactly as she did today. With practice tonight, I'm sure you can get her cooperation."

"She is absolutely right," said Lulu in another round of canine commentary.

Mentally begging the Havanese to be silent, Ellie grasped her muzzle. "Practice? Tonight?"

"Of course. I imagine they'll reschedule the sessions cut from today for tomorrow. That gives you plenty of time to take my baby through her paces. You and Rudy can come to my apartment and we'll eat one of my housekeeper's delicious dinners. After that, we'll move furniture and make a smaller version of a show ring. I'll set up a raised table and pretend to judge." She cocked her head, as if thinking. "I might even be able to convince a few of the tenants to play audience."

Audience? "Oh, but—"

"And I'll serve refreshments. Dog treats too. In fact, I'll encourage whoever can make it to bring their pets. With luck, you might even pick up a few new clients." Flora clapped her hands in glee. "I haven't given a party in quite a while. This will be so much fun."

"Sno mus fum," muttered Lulu, twisting to free her snout.

Releasing Lulu, Ellie frowned. She couldn't believe how thrilled Flora was, especially since she'd just lost a friend, but it was good to see her so animated. "I'm still not sure I can meet your expectations."

"All you have to do is lead me around the ring. I'll take care of the rest," Lulu said, settling back on her owner's lap.

Just then Sam strolled into the office. "Sorry I took so long." After getting comfortable in the desk chair, he ignored Ellie and gave Flora a pleasant grin. "If you're ready, we can begin." He glanced in his spiral notebook and said, "Mrs. Steinman, is it?"

Flora nodded.

"Tell me about your arrangement with Arnie Harris."

"My arrangement?" The woman hung on to Ellie's hand. "Why it was the same as any other agreement between a handler and an owner. There's a standard fee—"

"I'm aware of that, but I heard from a few of the officers who've finished their interviews. They said some owners make special deals, and Mr. Harris was usually on the collecting end, especially if the dog he handled won."

Flora bit her lower lip. "It's common knowledge that handlers receive a bonus if they bring in a victory. Arnie had his fair share, so he was worth the extra fee."

"Which makes the winning more a contest of dollars for the handler, correct?" Sam rested his forearms on the blotter and continued before she answered. "Tell me, Mrs. Steinman, how important was it that your dog came in first today?"

Flora's grip on Ellie's fingers turned viselike. "What are you saying, Detective?"

"Just wondering if you thought Arnie Harris would live up to his promise and take your dog to the winner's circle. Or maybe you'd found another handler, one you thought would do a better job, and didn't want to pay Mr. Harris for the work he'd done up to now."

"Of course I expected my girl to win with Arnie. And I didn't mind paying him more than some of the others received." Flora leaned forward in her chair. "Mr. Harris was an expert with years of experience. It was a coup when he agreed to accept Lulu as one of his charges."

"What about the man you fired? Did you and Edward Nelson have a falling-out? How did Mr. Nelson feel about losing a client to Mr. Harris?"

"Edward and I came to an understanding, but you'd have to ask him about his true feelings." When Flora balled her free hand into a fist and held it against her mouth, Ellie passed her a tissue. "I really don't have anything more to say about the matter."

Sam tapped the end of his pencil on the desk. "This is a police investigation, Mrs. Steinman. You have to answer whatever I ask or risk being brought to the precinct."

Ellie opened her mouth to speak, but Flora cut her off. "Surely you don't think that I—I had anything to do with his death?"

"It's my duty to question all persons involved with the victim."

"If I remember correctly, there's a good chance Arnie had a heart attack, so you won't even know if you have a 'victim' until the ME is finished with him," Ellie pointed out. "And Flora—Mrs.

Steinman—has been here all morning." Anyone with a double-digit IQ could see that the woman was frail and exhausted. "Can't the interrogation be done at her apartment? Tonight?" She gave herself a mental high five. If Sam agreed, Flora could kiss that practice session good-bye, and she'd be saved from making a fool of herself. "After you find out if a crime's been committed?"

Sam continued gazing at the senior citizen as if Ellie hadn't spoken. "It's best we get it over with now. The sooner I cross you off my suspect list, the sooner you can go home."

Ellie straightened in her chair. "Are you saying Mrs. Steinman and I are persons of interest in Arnie Harris's death?"

"Anyone on the floor at the time he keeled over is a person of interest, Ms. Engleman." Sam gave her his I-know-what-I'm-doing-so-back-off look. "No matter their age or reputation."

Inhaling a breath, she tried again. "Lulu needs to visit a straw box." Maybe taking the Havanese for a piddle would give her time to think. "Unless you want the dog to have an accident in Mr. Kincaid's office."

"You can take the dog as soon as I find a free officer to accompany you."

"Do you honestly think I'd leave the convention center without police approval?"

Sam heaved a frustrated-sounding sigh.

51

"You've been through this before. You know the drill."

Yes, she knew the drill, which is why she was positive he had no sound reason to question her and Flora so thoroughly. They had been at least fifty feet away from Arnie when he keeled . . . er . . . fell to the floor. They hadn't seen anything more than what the other hundred or so people in the Havanese ring had seen. "We can't tell you—"

"Are you trying to prevent me from doing my job, Ms. Engleman?"

"What? No!" Okay, sort of. "It's just that—"

Frowning, he raised his hand and stood. "Don't say another word and don't move. I'll be right back with that escort."

Ellie checked her watch. Sam had been in and out of the office a dozen times, but no patrolman had arrived to accompany her and Lulu to the straw box. She supposed he'd been assisting his partner and other officers with the investigation while she and Flora sat like birds on a wire waiting for him. In between, he'd questioned Flora about Arnie's personal life, asked who on the competition floor had known him, and requested that she name anyone who might have held a grudge against the dead man. When he asked about Arnie's health, Flora even gave the name of the handler's physician, who Sam promised to phone after he finished with them.

Though he'd lost his bossy attitude and had been pleasant in dealing with Mrs. Steinman, it was now three o'clock and Ellie could tell the older woman was ready to collapse. She'd grown tired of the interrogation, especially when Sam started asking Flora for information that Ellie considered an invasion of the woman's privacy. It was then that she offered to phone Flora's attorney, but the senior citizen was adamant. She had nothing to do with Arnie's death; therefore she had no reason to seek counsel.

The response seemed to give Sam the okay to continue the personal questions. And all the while the big idiot barely acknowledged Ellie's presence.

What was he thinking? He knew darned well that Flora had been standing beside her when the man collapsed. How could this sweet old lady have had anything to do with the handler's death? She was getting ready to protest his tactics again when there was a knock on the office door.

A patrolman opened it and peered inside. "Detective, you're needed out here. The boys from TARU just arrived and Fugazzo has a question."

Ellie made a mental note to ask Sam about "taru," then tried to convince Flora to give her a reprieve from the evening's so-called training session. Unfortunately the woman had only one thing on her mind.

"I'm sure Detective Ryder will let us go when he returns. Especially when I tell him we have much to do before tomorrow's competition."

With that, Ellie gave up arguing. Flora was a senior citizen who'd just been through a personal tragedy. Though she was certain it would be a mistake, she felt honor bound to do as the woman asked. "Okay, okay, I'll be at your apartment around six thirty, but you have to promise you'll take a nap when you get home. And if you feel ill, you'll cancel the evening."

Just then Sam returned, wearing a grim expression. "Mrs. Steinman, I believe we're done for now." When Ellie stood and took Flora's arm, he added, "Not you, Ms. Engleman. We still have a few things to discuss."

Ellie raised her gaze to the ceiling. "Besides the fact that Mrs. Steinman has just lost a dear personal friend, she's exhausted from all the questions. She needs help getting home."

"No, no, dear. Peebles is parked nearby. I just have to phone him, and he'll bring the car around."

Flora had a chauffeur? Ellie hid her surprise with a nod. She knew the woman owned pricey artwork and lived in an elegant high-rise, but a car and driver? No wonder she had all that cash to spend on Lulu.

"I'll find someone to escort you downstairs," said Sam.

With that, he again left the office, and Flora

pulled a cell phone from her purse. As she punched in a number, Ellie couldn't help but keep watch. Flora's face was pale, her features sunken, her demeanor subdued. Sam had no business grilling an elderly citizen for this long, and she planned to tell him so as soon as the woman went home.

"What time do you think Detective Ryder will release you?" Flora asked after finishing her call to Peebles.

"That depends on what he wants to know." Sam could be relentless when he thought it necessary. "Sometimes he's like a dog with a prized bone and won't let go until he's gnawed it down to a nub."

"Rudy says he's a pain in the balls." Lulu yawned as if bored with the entire business. *"Though I don't understand how he can say that when he doesn't have any—balls, that is."*

At that moment Sam returned, and Flora set the tiny pup on the floor, where she stood and gazed at Ellie as if confused.

"Ellie, will you answer a question?"

Ellie glanced at Flora and the detective, who were deep in conversation. Squatting in front of Lulu, she whispered, "Of course."

"Why don't you want to see me win?"

Taken aback by the Havanese's sincere attitude, she ruffled the dog's ears. "That is so not true. I'd love to see you win."

Lulu cocked her head, much as Mrs. Steinman had done earlier. *"Then why won't you be my handler?"*

It was then that Ellie realized how her protests must have sounded to the prissy pooch. "Is that what you think? That I don't want you to win?"

"Well, duh. What else am I supposed to think? I can't compete without a handler, and Flora turned down a bunch while we waited for you, so it's too late to find one I can work with. It sounds as if Flora's got tomorrow and the next day all figured out, so why disappoint us?"

"It's not about you or Flora. It's me. I'm—I—I get stage fright. Doing anything in front of a crowd scares the doo-doo out of me. The idea of being on display with all those people watching is—"

"But this isn't about you. It's all about me," Lulu reminded her. *"Aside from the judge asking you to take me around the ring, I doubt anyone will give you a second glance."*

Put that way, thought Ellie, it might not be so bad. If she got used to walking Lulu in front of a raft of wealthy people, she might be able to carry the memory forward and pretend she was doing the same thing on the convention floor. "I don't know. Let me think about it."

"Think about what?" asked Sam, staring down at her.

She stood and said the first thing that came to

mind. "I'm putting you on notice. If you don't let me leave right now, I'm going to—to—wet my pants."

"There's always the straw box," sang Lulu.

"Okay, fine," Sam said through gritted teeth. "Ask the officer escorting Mrs. Steinman if he'll take you to the restroom, but I want you back here immediately after you're through. You got that?"

"I've got it." She jumped at the knock on the door.

"That'll be Murphy." Sam took a look at his watch. "You've got fifteen minutes, not a second more."

When his personal bad penny left for the lavatory, Sam raked his fingers through his hair. God, what a mess. It was bad enough that Ellie had raised important eyebrows when a homeless guy she'd befriended had been whacked in the middle of Central Park. When the investigation into this death became public, she'd be smack in the middle of a third murder in less than a year, even after promising him she wouldn't get involved in another violent crime.

He took a deep breath and tried to realign his thinking. It was ridiculous to assume she had anything to do with the dog handler's demise, but he knew that only because he'd learned over the last eight months about what made her tick.

The fact that she loved Caramel Cone ice cream, never made smart-ass comments about his food choices, and laughed at his sometimes stupid jokes was endearing. She also showed more emotion for a sick mutt than an ailing human and wouldn't step on an ant.

But she had negative traits, too. She insisted on running headlong into a fray when she thought an injustice had been done, especially to a friend, acquaintance, or canine. That alone would set tongues wagging.

Though he'd grown to accept her quirks, he couldn't let that deter him from doing a thorough job on this case, which meant he had to keep her nose out of it. Because, according to the phone call he'd received a few minutes ago from Dr. Bridges, Arnie Harris's death was now officially classified a police matter. She'd found something in her preliminary exam that showed a sudden drop in the man's blood pressure, too quick to be considered normal. Pending forensics, toxicology results, and a full autopsy, she'd told Sam to handle the incident as he would any homicide.

In his initial questioning session with Flora Steinman, it appeared that she had divulged all she knew about the victim's death, but the old gal had been tired and obviously upset. Could be she'd overlooked something that might lead to a clue. He had to hope Ellie would remember more about the moments leading up to the crime than her aged companion—and that she would hold her impulsive streak in check.

She was observant and logical, with decent deductive reasoning skills. She and Mrs. Steinman might have viewed the same things, but Ellie would probably interpret them in a more sensible manner, or at least sensibly enough to give him something to work with.

He still couldn't believe his partner had been right. But who the hell would commit murder at a dog show?

Sam shook his head. He'd never run up against a bigger group of fanatics than dog lovers and the criminal element that sometimes attached itself to their circle. In the past year, he'd met an assortment of sleazeballs—men who stole, sold, and shipped canines to foreign countries and creeps who kidnapped dogs and held them for ransom. In his line of work he'd learned that people would do most anything for personal gain, but it was still hard to believe there really were folks who would kill to achieve a big finish in a dog competition.

The office door swung open and Ellie marched into the room, plopped into a chair, and glared at him as if he'd been the one to murder Arnie Harris.

"What do we need to discuss?" she asked, thrusting her chin in the air. "And hurry it up. I have things to do tonight."

"So I heard," he replied, biting back a smile. "You're going to practice being a handler."

She slouched in her seat. "It isn't funny."

So much for holding back a grin. "I never said it was."

"I don't want to do it, you know."

"I thought you were jazzed about being here. Said it was a great opportunity."

"I said it was a great opportunity to meet champion canines and find out how the other half of the dog world lives, not put myself on display."

"Just think, you might be on television," he goaded, knowing she had a problem doing anything in front of a crowd. "Imagine millions of TV viewers focusing on your every move."

She crossed her arms and stretched out her legs. "I really don't appreciate your lame brand of humor, Detective."

"Sorry. I couldn't resist." He opened his spiral notebook. "So, clue me in on what you found out about the 'other half' of the dog world."

"First, I learned that it takes a lot of money to compete at this level. And handlers make a good living working a show, more if they board the dog and train with it beforehand."

"I got that impression, too. What else?"

"I walk a few purebreds, but Lulu is the only one who actually does this sort of thing. I watch all the televised events, but I've never been this close to stiff competition. I'm still taking it all in."

Sam frowned. "These people are crazy."

"There you go again, knocking something you know nothing about."

"Hey, I know a group of nut job fanatics when I meet them. The other officers have been filling me in, and—well, let's just say most of these people aren't playing with a full box of biscuits."

"Ha-ha. You're a regular laugh riot today." Ellie shifted in her chair. "Okay, so what else was it you wanted to ask me?"

Flipping a page in his spiral pad, he glanced at his notes. "Mrs. Steinman said you met Arnie Harris."

"Flora introduced us when Arnie came to the holding area. We talked for a few minutes, then walked to the ring together."

"Did you see him eat or drink anything, either on his way to you or while he was with you, other than that piece of liver?"

"No."

"Did you discuss anything special—anything out of the ordinary?"

"Not really. It was all about Lulu and the big win."

"So you think that little bit of fluff actually has a shot at the title?"

"I'm no expert, like Arnie or Flora, but they said yes. And the oddsmakers agree with them."

"Oddsmakers?" He wrinkled his brow,

annoyed that he hadn't thought of the possibility himself. "Are you telling me people bet on the outcome of these events?"

Ellie smiled, the first one she'd given him since he'd arrived at the center, as if proud of the fact that she'd thought of something he hadn't. "I don't have any proof, of course, and I haven't placed a bet, but I'm sure they do. Don't fans bet on anything these days? College ball, Little League games, just about every sport there is. And canine competitions fall into that category."

"This isn't college ball. It isn't even a sport."

"But it is a contest. And you know people. If there's a dollar to be made . . ."

Sam couldn't argue with her there. "Did anyone come around while you and the victim were talking?"

"Why do you keep calling Arnie the victim? I thought he had a heart attack."

"I can't say," he muttered.

Her eyes opened wide. "Oh, my gosh, he didn't have a heart attack, did he? He was murdered."

Sam raised a hand. "You know I can't divulge that type of information. It's too early in the investigation."

"You don't have to say another word." She stood and began to pace. "Someone murdered Arnie Harris."

"Hey, stop it right now," he almost shouted.

"The question is why. And the answer is obvious."

Standing, Sam came around the desk and walked to her. "Obvious? Okay, Nancy Drew, let's hear your theory."

Ellie crossed her arms and faced him. "It's simple. The killer wanted Arnie dead so they could handle Lulu and get the victory."

"It's a possibility, but your point about the oddsmakers gives me another idea."

"Oh?" When he didn't answer, she huffed out a breath. "Come on, Sam. You owe me one, especially since I gave you the original clue."

She had him there, and besides, it couldn't hurt to tell her what he was thinking. "What if someone didn't want Lulu to win? Without a handler she'd be out of the competition, leaving the door wide open for another dog to take home the trophy."

"It's a possibility," she agreed.

Sam held her by both elbows and drew her near. "If that's the case, and you're the dog's next handler, you could be in danger too."

Ellie gave him a who-are-you-kidding stare. "Nope, not me. Once word gets out that I'm the one responsible for Lulu, she'll drop from the favorite spot like a lead balloon. All they have to do is take a good look at me to know I'm not a threat."

"Maybe so, but I don't want you to take that chance."

"What do you mean, *you* don't want me to take that chance?"

"Just what I said. We're a couple now, and I'm forbidding you to accept the job," he blurted. "Under no circumstances are you to handle that dog tomorrow."

Chapter 4

Ellie grabbed her mail from the box, snapped the lock, and charged up the steps to her apartment. "Stupid jerk, telling me what I can and can't do. Who does he think he is?"

Poised to knock, she stopped at Vivian's door and glanced at her watch. Damn, it was too early for her best friend to be home. Taking the next flight two steps at a time, she continued to rant. "So he thinks we're a couple, does he? Well, couples support each other. They do not set boundaries or give ultimatums."

Unlocking her apartment, she stormed inside and slammed the door. It had taken her ten years to get rid of the first dickhead in her life. Losing dickhead number two wouldn't take more than ten minutes.

"Did she win? Did she win?"

Stomping past Rudy, who was dancing on his hind legs, she headed for the kitchen and pulled a bottle of brandy and one of crème de cacao from the pantry. After adding a splash of both to her blender, she tossed in a couple of ice cubes, set the contraption to high, and turned it on.

"Jeez, what got into you?" Rudy asked, circling her ankles.

When the drink turned fluffy Ellie retrieved a glass and poured the creamy concoction. She didn't drink alcohol often, but sometimes a girl needed a kick-ass jolt to keep her brain on track. Heaving a breath, she raised the glass.

"Hey, a little attention here."

She ran a hand through her curls and stared at her four-legged pal. "I've had a hell of a day, so be careful how you talk to me."

"I only want to know one thing. Did my girl win?"

Ellie drained the glass, set it in the sink, and plopped into a kitchen chair. "Lulu didn't finish the competition."

"Oh, brother. I should have known something terrible went down. That's the only time you bring out the hard stuff." Rudy rested his paws on her knee. *"Did a bad thing happen to Lulu?"*

Taking a second calming breath, she realized she had to get a grip. Her fuzzy buddy was so in tune with her emotions, he'd be as upset as she was in a couple more seconds. They were due at Mrs. Steinman's in less than sixty minutes, and she needed a shower and a change of clothes . . . and maybe another drink.

"Pay attention, Triple E. What happened to Lulu?"

Gazing at her yorkiepoo, she ruffled his ears. "Sorry. I'm upset for a couple of reasons."

"I got that when you polished off the booze in a single swallow. Now what about my girl?"

Ellie leaned back in the chair, and he jumped into her lap. Stroking his head, she said, "First off, Lulu is fine, even though the Havanese competition has been postponed until tomorrow. But something happened that directly affected your bitty buddy."

He gave her cheek a sloppy lick and reared back. *"Don't keep me in suspense. What went down?"*

She raised her eyes to the ceiling. "Would you believe another dead body?"

"Another one?" Rudy yipped. *"Human, I hope."*

"Yes, human, you knucklehead. Her handler, Arnie Harris, died on the competition floor."

"The guy who drags her around the ring?" His doggie expression turned wary. *"Wait a second. Are you gonna tell me that somehow we're involved?"*

She moaned in protest. "I barely knew the guy, and Sam only *thinks* it's foul play. He won't know for sure until the medical examiner finishes the autopsy."

"Are you saying Detective Doofus is in on it, too?"

"He and his partner got the call. I almost

fainted when he walked onto the Javits Center floor. You had to be there to believe it."

"It's not my fault I wasn't with you. I offered to come along, and you said no. I told you I should be allowed inside."

"Enough. We have things to do." They'd had this discussion a dozen times before, and Ellie refused to argue about it. Setting Rudy on the floor, she walked to her bedroom as she talked, positive that her boy was following. "I need a shower and clean clothes, and you have to be fed." She hung up her wool jacket and matching slacks, then tossed her pale yellow turtleneck in the hamper. Wrapping herself in a robe, she headed for the bathroom.

Ten minutes later, refreshed and clearheaded, she returned to the bedroom. After pulling underwear from a dresser drawer, she chose jeans, a red sweater, and loafers from her closet, sat on the bed, and dumped the clothes beside her.

Panting in anticipation, Rudy hopped on the mattress. *"I'm waiting,"* he singsonged, climbing into her lap again.

She couldn't blame her patient pooch for wanting the details. He'd been crazy about Lulu since their first meeting, no matter her self-absorbed personality or canine quirks. Nuzzling her nose on the top of his head, she sighed. Snuggling with her dog had a calming effect, not only because she was angry with Sam but also because holding her fuzzy buddy always seemed to give her a better perspective on her problems.

"It was a difficult day. I don't even know how to start the story."

"How about at the beginning? And don't leave out a thing."

Ellie gazed at her bedside clock, noting they had a few extra minutes before they were due at the Beaumont. "Okay, from the beginning. I got to the Javits Convention Center on time. The place was jammed and the air electrified, just like opening day at Yankee Stadium or the start of the final round at the U.S. Open. You should have seen the high-class canines, all there to compete, each one more beautiful than the last."

"What about my girl? How did she look?"

"Adorable. Groomed to perfection. And she was a well-mannered lady—most of the day."

"Okay, so what happened?"

"First off, I met her old handler. Did you know he lives in Flora's building? Claims he's a dog walker too, but I've never seen him with a pack."

Rudy sneezed, then raised his muzzle. *"Is that the guy who wears too much aftershave? Nelson somebody?"*

She scratched his favorite spot, the underside of his chin. "That's the one."

"But Lulu likes the new guy better. The guy who died."

It always amazed Ellie how much the

yorkiepoo knew about her charges. He seemed to stick his nose into every corner of their lives, and their owners' lives as well. "Give the dogster a biscuit," she teased, still scratching. "You're a regular mind reader."

"I know. So go on."

Using both hands, she gently held the sides of his head and met his questioning gaze. "Arnie died as they started their strut around the ring."

"What? No." He shook from her grasp and hopped to the floor, where he pranced in a circle. *"How did it happen? What did Lulu say?"*

"Lulu didn't act nearly as upset as you seem to be, but Flora was totally rattled. Apparently she and Arnie—"

"Planned to do the horizontal mambo—at least Flora did."

"Is there anything you and Lulu don't talk about?" She could only imagine how much the Havanese knew about her dog walker's private life.

He gave her a doggie grin. *"Truth?"*

"Of course I want the truth. Why would you lie to me?"

"I'd lie if I thought the truth would get you all bent out of shape. But that hasn't happened in a long time."

"So you and Lulu tell each other everything."

"Uh-huh. Now get on with it."

"How about if you eat dinner while I finish the

story? We have to be at Mrs. Steinman's in less than thirty minutes."

"We're going to Lulu's apartment? Tonight?" He rose on his rear legs and danced with excitement. *"Don't just sit there. Let's get movin'."*

"I'm glad to see something's made you happy." Ellie tugged on her clothes and headed for the kitchen. "You listen while I talk, and then we'll leave for Lulu's."

Ellie and Rudy arrived at the Beaumont at six thirty on the dot. The twenty-minute trip broke their previous twenty-two-minute record because Rudy had dragged her down the sidewalk at breakneck speed, causing her to cheat at crosswalks and bump into pedestrians while she tried to control him. She'd explained Flora's plan while he gulped his kibble, but it was clear he didn't understand the importance of this visit. All he cared about was getting to Lulu.

Now, as they took the elevator to the correct floor, Ellie caught her breath as the yorkiepoo talked. The pooch was so nervous, his words jumbled into one long string.

"How do I look? Maybe you should have brushed me before we left home—I gotta show my soft side—let her know how bad I feel." He pushed his snout against the elevator door. *"Come on, open up."*

"Stop fussing. I gave you a bath just a couple

of nights ago, remember?" They stepped out of the elevator and into the hall. "I think you'd better calm down. I don't know who Flora invited to this shindig, but I'm sure there'll be some strange dogs. Probably a few strange people, too. I expect you to be on your best behavior, unlike the way you were on our drag race over here."

"Yeah, yeah, yeah. Okay, fine. Best behavior. I've got it," he panted. *"You don't have to tell me twice."*

Ellie knocked on the door, and a woman who sometimes answered when she came to walk Lulu greeted them. "Come in, come in. Mrs. Steinman will be happy to see you." The woman held out her hand. "My name is Nelda, by the way, and I'm Mrs. Steinman's housekeeper. I should have introduced myself long before now."

Nelda's pleasant tone reminded Ellie of Corinna, her mother's loyal right hand. Was there a special school that housekeepers attended before they hired out as help to the wealthy? One that gave them the patience and personal skills to manage all aspects of their employers' high-dollar lifestyle?

"Follow me, and meet everyone," Nelda said. "They've been waiting for you."

Trailing after the housekeeper, Ellie crossed the pale pink marble foyer with its pale pink silk-covered walls and impressive artwork. She'd checked the paintings when she first started this job, and she knew she was in the presence of a signed Matisse and Monet, plus a few costly sculptures. Mrs. Steinman had once told her that her dead husband had been a hedge fund manager, while she'd been born teething on the proverbial silver spoon. While Ellie's mother had enough money to fire up a barbecue pit, it seemed Flora had enough to charbroil the entire state of New York.

Ellie cringed when she heard the din of voices. What had happened to Flora's promise of a small, intimate dinner before the evening practice session began? She and Rudy followed Nelda to the arched entryway that led to the dining room, where the housekeeper left them with a polite "Enjoy dinner."

Taking in her future "audience," Ellie counted about twenty guests, both human and canine, circling a huge table filled with delicious-smelling food. Rudy tugged at his leash, and she squatted to speak to him. "Calm down, please, and exercise a bit of self-control or I'm taking you home."

"But Lulu's over there, rubbin' noses with that Poodle. Next thing I know, they'll be sniffin' butt. I gotta protect my turf."

She took note of the freely wandering dogs and unsnapped his lead. "Remember, best behavior," she reminded him as he raced to the far side of the room.

"There you are," said Flora, approaching as Ellie stood up.

"Mrs. Steinman. I'm—I didn't think—this is so much more than I expected."

"Blame it on my housekeeper. Once I told her what I wanted to do, the woman simply took over." She grasped Ellie's hand and led her to the feast. "Nelda called some fancy catering service while I phoned a few guests, and here we are, eating a dozen different appetizers, caviar on toast points, lobster salad, some sort of filet mignon on a stick, and the yummiest vegetable ragout I've ever tasted. They even sent a trio of waiters to set up, break down, and serve dessert."

Ellie took in the portable bar in the corner, complete with a bartender, and gazed again at the overladen table large enough to seat twelve. "This is some spread. How did she get it done in just a few hours?"

"Nelda says all it takes is money, and since I have more of that than I know what to do with, I don't mind." Flora handed her a china plate. "Help yourself while I check on things. The first crew was supposed to arrange the living room for our exercise, and I'm going to make sure they did it in the proper manner."

Flora left and Ellie perused the table offerings. She passed up the fish eggs, a delicacy she'd never developed a taste for, and helped herself to the vegetables and lobster salad. Might as well get her fill, she thought. Even a condemned man has a last meal before going to the gallows.

A woman wearing pale blue Carolina Herrera loungewear neared, her face a testimony to the wonders of plastic surgery. "Are you the reason Flora called us all together?" she asked, helping herself to the caviar. "The newbie handler?"

Ellie's smile tightened. "I'm Ellie Engleman, Mrs. Steinman's dog walker, but I plan to take care of Lulu tomorrow. And you are . . ."

"Mitzi Nelson. It's nice to meet you."

Nelson? As in Edward Nelson, Lulu's ex-handler? If Mitzi was his wife, Edward was probably here, too. Great. Just what she needed to boost her confidence—a professional she couldn't hope to emulate tracking her competence. Unsure of how to proceed, she decided to continue the conversation as if it didn't matter. "I take it you're a dog lover?"

Mitzi raised a sculpted brow, though her forehead didn't move. "Heavens, no. I hate the little pissers. Give me a good cat any day." She took a nibble of her toast point. "I'm only here for the food—and to support Flora, of course."

With such a lousy opinion of dogs, Mitzi couldn't possibly be Edward's wife. "Oh, uh, well . . . so you live with cats then?"

Felines didn't bother Ellie, but they were nothing like dogs. Cats didn't do a happy dance when you came home from a hard day's work, didn't commiserate when you were miserable, and they never seemed to care if you were in the room or not.

"Who, me? Not on your life. They tear up the furniture and do their business in the house." She sipped her flute of champagne. "No, no, no. We have pets of a different sort at our house."

The confusing answer sent Ellie's head reeling. What did she mean by "different sort"? "Then you have birds?"

"Birds?" Mitzi's surgically remodeled nose wrinkled. "Lord, no. They make a ton of racket—dirty cages, too."

Okay, time to throw in the towel. "Well, it was nice meeting you." Not. "If you don't mind, I need to find Flora. There's something we have to discuss."

Mitzi didn't bother saying good-bye, and Ellie didn't care. She picked up her plate and headed for the living room. She would have to face the gallows sooner or later. Might as well check out the execution site while she had the chance.

When she arrived in the stadium-size living room, Flora wasn't there, but the room appeared to be ready. Antique dining chairs were arranged on either side of a mammoth sofa, and a waist-high table covered with a damask cloth stood on the sidelines, while a small show ring encircled by a few footstools and what looked to be an umbrella stand took center stage.

Impressed that Flora had thought of everything, she sighed in resignation. Once she did a couple of practice runs, there'd be no turning back. She'd be locked into the competition. Locked into trotting around the Javits Center with a pampered pooch who would probably bask in the limelight while her idiot handler made an absolute fool of herself.

Ellie skirted the perimeter and sat on the silk-covered pale pink sofa. With her luck, she would put her fanny on one of those irreplaceable antique chairs and it would fall to pieces beneath her. She picked at her food, barely tasting the lobster salad or the medley of baby vegetables. The only thing that could complete the evening was a visit from Detective Dreamy, as Vivian liked to call Sam Ryder. Though Rudy's favorite name, Detective Doofus, would be more appropriate after the ultimatum Sam had tossed at her today.

When the doorbell chimed, she rolled her eyes. More witnesses to her fiasco. Moments later, Flora walked in, a smile replacing her frail expression. Blinking, Ellie sucked in a breath.

"There you are," Flora announced. "And look who just rang the bell."

"Ms. Engleman," Sam said, his handsome face set in a frown. "I thought I might find you here."

"Detective." Ellie glanced around the room. If only there were some place to hide.

"Looks like I'm just in time for your lesson." He gazed at the faux competition ring and seating area, then at Flora. "I was in the building talking to someone about another case. Thought I'd stop by and see the show."

Ellie could tell from Sam's tone and the imperious look on his face that he was lying, the rat. But she knew better than to call him on it in front of Mrs. Steinman.

Flora nodded in approval. "I'm delighted you're here. Ellie can use the encouragement. I'll gather the guests and be right back."

Almost three hours later, Sam stood with Ellie and her dog in the Beaumont foyer. His car was parked right out front, its blue light flashing, but Ellie hadn't answered when he asked if she wanted a ride home. Instead, she seemed ready to bolt out the door and hail a cab.

"I think tonight went just fine," he said, hoping he'd get the words right. "By your third time around that miniring, you looked like a pro."

She raised her nose in the air and continued walking.

"Mrs. Steinman thought you did great."

Ellie didn't say a word.

"Come on. Stop acting like a spoiled brat and say something."

Nodding at the night doorman, she and her dog headed into the street, where she signaled a passing taxi. "I've talked," she told him. "But you haven't been listening."

Waving away the stopped cab, he took her elbow and steered her to his car. "I don't mean talk like you did with those nutty dog lovers. I mean talk to *me*. Let me take you home."

Ellie shrugged out of his grasp when they reached the passenger side of his vehicle. Ignoring her, he opened the rear door. When Rudy refused to jump in, which was par for the course, Sam picked up the mutt, set him on the backseat, and slammed the door. Then he opened Ellie's door and waited until she settled inside.

"There are a few things we need to go over."

"Unless it's an apology, we have nothing to discuss."

He went around the front of the car, removed the roof light, and slid behind the wheel. *Women!* He hadn't done anything he needed to apologize for, at least not from his point of view. Too bad if he'd ticked her off today, but giving her a direct order was the only thing he could think of that would get his point across.

He pulled into traffic and made a right on Seventy-second. "Just so I have it straight, you expect me to apologize for advising you to stay out of this mess?"

She swiveled in her seat. "This 'mess,' as you call it, involves a client and a friend. Mrs. Steinman and Lulu need me. I had to say yes."

"That's not the way I heard it," Sam told her, taking a right onto Second Avenue.

"Oh, and how did you hear it?"

He'd had a feeling this might happen. As soon as he tried to explain himself, Ellie was going to do her best to drag information out of him that was police business only. He drummed his fingers on the steering wheel.

Sniffing, she stared straight ahead. "Just like I figured. You're going to keep me in the dark any way you can."

Oh, brother. Sam made a right on Sixty-sixth and a few blocks later parked in front of Ellie's apartment. She grabbed the door handle, and he put his palm on her shoulder. "I'm sorry if you took my suggestion the wrong way." Then he left the car and walked to her side. She was already out and unloading her dog. "I want to come up."

"Double parking is illegal." She took hold of Rudy's lead and glared. "And you didn't make a suggestion. You gave an ultimatum."

She and her fuzzy pal began walking toward Lexington, their normal nightly route, so, like any contrite male, he followed. He'd put a lot of time and effort into this relationship, and he wasn't about to back out now. Ellie was perfect for him, in every way. He'd planned on wearing her down, deflecting her excuses, and getting her in the sack this coming weekend. It was his fault that she was wary about the sexual side of their dating, but he'd paid his dues with four months of dinners, a couple of bouquets of flowers, and two sets of theater tickets. He'd even made friends with her dog . . . in a manner of speaking.

At the corner, he waited patiently while Rudy did a squat and drop, then plucked the plastic bag from her hand and collected the waste. Thank God Vince wasn't here. He'd laugh his ass off if he saw the lengths his partner went to just to keep his woman happy. But Ellie loved her dog, and he cared about Ellie. Short of allowing her to put herself in danger, he'd do whatever he could for her.

Standing, he tossed the bag in a trash can and gave her a look, noting the hint of a smile on her face. He cleared his throat. "Something funny?"

"Not exactly." She turned and headed for home.

"Then why are you grinning?"

"This is an expression of approval, not a grin."

"You mean I actually did something you approve of?"

Ellie waited while Rudy watered the base of a tree. "You've come a long way since we first met. Eight months ago you acted as if scooping poop was akin to swimming in a cesspool. Now, you simply take over for me."

"No big deal. I figure if you can do it all day, I can do it when we're together."

Sam reached for her hand, but she brushed past

him and aimed for her apartment building. Shaking his head, he followed, still seeking forgiveness. Trouble was, he didn't know what he wanted to be forgiven for.

They arrived at her complex and stood at the foot of the stairs. "Are you going to invite me in so we can talk?"

When she raised a brow, he figured he had one shot left. "It's important."

Her world-weary sigh ruffled the copper-colored curls on her forehead. "Okay, sure. But not for long. It's almost eleven, and I have a lot to do tomorrow."

Chapter 5

"After all the moaning and groaning, I can't believe you're letting the despicable detective in our apartment," Rudy groused as they climbed the stairs.

Ellie jerked his leash, a warning that her dog darn well knew demanded his silence. He'd been fairly good at keeping his muzzle shut whenever Sam had come to the condo for dinner these past few months, and she didn't want tonight to be any different.

"What happened to your rant about kicking him out of our life?" the yorkiepoo continued, ignoring the yank.

"*Our* life?" she muttered.

"Whose life?" Sam asked.

She stuck her key in the lock. "Mine, not that it's any of your concern." She pushed the door open and walked inside. "Especially since you have so little regard for my opinion."

"How many times do I have to say it? I gave that order because I don't want to see you hurt." He followed her into the kitchen. "Why is that so difficult to understand?"

Ellie unsnapped Rudy's leash and set it on the table, then pointed at her pal. "You, off to bed."

With a look of doggie disapproval, he parked his butt on the floor and gazed at Sam.

She frowned. "You are *so* done for the night." Scooping up the recalcitrant pooch, she carried him into the bedroom and dropped him on the mattress, talking the entire while. "I have enough crap on my mind. The last thing I need is for you to be difficult." She wagged a finger. "And stay here. I can take care of Sam by myself."

"Uh-huh, sure." Rudy circled his favorite sleep spot, a pillow at the top of the bed, and curled into a ball. *"Don't be fooled by the blowhard's sweet talk, Triple E. You might think he's changed for the better since you first met him, but I say he hasn't."*

She placed her hands on her hips. Sam *had* changed since the Albright case. He called when he said he would, made dates in advance and kept them, even surprised her with flowers once in a while. And he didn't pressure her to have sex, though she knew it was what he wanted. Instead, he accepted that she wasn't ready to dive into bed with him after what he'd done, and he didn't blame her . . . at least, that's what he kept telling her. He wasn't the most romantic guy around, but he'd seemed to be shaping up, until today, when he'd given her that stupid ultimatum.

"I know he has flaws, but so do I. And I pride myself on my forgiving nature. I could—" Great. She was talking herself out of being mad at the big idiot. "I plan to use my best judgment in dealing with Sam and make the decision I think is right for me. And you, my cranky four-legged kibitzer, will just have to live with it."

Returning to her guest, Ellie decided Rudy was right, not about her and Sam's relationship but about how she allowed herself to be treated like someone who didn't have a brain. This was no time to fall for the detective's sappy excuses or let him boss her around. She turned the corner into the kitchen and found him sitting in a chair, nursing a beer.

"Help yourself, why don't you."

He quirked up a corner of his mouth. "You've told me a dozen times that I'm welcome to whatever I find in the fridge. Unless I'm no longer welcome here?"

Ellie took a deep breath and sat down. She'd

realized four months ago that she would always want Sam in her apartment and her life. And that was the problem. "Say what you want to say, while I think about it."

He upended the beer, then went to the recycling bin and deposited the empty bottle. Sitting across from her, he said, "First off, Arnie Harris's death is now officially listed as a homicide."

Blinking, Ellie searched for a way to ask the next question and still stay out of trouble. "What makes the ME think he was murdered?" And how was she going to explain it to Mrs. Steinman? "What happened to the heart attack theory?"

"Dr. Bridges performed the autopsy and saw no sign of a heart problem, but she did seem to think that something caused a fast and unnatural drop in his blood pressure. That rang a warning bell, so pending toxicology and other test results, she's labeling it homicide, which means I move forward with the investigation until I hear otherwise."

"But Arnie was older. It could have been an aneurysm—"

"Maybe so, but that's not up to me to decide. The doc's just covering all the bases."

"What about adult sudden death syndrome?" She dug into her memory bank, trying to recall where she'd picked up that bit of trivia. "I knew a girl in college, Mary Ellen Mayer, and her brother dropped dead while watching television at home. After six months of testing they never found a reason for it. Same thing happened to some movie star's son a few years back, only he was playing tennis. I can't remember the actress's name."

"I've heard of it, too, but it's still the ME's call." He gave her a pointed look. "I'm just following orders."

Subtle, Sam, very subtle, Ellie thought. And a direct dig at the reason they were at odds. "What do you think I should tell Mrs. Steinman?"

"No one has to tell Mrs. Steinman anything."

"What?" she squeaked. "Are you saying I can't—that no one is going to notify her?"

"She isn't a relative, so there's no official need for her to know."

"And you always do things in an *official* capacity."

"I try." He heaved a sigh. "It's just that sometimes certain people force me to bend the rules."

Hearing his second dig, she straightened in her chair. "I'm going to tell her."

"Now there's a surprise. I had no idea you'd do that."

Folding her arms, she stuck out her lower lip.

Sam threaded his finger through his hair. "Hell, Ellie, tell her whatever you want. Just remember, she's not family. She has no right to ask questions and no need to be informed of the progress of the investigation, and neither do you."

Ignoring his last remark, she concentrated on Arnie. "Have you been in touch with Mr. Harris's family?"

"I talked to his son in California, who promised to phone his sister in Chicago. Seems the family isn't close, but they'll take over burial arrangements when we're through with the body."

"I can't imagine losing a father and not knowing how or why he died." She held back a sniffle. "Especially if he was murdered."

"Giving sympathy isn't part of my job. Finding out who killed the man is."

Thinking, Ellie rubbed her nose. She hated to admit that Sam was right about his professional obligation. Which meant it was up to someone else to give the family, including Flora, a bit of consideration. And that someone could only be her. "Do you have any suspects?"

"I haven't heard from RTCC yet, but—"

"That's the second set of initials I've heard you use today. What the heck is 'RTCC'?"

"It's short for the Real Time Crime Center. They assisted with the questioning of the attendees, and it's their job to do a background check on anyone who raised a red flag."

"And that other thing? 'TARU'?"

"Technical Assistance Response Unit. They're reviewing the surveillance tapes with Vince."

"I see. Have they found a reason someone might have wanted to do Arnie in?"

He shook his head, his expression one of amazement. "I can't believe you're asking me these questions. Worse still, that I'm answering them."

Not to be deterred, she forged ahead. "What about the reason I came up with? The one about another handler making sure Arnie was out of the picture so he could take over Lulu's competition?"

Sam shrugged. "I talked it over with Vince, and he doesn't buy the whole murder setup. He's positive the test results will point to something natural."

"So the two of you don't see eye to eye on this?"

"In a manner of speaking, though Vince is a by-the-book kind of guy. If the ME says it's suspicious, he'll continue to work the case with RTCC and TARU."

Boring, boring, boring, Ellie decided. "While you do the brainy stuff, talk to the most obvious suspects, go over the clues, that sort of thing."

"You got it."

She recalled Mitzi Nelson and the obscure answers the woman had given when asked about pets. Too bad she hadn't asked Mitzi if she and the ex-handler were related. Edward Nelson was definitely someone the cops should investigate. "Have you spoken to Lulu's last handler?"

"The big guy Mrs. Steinman fired?"

"Yes."

"He'd been released by the time I heard about him today. He was one of the reasons I was in the Beaumont."

"Then you lied when you said you were there to speak to someone in the building about another case." The idea that she was getting good at reading the man made her bite back a grin. "You were really there to talk to Mr. Nelson."

"Yeah, only no one answered when I knocked on his door."

Hmm. So maybe Edward and Mitzi weren't related. "He was probably doing something with Fidel."

"Fidel?"

"The Havanese he's handling. After today's fiasco, I'm sure he and the dog's owner are planning a new strategy."

"I'll talk to him tomorrow. And it wasn't a complete lie. I did hope to catch you at your training session."

Ellie grabbed a paper napkin from the holder in the center of the table and began pleating it into a fan. "Then you knew I wouldn't take your advice?"

"From the way you stomped out of the office this afternoon, there was never a doubt in my mind. In fact, discussing your next plan of action was at the top of my to-do list."

"Excuse me?"

"I want to talk to you about this harebrained scheme of being a handler."

Ellie narrowed her eyes. It might be harebrained, but she had to do it. "I did okay tonight."

Sam grinned. "Far as I could tell, you did great, but that's not what I want to talk about."

"I know, tomorrow will be the worst." For her. "This is a terrible thing to say, but I actually hope Lulu loses."

"I never thought I'd hear you say that about one of your oh-so-perfect charges."

"I only feel that way because of me, not my dogs. It's going to be agony parading around that ring in front of a million people. If I'm lucky, I'll fall on my face and it'll be the end of Lulu's competition. I just can't stand the fact that she'll suffer because of my shortcomings."

"If the dog loses, Mrs. Steinman will be the one who suffers. The way I read her, that mop of fur is her reason for living."

"Lulu is, sort of, and I'm the last chance Mrs. Steinman has to see her baby win big." Ellie smoothed the wrinkled napkin on her thigh. "I tried to convince her to drop this competition and wait until Westminster in February, which would give her time to hire another handler, but she's adamant. She paid Lulu's entry fee for this event, and she found someone she thinks will carry her girl to the finish line—period."

Sam leaned back and stretched his legs. "Care to tell me what happened in your life that made you so fearful of performing in front of a crowd?"

They'd talked about their teen years, their time in college, even shared family secrets, but there was no way she would ever tell him about her debacle of a dance recital when she was six and she fell on her fanny wearing a goldfish tutu. Or the embarrassing flute competition when she was ten, where she'd gotten her sheet music mixed up and ruined the number with her off-tune screeches. The final humiliation had been her disastrous attempt at walking down the runway in some stupid junior miss modeling competition that her mother had arranged when she was twelve. Tripping out of her shoes and wrenching her ankle made that the day she'd ended her public appearance career for good.

"I—I don't remember a specific event," she lied. "Why does it matter?"

"I just wonder if there's some way you can overcome your stage fright and be comfortable tomorrow." He reached out and took her hand. "There's a lot of stuff out there: self-hypnosis, or maybe some type of relaxation technique that would help you prepare." Standing, he walked to her side of the table and pulled her to her feet. "Since you're determined to do this, I hate to see you put through anymore misery."

No fair, Ellie reminded herself, gazing up at

him. No fair that he was being kind . . . caring . . . considerate of her feelings. "Thanks for the concern, but I'll be all right."

He placed his lips on her forehead. "I know you will. That's one of the things I like about you."

She drew back and smiled. "Gee, and here I thought you liked me because I let you win at Scrabble."

"I've beaten you what, two times? It's not my fault you get all the high-point letters." Sam's gaze softened. "It's also because you make the best of things, even when you know the situation is hopeless. I didn't say it was smart, but I do approve of your tenacity."

She laid her head on his chest. "Then you understand why I have to do this?"

"Yeah, I understand why you want to take the dog through its paces, but I want you to be careful. Don't get close to anyone unfamiliar. Speak only to people you know. And by all means, watch your step."

Wrapping his arms around her back, he nuzzled her neck. "But I still don't want you sticking your nose in the police proceedings. It's a matter for the cops, not you." He gave her a squeeze. "It's time for me to leave. Tomorrow's a big day."

Ellie stepped back and they walked to the door hand in hand. "Are you going to be there?" she asked.

His smile stretched from ear to ear. "I'll be on

the job, but I'd be there even if it wasn't part of the investigation."

Leaning forward, he kissed her with gentle passion, and Ellie's heart raced in response. This was the man she'd come to know, the man she'd come to respect.

Heaven help her, he was the man she loved.

The kiss grew in intensity, until he stepped back and heaved a sigh. Touching her cheek, he cupped her jaw. "Get some sleep. I'll see you in the morning."

Ellie rose at seven and took Rudy for his first walk of the day, frowning at his uncommunicative demeanor. Fine, let him be that way. She had too many other things to worry about. He'd get over his being mad by the time she came home, and they'd discuss her sure-to-be-disastrous performance then.

In the kitchen she poured a morning nibble into his food dish and gave him fresh water. If she'd had a Valium, she would have taken it. Lord knew, she needed something to calm her nerves. It was too early to call Vivian, but she had to have something to cure sweating palms and a frantically pounding heart.

She took a few deep breaths and started a pot of coffee. Then she phoned her assistant.

"Joy, it's Ellie. How did things go yesterday? Were any of the dogs a problem?"

"Grade-wise, I'd give the day a B+. If I didn't know better, I'd swear a couple of them gave me a grumpy who-the-hell-are-you look when I opened the door, but once they got outside, they were fine. They just need to get used to me. One thing's for certain, those little guys are a hunk magnet. I met some fine-lookin' brothers on the walks."

Ellie smiled at her assistant's take on things. Joy was a tall, shapely, and very pretty African-American woman with a sunny disposition. It was normal for her to come in contact with men while doing her job. "That's great. And you were able to work around your class schedule?"

"Sure, but I can't do it too often. Hauling that many dogs is a killer on my feet, and it takes away from my study time. What about you? Did that Havanese win?"

"Um, not exactly. There was a death at the show, so things got postponed. That's why I called. I can take the morning run today, but I still need you to help with this afternoon."

"No to this morning, and yes to this afternoon. Got it."

"Um, and one more thing." Ellie wasn't sure how this latest request would go over. "I'm not certain, but I might need help with tomorrow afternoon's runs, too."

Joy's silence was deafening.

"I'll give you a bonus on top of the regular amount, if you say yes."

"How big a bonus?"

Ellie's business had taken off over the summer and was doing well. And even if it weren't, she'd have found a way to pay someone for covering her schedule. Flora had offered to recoup her losses, of course, but Ellie already had decided money was no object where her charges were concerned. "How does a hundred dollars sound?"

"Like a plan," Joy told her. "But make sure it doesn't happen too often. I have a life, you know."

So do I, thought Ellie. And right now it's in the crapper. "Trust me, I don't intend to be in this position ever again."

"Gotcha," the girl said in a cheerful tone. "I'll call you tonight to report in. 'Bye."

The line went dead and Ellie closed her cell phone. After Hilary had left for Florida, she'd found three dud assistants. As a smart and energetic young woman, Joy seemed the most promising to date. She hated dumping so much on the girl this early in their relationship, but there was nothing she could do about it except cross her fingers and add that bonus to Joy's next check.

She dropped two slices of cinnamon swirl bread in the toaster, poured a cup of coffee, and sat at the table, mulling the day ahead. If she did a competent job and the judge actually named Lulu Best in Breed, she'd have to prepare for the next step. She assumed Best in Group would take place tomorrow afternoon, which is why she'd lined up her assistant. Unfortunately, a win today would also give her the chance to screw up again.

And if by some miracle Lulu won Best in Group, she'd be responsible for leading the petite pooch through Best in Show. The idea of taking part in such an important event tied Ellie's stomach, and her brain, in knots.

Last night, she'd told Sam that she would be lucky if she fell on her face today and ended Lulu's chances at the top prize, but she hadn't meant it. Not really. Lulu and Mrs. Steinman had worked hard to arrive at this point. It wasn't fair that her klutz quotient should turn their dream into a nightmare. Now that she'd committed to the position, she owed it to both females to give the outing her best shot.

The toaster dinged and Ellie walked to the counter, buttered the crisp slices, and brought them to the table. While draining her coffee mug, she thought about adding a shot of Baileys to the next cup. She'd heard it said that alcohol some-times gave the drinker courage. And courage was definitely something she was going to need to get through today.

"So, what are you planning to wear for the show?" asked Rudy, interrupting her musings.

She went to the coffeemaker and poured an additional half cup, added sweetener and milk, and returned to her chair. If he was willing to talk, she wasn't going to tease him about his earlier silent treatment. "I haven't given it much thought. Got any ideas?"

"Something tasteful yet fun," said the yorkiepoo, the tenor of his voice a direct copy of a fashionista doing "Best Dressed" commentary at a red carpet event. *"Not too bright, but not somber either."* He cocked his head. *"How about the gray blazer and slacks, and your turquoise blouse? That color really brings out the blue in your eyes."*

"The blue in my eyes?" She stifled a grin. "I thought dogs were color-blind."

"So what. Every time you wear that blouse, the doofus detective makes a sappy comment. It might be enough to sway a judge."

"Yesterday's judge was a woman, and she'll probably be there today, so I doubt that will happen. Besides, it's not about how I look. The focus will be on Lulu."

"And Flora will see to it that she's in top condition, but you have to present a winning image too. Can't hurt to look your best when my girl struts her stuff."

Ellie shrugged. "I guess I should shower, put on makeup, and maybe use that volume-building mousse on my hair."

"I like the glop that makes your curls shiny. Your hair will catch the lights when you're on camera."

On camera? Just what she needed to hear. "Cameras are supposed to add ten pounds. Are you sure I look all right in that gray suit?"

Rudy trundled over and laid a paw on her knee. *"You always look great to me, Triple E."*

His "doting dog" stare made her heart melt. She believed that Rudy would care for her no matter how much she weighed or what the color of her eyes was. His unflagging loyalty was the reason she thought so highly of canines. They gave love and devotion no matter how their owners treated them.

"That's very nice of you to say."

"Was it nice enough to earn me a Dingo bone?"

She ruffled his ears, then carried her plate and coffee mug to the sink. Turning, she rested her backside against the counter. "You are shameless. Of course you can have a rawhide chew, though I'd give you one even if you weren't so sweet. But I love it when you flatter me."

He trotted after her as she walked to her bedroom. *"Then you'll do your best today, and make sure my gal wins, right?"*

Ellie pulled the gray suit and turquoise blouse from her closet and laid them on the bed. "So that's what this is all about? You want me to guarantee Lulu will take home the blue ribbon?" Back in her closet, she dug until she found her most comfortable pair of black flats. "Sorry, the best I can promise is that I'll give it my all."

"Guess a guy can't ask for much more," he said, sounding resigned.

"I'll try, really I will." She retrieved clean underthings from her chest of drawers. "Just remember, I have no control over the judge's opinion, and that's what really counts."

"All I'm asking is that you give it one hundred percent."

"Certainly. It's the least I can do for Lulu—Mrs. Steinman, too. But I want you to promise that you'll think of me today, and send a few of those good doggie vibes my way."

She stripped off her sleep shirt and put on her robe. "You wait here. I'll be out in a couple of minutes to get dressed, and then I'll find that Dingo bone. Oh, and I'm stopping at Viv's on the way out. She left half a dozen messages on my cell, so I want to fill her in on yesterday. I'll ask her to come home for lunch so you and Mr. T can have a midday stretch. That should do you until tonight."

Chapter 6

"Good morning, Natter." Ellie nodded at the Beaumont's middle-aged doorman. "How are things going?"

He smiled a greeting. "I talked to Mrs. Steinman and she told me what happened yesterday. Too bad about Mr. Harris."

"Did you know Arnie?"

"I met him a couple times when he came to visit. Seemed like a nice old gent to me."

"Me, too. I don't have time to talk about it this morning, but I was hoping that maybe later in the week you could tell me what you know about Edward Nelson."

"Ah." Natter ran a hand over his thinning brown hair, worn in an obvious comb-over. "I see."

"What's that supposed to mean?"

He raised a craggy brow. "Just 'Ah, I see.' Nothing more."

Great. Another mystery to solve. "How about reaching into that memory bank of yours and pulling out some info on the man?" I am not doing Sam's job, merely feeding my curiosity, she told herself. "I promise I won't breathe a word about what you say to anyone."

"Good, because if it got out that I spilled stories about my tenants, well, let's just say I'd be in hot water." He tipped his hat to a woman walking through the lobby. "Morning, Ms. Lewis." After Ms. Lewis entered the elevator, he said, "Do you think Mr. Nelson had something to do with the incident?"

Did she? "Probably not. It's just that—"

"Something about him is off?"

"I guess that's a nice way to put it. I gather you think so, too?"

"I do. Oh, and before I forget, Mrs. Steinman asked me to tell you that she'd meet you at the convention center at eleven a.m. sharp. She and the little hairball left about thirty minutes ago." His grin returned. "She said you were going to handle Lulu."

Ellie slipped into the elevator. "I am, but I doubt I'll have any success. See you in a few minutes." She pressed the button for her usual first pickup floor. Cheech and Chong, a pair of uncommunicative Chihuahuas, gave Rudy something to complain about every day. Without him by her side, she could tackle the morning job in peace.

She rang the bell on the penthouse suite to warn the Fallgrave sisters of her arrival, and when no one answered, let herself in. Jan had a gig at a club in the Village this month, and she'd probably been out late. Patty was supposed to be in town, too, but her supermodel schedule seemed to change from day to day. "Cheech! Chong! You two ready to go out?" she called after opening the door.

"Be right there," a woman shouted. A moment later, Janice Fallgrave entered the room, carrying the Chihuahuas, and set them on the tiled floor. "You're early this morning. Does it have something to do with what happened yesterday?"

"Yesterday?"

"At the convention center."

Ellie was amazed at the speed with which the news had traveled. "How did you know?"

The petite singer held up a newspaper. "It's on the front page. I haven't read the whole article yet, but I bet Mrs. Steinman is a wreck."

She stepped closer to examine the paper. The headline—murder at local dog show—sent chills up and down her spine. "This isn't the worst part—I mean, it is for Mrs. Steinman and Arnie, but I'm on the hot seat, too. Guess who has to take the dead man's place at the MACC today?"

Janice blinked her big blue eyes. "Oh, my God. You're kidding."

"Believe me, it's not something I'm looking forward to, especially since all I had in the way of practice was a quick view of the show yesterday and a fast round of how to do it at Flora's last night." Ellie shrugged. "I did okay, and now they're stuck with me."

Janice handed Ellie the dogs' leashes, commenting and asking questions as the Chihuahuas were hooked up to go. On her way out the door, Ellie said, "Let me know when Patti gets home, and I'll stop over to tell you more about it."

She guided the boys to the elevator in silence. Cheech and Chong had never communicated with her, and she often wondered if Rudy was right. Did the tiny guys really have no understanding of the English language? Were they here illegally? Impossible, she decided as she rode to the next floor. Rudy was just cracking wise, as usual.

She picked up the rest of the Beaumont dogs, waved at Natter as they passed in the foyer, and took them to the corner where they crossed Fifth and aimed for the park. As soon as they reached the other side, Bruiser, a timid Pomeranian, spoke.

"Did Lulu win yesterday?"

Ellie heaved a sigh. The Havanese was a member of this pack, and the other dogs had talked of nothing but Lulu's big win for weeks. "The competition was postponed," she said, quickly changing the subject. Knowing someone close to Lulu had died could upset them. "How did you like Joy?"

"Mind telling us the reason for said postponement?" Boscoe, a feisty fox terrier with trouble in his eyes, demanded in a shout.

"There was an accident," Ellie answered, hoping to keep the rest of the details a secret.

"Did Lulu get sick?" asked Ranger. Her newest Beaumont client was a chocolate brown miniature Poodle with a woe-is-me personality and a tendency toward hypochondria. *"Maybe she caught my roundworms."*

"You have roundworms?" Ellie rolled her eyes amid commentary from the other dogs.

"Ee-uww, ick," said Peanut, a small fuzzy dog

of untraceable origin. *"You better tell my mom, so she can take me to the vet."*

"Well, don't tell mine," yipped Harvy. *"Last time I had worms, she threatened to drop me at a shelter."*

Ellie listened to their complaints, trying to remember if Rudy and the Poodle had sniffed butt last week. "Ranger, are you on medication?"

"Ate the pill in my dinner last night, and I'll get another in three weeks. I heard the diva tell the boy I'm not contagious anymore."

Diva was the way Ranger referred to his owner, an opera singer of some renown named Sunny Russo, and "the boy" was her son, John, a quiet twentysomething Ellie rarely saw. Happy that the dogs were no longer focused on Lulu, she made a mental note to have Dr. Dave check Rudy's poop when the dog made his next drop, Mr. T's, too. The yorkiepoo and the Jack Russell would be mortified if they got parasites, no matter how common it was.

After she returned her charges to their homes and left notes, she headed north toward Seventy-third and the Davenport. Randall was there, as always, and he too held a newspaper in his hand.

"Please don't tell me you're involved in another murder," said the doorman, his brow wrinkling.

Ellie had known Randall since she was in grade school. Over the years, he'd become her friend, her confidant, and her biggest supporter. She owed most of the customers in this building to him, and she knew she could count on him for anything, including advice.

"How do you know I had something to do with it?" she asked.

"You told me last week you were planning to attend and assist a woman with her Havanese, and the report said that's the type of dog the victim was handling when the death occurred." His grin was a bit too smug. "Knowing your attraction to trouble, I'd be shocked if it wasn't you."

"I didn't do a thing, honest. It just . . . happened."

"Well, I certainly hope you're going to stay out of it this time, though it didn't sound that way in the article. The reporter said there were rumors there would be a surprise replacement handler. Would that be you?"

Who the heck had spread that rumor? Ellie wondered. Surely not Flora, but if not her . . . "She asked and I had to say yes. She claimed she didn't have anyone else."

"Please keep in mind that locating a killer is the job of the police, not you," the doorman said in a lecturing tone of voice.

"Jeez, you sound like Sam."

"Detective Ryder is in charge?"

"The way my luck runs, who else would it be?"

Ellie heaved a sigh. "And he's furious that I'm in the mix, even though I had nothing to do with it."

"I can only imagine how unhappy your involvement makes him," Randall said, as if talking to a child. "He worries about you, as do I."

The dapper doorman knew that she and the detective had dated a couple of times; the two men had also joined forces as her unofficial protectors—the overconcerned idiots. Neither one of them thought she had enough smarts to take care of herself, though Randall, unlike Sam, did give her credit for having a brain.

"He'll live with it. Just don't worry about me. I'm more concerned about taking Lulu through her paces." Ellie entered the elevator. "I'll see you in a few minutes."

On the ride upstairs, she realized that the dogs from the Beaumont had gotten so wound up in the roundworm discussion they hadn't commented on Joy. Oh, well, she'd just ask this group. They would answer her directly and probably badger her for those promised "special" treats. Striding from the elevator, she walked to Sweetie Pie's door. One more building after this, and she'd be on her way to the show.

Ellie pushed through the packed convention center, marveling at the number of people still crowding the admission area. She had cab fare hidden in her bra, her cell phone in one pants pocket, and her apartment keys in the other, so she had no worries there. Then she recalled the probable reason that there were more fans today than yesterday: More than half of the previous day's competition had been canceled. That meant double the number of breeds had to be worked in today, and she still wasn't sure when Best in Group and Best in Show would be held.

Riding to the competition floor, she recalled the newspaper article and wondered if some of the spectators might actually be here to focus on her and Lulu. She'd picked up a morning paper before taking the subway, and read the entire story of Arnie's death. Would non–dog lovers really pay for the chance to see a substitute handler get killed on the competition floor?

Though the idea was hard to swallow, this city was home to many curiosity seekers. People loved to gawk at hit-and-runs, pedestrian brawls, traffic accidents, even window washers hanging precariously from scaffolding twenty stories high. The ghouls might be here in full force today, thanks to the newspaper's sensationalized story.

Wouldn't happen, Ellie decided after stewing on the ride up. No one would pay good money just to see if she'd be next on a murderer's hit parade. Spectators in the stands would focus on their favorite canines. There wouldn't be any more people in the Havanese ring this morning than there had been when Arnie died. She could handle a hundred dog lovers staring at her as she jogged around the ring with Lulu . . . couldn't she?

Jostled by fans as she stepped off the escalator, she figured the attendees were merely hoping to get a good seat, hook up with friends, and watch the show, just as she'd done yesterday. Approaching the Havanese area, she spotted Lulu, again relaxing on her pillowed throne while Flora talked to a well-dressed woman Ellie didn't recognize. And judging from the unhappy expression on the matron's face, their conversation was unpleasant.

"You're making a big mistake," Ellie heard the strange woman say as she neared. "And ruining your chance for a major win."

With her papery cheeks flushed a deep pink, Flora stared up at the newcomer. "I know what I'm doing, and even if I didn't I don't want your opinion."

Straightening, Ellie shouldered aside those blocking her path. How dare anyone push Flora around after what she'd been through? "Is this person bothering you, Mrs. Steinman?" she asked as she glared at the stranger.

The middle-aged woman, thin with a bony face and sunken brown eyes, appraised her from head to toe. Not comfortable with being viewed like a specimen under a microscope, Ellie gave her best impression of polite. "Maybe I can answer your questions. I'm Ellie Engleman, Lulu's new handler."

The woman gazed at her as if Ellie had just said she juggled live snakes. "I wouldn't be so cocky if I were you, young lady. You have a lot of nerve, taking advantage of this sort of situation to break into the business."

"Now, Felicity." Flora placed a palm on the woman's forearm. "The decision was mine, not Ellie's."

"Excuse me, Flora, but if this person has a problem with me, I can speak for myself." Was this the woman Flora had told her about? And why was she ordering them around? "If you have something to say to me, Felicity"—she exaggerated the pronunciation of her name—"I think it best you get on with it and leave Mrs. Steinman alone. She's been through enough."

"Precisely," Felicity said in a venomous tone. "That's why she doesn't need an upstart blowing her prized bitch's shot at a win here."

Flora took control before Ellie could speak. "I've had enough of your interference. I want you to leave. Now." She waved her hand as if shooing a fly. "Ellie knows what she's doing, and I trust her."

Shrugging her thin shoulders, Felicity skulked away without a backward glance.

"Wow," Ellie said, watching the woman disappear into the crowd. "Talk about rude. I take it that's the woman you mentioned yesterday?"

"Felicity Apgar. A handler who has pestered me before."

Ellie nodded. "She was someone else who wanted to show off Lulu in the ring."

With a shaky hand, Flora fingered the double strand of pearls draped around the collar of her navy blue suit. "We've never been friends, but she's usually congenial. She's even complimented me when Lulu bested a dog she showed. Before I decided on Arnie, I actually considered hiring her, but then I heard a rumor, something about unethical behavior, and I rejected her offer to take care of my girl. This temper tantrum came out of the blue."

Unethical behavior? "Do you know what she was accused of?"

"I don't remember, and I hate gossip, so I simply told her no."

Ellie added Felicity to her list of suspects, and decided that the woman probably wasn't the only handler who was jealous of her. Those two boys, Josh and Jim, had to have been annoyed when they heard who was replacing Arnie. If this kept up, she'd be on all the handlers' hate lists before she ever met them.

"I'm so sorry," she began. "I had no idea the amount of grief you'd take for giving me the job."

"Nonsense," the woman replied, taking Ellie's hand. "Now come along and say hello to my baby. The two of you worked so well together last night, I just know today is going to be perfect."

"Thanks for trying to protect the old girl," said Lulu when they approached, *"but she's a tough bird. She can take care of herself."*

"I think so, too," said Ellie. Then she coughed. "I mean, I think Lulu is ready. What about a bow for her hair?"

The Havanese yipped at the same time Flora said, "Oh, no. Never. Bows would disqualify a Havanese. Only two small braids are allowed, but when Arnie and I tried that look, Lulu refused to sit still."

"Braids? Hmmph. Who did she think I was? Johnny Depp playing Jack Sparrow?"

"Okay, no bows and no braids," Ellie said with a grin. "I think she looks great."

"I always look great." Lulu preened, taking in Ellie's outfit. *"You look nice, too, but remember I'm the one on display. All you have to do is guide me around the ring."*

"So nice to hear you approve of the color of my suit."

"I certainly do," said Flora, unaware of the other conversation. "You look like the consummate professional."

"Um, thanks," said Ellie, mentally kicking herself. It was important for her to remember that people would be watching her every move; she had to be careful what she said and whom she said it to. "I haven't checked in yet. Do you know where I go to get my armband and whatever else I'm supposed to have?"

"Certainly, but please let me take care of it for you."

"Oh, but I can—"

"No, no. Allow me. I'd rather you stay with Lulu and plan strategy for the competition, get comfortable with each other, that sort of thing. I'll be back in a few minutes." Flora flashed a smile and headed into the crowd.

"She's a nervous wreck. She needs something to do," said Lulu when her mistress walked away. *"I had to sleep right next to her on the bed last night . . . almost got smothered."*

"Did anyone make a comment after I left the training session?"

The Havanese sneezed. *"Not about you, but they did praise me. Said I was very brave to venture into a championship situation with a novice."*

"Gee, there's a confidence builder."

Lulu snorted, her version of a laugh. *"It is all about me, you know."*

"So you keep saying." Ellie stood on tiptoe, checking the crowd to be certain Felicity wasn't hanging around. Edward Nelson, only three booths away, gave her an odd look and a too polite grin. A bald-headed man standing at his side nodded in her direction, then tapped Edward on the shoulder, and both men bent to fuss over Fidel. The more she saw of Edward Nelson, the less she liked him, and she got the impression that Fidel's owner or whoever the guy was wasn't too happy about her either. "What did Felicity say before I arrived?" she asked, returning her gaze to Lulu.

"Just the usual. She's got years of experience. She's always admired my conformation. A lot of yadayadayada."

"And you don't like her?"

"I don't like most humans."

True, but Lulu had never professed to being a lovable or softhearted canine. "Only Flora—and me, I hope."

"Rudy thinks you're the sun, the moon, and a Dingo bone all rolled into one. It's his opinion I respect."

Unhappy that she'd lost out to her dog, Ellie heaved a sigh. It was tough soaking up criticism, especially since she hadn't wanted this job in the first place. Now she was stuck in an enormous arena, preparing to make a fool of herself for the hundredth time in her life.

"Stop frowning, and remember to show lots of teeth when we're in that ring. I told you I'll take care of the rest."

"Okay, fine. I get the message. Smile big, fluff your feathers, and guide you around the oval. The winning or losing is on your shoulders." Too bad no one would know it but her and the Havanese. "Now quiet. Here comes Flora."

"Here's your identification band," the woman said, handing Ellie a swatch of stretchy cloth.

She stared at the printing around the band. "I never took a good look yesterday. What's all this gibberish printed underneath the number?"

"It's a list of Lulu's credentials," Flora explained. "The top line is the name she's registered under on her American Kennel Club papers. Below that was Arnie's name, which I had changed to yours, then the kennel she's from and the championships she won that led her to this moment. It's nothing you need to worry about."

Ellie slid the armband over her left hand and straightened it just above her elbow. If Flora said she didn't need to worry about it, that was fine. She had enough bits of trivia rolling around in her mind: conformation, gait speed, stacking style, baiting—

"Attention, group twenty-seven," said a voice over the loudspeaker. "All handlers and their dogs, please head to show ring number one. Competition will start in ten minutes."

Flora lifted Lulu from the pillow and passed her to Ellie. "This is it. Stay calm and take a deep breath." The older woman inhaled, as if

demonstrating how it was done. "And whatever happens, know that Lulu and I are very
grateful."

Sam had left Vince with the RTCC boys and the
tapes of yesterday's crime scene. His partner
had already decided this would be his last look
at the videos unless he or one of the experts
spotted something that made it necessary to question any persons of interest.

He had more important things to do, and the
first was finding Ellie. He'd learned a few tricks
of the handler's trade during his early-morning
interviews and wanted to make sure she knew
them, too. She was nervous enough about today,
and she didn't need a disreputable competitor
interfering in her debut.

Not that he thought she would ever do this sort
of thing again. In fact, he was surprised that
she'd given in to Mrs. Steinman's demand to
begin with. Ellie was stubborn and impossible to
win over once she made up her mind. Either
Flora Steinman was a magician or Ellie liked
her so much she'd decided to compromise her
standards just to make the woman happy.

He walked onto the floor as the announcer
called the Havaneses to the competition area. One
by one, he locked gazes with each of the patrolmen posted around the ring and nodded, reminding them that the main event was about to begin.

Standing in the entry, he watched the previous breed, hairy behemoths the size of Shetland ponies, file out, and the new group file in. He smiled when he saw Ellie, and he didn't give one good goddamn who noticed. Her copper curls gleamed in the bright lights beating down on the competition area. Dressed in a tailored suit and wearing the blouse he thought complemented the color of her eyes, she looked exactly as she should—personable and professional.

The pack of nine dogs made a single pass around the show ring's oval, then came to a stop in number order. Sidling near, Sam took hold of her elbow and drew her a few feet away from the number eight dog and Edward Nelson. "You hanging in there?"

"I can't talk to you right now. I'm concentrating."

"Sorry. I'll leave in a second. I just want to know if you're okay."

"I am if that's what you call terrified." Huffing out a breath, she peered into the ring. "I can't believe we're using the same section as yesterday. Whatever happened to preserving the crime scene?"

He shrugged. "No point to it. So many people tromped over the area before we got here, there wasn't much left to preserve." A moment later, the judge called the first dog to the table. "That's the same woman you had yesterday. I spoke to her then and again this morning, and she seems genuinely upset that someone died on her watch."

Ms. Dickens examined Havanese number one, then instructed the handler to take the dog up and back.

"Still got the jitters?" Sam asked, noting that Ellie's breathing had slowed.

"A little. Why? Do I look nervous?"

He held off giving her the hug he knew she needed. "You look good to me. By the way, I learned something about your fellow handlers. Do you know the 'bait dropping' trick?"

Fixated on the judging table, she nodded. "Nasty, isn't it? Dropping a treat to lure the next dog on the floor into breaking stride."

"Are you ready for that?"

"Bigger question—is Lulu ready for it?"

Sam lowered his gaze to the furball sitting at Ellie's feet. "She seems to be concentrating. Do you think she knows what's going on?"

Ellie faced him, wearing a feeble grin. "Lulu knows exactly what's going on. She's here to win."

"Let me guess—the two of you had a talk."

"You bet we did." The judge motioned for dog number two, and Ellie frowned. "Six more, then we're up. I think I'm going to be sick."

"No, you're not. Just take a couple more deep breaths."

She did as he suggested, but her eyes never left the waist-high table. A few minutes later she said, "Three more. I feel as if I'm having one of those out of body experiences, watching everything as I float high above."

"Trust me, this is not a near-death ordeal. Maybe if you pretend the judge is naked—better still, pretend everyone in the audience is—it won't be so bad."

The comment made her giggle. "Okay, that's enough of a pep talk for the morning. I appreciate it, but—" Straightening, she trained her eyes on the next competitors. "There go Edward and Fidel." The tall handler and his canine strode toward the judge, as cocky as they'd been yesterday. "I wish I had his confidence."

"You don't need confidence, babe. You have something much better," Sam said. "You have heart."

Ellie's smile grew brilliant. "That's such a sweet thing to say." The crowd applauded, and she eyed the male Havanese. "I can see why Fidel and Lulu have battled it out a time or two. The little guy's a ham."

When she glanced down, Sam realized she was staring at Lulu as if the canine had something important to say.

"Okay, okay, I'm paying attention," she muttered.

He shook his head. This was not the time to hold an out-loud conversation with a dog, but it looked like that was exactly what Ellie was doing. He raised his gaze and watched Havanese number eight strut around the ring. Squeezing her elbow, he said, "You're next."

"What? Uh, oh. Right." She again looked at Lulu. "You ready? Here we go."

Ellie swallowed her fear, slapped a grin on her face, and stuck to Lulu's side as the dainty dog trotted toward the judge. When they arrived at the podium, she lifted the Havanese onto the examining table, and Lulu immediately stood in the "stack" position, showing off her perfectly proportioned body.

Alleyne Dickens glanced at Ellie and smiled as she began her inspection. "Word has it this is your first show."

"Yes, and I'm overwhelmed."

"Not to worry. You have an excellent bitch. Show me her bite, why don't you?"

Ellie put a finger and thumb on Lulu's muzzle and Lulu gave a doggie grin, showing her perfect teeth.

Ms. Dickens ran her hand over Lulu's head and neck, down her spine to her tail, then did the same to Lulu's underbelly. Nodding, she said, "On the floor, please, and take her up and back."

Grasping the dog under her chest and tail, Ellie lifted the Havanese and set her down.

Lulu raised her nose in the air. *"Hang on to your hat,"* she pronounced.

Ellie knew what that meant, and she let the dog do her thing. Lulu trotted in a circle, as if modeling a designer original, then executed her trademark move: a high back flip.

The crowd roared and Lulu tugged on the lead. *"Keep up, kiddo. Time to show them what I'm made of."*

Ellie moved into the preferred "gait" mode and glided alongside Lulu while she pranced across the ring. On their way down the oval, Ellie made sure to keep the leash loose, so it appeared as if Lulu was in charge. When she spied a small piece of liver directly in their path on the floor she almost skidded to a stop. Good Lord, someone was trying to ruin their stride!

"Lulu, ignore," she commanded in a stern but soft tone.

Muzzle raised high, the petite pooch trotted past the treat as if it were invisible.

Now at the far side of the ring, Ellie turned on toe—who knew she'd actually use those stupid dance lessons in real life?—and headed back to the judge.

Ms. Dickens gave them a long look, then waved them down the line to their original spot while the crowd cheered. Ellie grinned when Flora gave her a thumbs-up. So far, she'd survived. It was just a matter of waiting.

Each pair of competitors stood at attention as the judge walked slowly past, awarding every canine a second inspection. She stopped at Edward and Fidel and narrowed her gaze, then sidled to her right and did the same to Ellie and Lulu, who was again stacked perfectly.

Walking backward, the woman made a motion with her hand. "Once more around the ring, if you please."

Ellie concentrated, aware that the judge was watching each dog's every move. This was her final chance to show off her charge, and she wasn't going to blow it. She was so involved in getting everything right that she almost ran into Edward's back, but she caught herself in time to adjust their stride.

What the heck was wrong with the man, slowing down in the middle of the parade?

Back at where they'd started, the pooches again stopped, and Ms. Dickens took another stroll down the line, giving each dog a final look. Then she pointed at Lulu. "One," she announced, and the crowd roared in approval.

Chapter 7

"Come on, work with me here!" Lulu shouted, pulling Ellie into the center of the ring.

Unable to speak, or smile, or think rationally, Ellie followed the Havanese and, in shock, allowed the fuzzlet to take the lead. Ms. Dickens was still calling out placements, but she had no idea who'd come in second or third. Her dog had won Best in Breed! Certain that her face was frozen in surprise, she could only try to keep up as Lulu took her victory lap.

A moment later, just as she'd seen on television, the other handlers and dogs gathered to offer best wishes. Ellie heard their words, but she couldn't respond. Her chest felt constricted, her throat had closed, and her eyes were brimming with tears. Swiping her cheeks with her free hand, she squatted in front of Lulu.

"You did great."

"Just like I said I would," the prissy pooch reminded her.

A hand clasped Ellie's shoulder and she stood to accept the blue ribbon. "Congratulations. Please leave the ring the same way you entered," said the MACC steward.

Ellie's head was filled with helium, and her heart still pounded like a kettledrum. Scooping up Lulu, she did as the steward requested. When she reached Flora, she put the dog in her arms and guided the older woman into the hall, where she pulled her aside.

Flora snuggled Lulu against her lips, muttering in the scruff of her baby's neck. "My precious girl, I knew you could do it. I am so proud of you." Then another round of kisses. "You are wonderful."

Holding the blue ribbon to her chest, Ellie

caught her breath, nodding at several handlers who grinned at her as they marched past on their way into the ring. It was obvious that word had spread: the novice had taken a first.

Flora set her dog on the floor and gazed at Ellie, her face bright red but composed. "Thank you, dear. I knew we could count on you."

"Don't thank me. Lulu did all the work," Ellie told her, still gasping for breath.

"She's a trouper, but without you we wouldn't have made it this far. We need a plan for tomorrow."

A plan? Flora had to be talking about Best in Group, where she and Lulu would compete against three times as many canines as they'd beaten here. More dogs meant a longer wait to be judged, which meant more time to hyperventilate, get sick to her stomach . . . do her worst.

"Let's go to the holding area and collect Lulu's things," Flora suggested. "We've been told to move quickly so they can get all the dogs through the preliminaries today."

Still dazed, Ellie followed her to the packed staging area. There they met Sam, and she knew from the set of his jaw that he was back to business.

"Congratulations." Though his tone was reserved, he wore a smile in his eyes.

"Thank you."

"I've made arrangements for both of you to go to one of the interrogation rooms."

"I'd planned to leave my girl with a friend and take Ellie to lunch," said Flora. "All the excitement's made me hungry."

"I can have sandwiches brought in, if that's all right with you," he offered.

"Is that really necessary?" Ellie asked.

"Afraid so. We have things to discuss, and it has to be done before the show is over." Nudging through the mob, he called over his shoulder, "Follow me."

Ellie handed Flora the blue ribbon, plucked Lulu from her arms, and let the woman go ahead of her. Before she could follow, there was a tap on her shoulder and the bald-headed man she'd seen standing with Edward earlier gave her a nod.

"Congratulations. That's the third time your dog bested mine in the ring. I was hoping things would turn out differently today, but . . ." He shrugged. "Better luck next time."

Unable to comment, Ellie raced to catch up with Flora. Sam needed to be told about Felicity Apgar, but did it have to be now? She'd barely caught her breath. Her head was still fuzzy. She had to prepare for whatever came next.

"I hear the wheels turning," said Lulu, radiating calm. *"What's the problem?"*

Impressed at Lulu's cool demeanor after such a big win, she said, "Too many things to name."

"If it were me, I'd start by telling the detective

about that piece of bait someone dropped on the ring floor. Lucky for me, I'm so focused. It would have totally broken a lesser dog's stride."

Ellie was so jazzed about the win that she'd completely forgotten the sneaky trick. And logically, there was only one person who could have done it. The handler who'd competed directly ahead of them. Edward Nelson.

"Do you think Edward did that stride slow-down thing on purpose, too?"

"Well, duh. Of course he did."

Annoyed, Ellie pulled back her shoulders. "Are you thinking what I'm thinking?"

"I think Edward is jealous of the fact that you took over for Arnie instead of him."

"That's stupid. Edward couldn't have shown you. He was already committed." A man and woman stared at her, and Ellie realized she was again holding an open conversation with a canine. "Let's talk about it later."

They caught up to Sam and Flora at the hall that led to the business center, where Sam stopped at the manager's office and held the door wide. "Wait here. I'll be back with lunch."

Inside the room, Flora collected her baby and took a seat. "Let me hold her for a while," she said, nuzzling Lulu. "What do you think the detective has to tell us?"

"I don't have a clue," said Ellie, taking the same seat she'd been in yesterday. "But we're going to find out. In the meantime, there's a couple of things I need to ask you."

Flora nodded. "Go ahead."

"Best in Group is next, correct?"

"Yes."

"Will the rest of the competition happen today or tomorrow?"

"The way I understand it, the officials juggled the schedule until their eyes crossed, but there was no way they could finish the show today. They expect the seven Best in Group finals to take place at three o'clock tomorrow. After a two-hour break, Best in Show will go on as planned." She ran a hand over Lulu's head. "Unfortunately, they can't make a final decision until they get all the owners and handlers on board, even though they've already cleared it with the television station. If there's a change, I'll be notified and it will be my responsibility to call you. They also plan to announce the times on the television news and in the morning papers."

Ellie heard "television" and the rest of Flora's explanation grew dim. If her mother found out that she'd appeared on TV and hadn't told her, there'd be hell to pay. The problem was, Georgette would give an unasked-for critique on her daughter's hair, makeup, and wardrobe if she watched. Ellie was damned if she did and damned if she didn't.

Flora sighed. "I don't know how I'll ever repay you for doing this. You are a dear."

Drowning in guilt, Ellie frowned. If Mrs. Steinman only knew how many times she'd wanted to back out, how many excuses she'd formed but hadn't uttered, she wouldn't think her dog walker was quite so "dear." "Lulu is a part of my family. I'll always be there, for both of you."

"Give her the lowdown on Edward," the Havanese encouraged. *"She should know what that bum did."*

"There's something I have to tell you, though I'm not positive of it," Ellie began. "It's about Edward—"

The woman patted her hand. "He's a stinker."

"You know what he tried to do?"

"I might be old, but I'm still in control of all my faculties. I've seen Edward use that bait-dropping trick before, even told him not to do it when he was handling my girl. He didn't because he knew better than to cross me, but I never thought . . ." She heaved another sigh. "I failed to warn you because I didn't think he'd have the nerve to use it against my dog."

"Then I was lucky that Lulu was too focused to pay attention."

"She's a professional," Flora agreed. "Right down to her toenails."

"Told you so." Lulu snorted to emphasize the point.

"I know you did—er—I mean, you're right." Ellie stroked the dog's muzzle. "She's quite a canine."

"What do you suppose is keeping Detective Ryder?" Flora asked. "It's past my lunchtime."

"If you can't wait for Sam, I could always run to the concession stand and—"

Just then the detective walked in bearing a tray. "Here you go, ladies. Sorry it's not gourmet fare, but it's all I could find on short notice. Help yourselves."

"Hot dogs," Flora said, sounding like a six-year-old. "I haven't had a frankfurter in ages." She set Lulu on the floor and walked to the desk. "These look delicious."

Ellie pushed their chairs closer to the food and smiled at Sam. "Thanks."

"Don't mention it." He chose a hot dog, added mustard from a small packet, and took a bite. "We can eat while we talk, if that's all right with you."

After choosing a wiener, Ellie added mustard and grabbed a can of Diet Coke. "Who goes first? You or one of us?"

"Let me ask questions and you answer. Mrs. Steinman can comment if she knows more or disagrees." He flipped open his spiral notebook. "Tell me about this morning."

"When I arrived at our stall, a woman named Felicity Apgar was making trouble for Flora. She

127

took a couple of shots at her and one at me, too. She'd already pestered her about handling Lulu when Flora was alone yesterday."

"I already talked to her and didn't get a bad vibe—"

How come Sam never checked things out when she got a "bad vibe"? She gave Flora a sidelong glance and saw that she was feeding Lulu a bit of her hot dog. "There was talk of Felicity doing something unsavory a couple of months back. If you ask me, she's a prime candidate for wanting to get rid of Arnie."

"I'll check with Vince, see if he's heard anything of it, but I don't think—"

"You do that, and bear in mind that women who want to get ahead in their field can be just as unscrupulous as men."

Sam swallowed the last of his hot dog and took a drink of coffee. Then he turned his attention to Flora. "Mrs. Steinman, do you have anything to add to this discussion?"

Flora dabbed her mouth with a napkin. "I still don't believe all this. Ellie told me the medical examiner was now fairly certain that Arnie had been murdered, but it simply doesn't make sense. I can't imagine anyone killing someone over a canine competition, especially a man as sweet as Arnie."

"Care to give me your thoughts on this Apgar woman?" he reminded her in a patient tone.

"Felicity is excitable, but so are many people, and what I heard was nothing more than rumor. I don't even remember what was said." She fisted a hand against her pale lips. "I simply don't understand how a person can take another person's life."

"Trust me, killers have a million excuses," Sam intoned. "I've investigated a couple hundred violent deaths, and I've learned that money, jealousy, and a thirst for revenge can bring out the worst in a person. I need help pinpointing who might have one or more of those intentions."

"What about those two young guys, the J brothers?" asked Ellie when she realized Flora wasn't focusing on Sam's question. "And let's not forget Edward Nelson. If you ask me, they're our best suspects."

Sam upended his coffee cup, set it on the tray, and stood. "Mrs. Steinman, would you excuse us for a minute?" He clasped Ellie's arm. "We'll be back in a second."

Ellie raised her eyes to the ceiling as she followed him out. Now what?

Sam's gaze swept the hall before he drew her into the office across the way, where he sat her in a chair. "Take the load off, Nancy Drew, and listen up for a second."

Oh, boy. She'd heard him use that long-suffering tone before. "Don't start with me, Sam. Like it or not, I'm involved in this case, especially if I'm next on the killer's hit list."

He stepped closer. "I know Edward Nelson is a person to watch, but what about those two younger men? Did either of them give you a hard time? Threaten you or make you uneasy?"

"No, but they should still be suspects in this case."

He shook his head. "You are one pain in the ass, you know that? How many times do I have to say it? For you, there is no case. And now that I've done some homework, I'm not sure you're in danger."

Humph. Nice way to let me know, she thought. "Care to explain your thinking?"

"For one thing, the competition is over and your dog won. Since everyone saw you do a good job, it's too late to get rid of you."

"There's still the Best in Group and Best in Show trials. Felicity Apgar would probably sell her own mother to take Lulu around for those segments. Ditto the J guys and Edward."

"Maybe, but they have to know we'll be here to keep an eye on things. Plus, you're aware, too. After what happened, you'd be an idiot to let someone catch you alone, and you'd never eat anything a stranger handed you."

"Eat something? Are you saying Arnie was poisoned?"

"Considering the way he died, it's a logical deduction. The ME had to send that piece of liver and the rest of the treats in the victim's pocket pouch to Albany for analysis. Seems there are a couple of substances that cause a sudden drop in blood pressure, and our lab can't identify all of them."

Ellie opened and closed her mouth. "But Arnie told me he made those treats himself. Why would he deliberately swallow something that would harm him?"

"Beats me, but right now that's all we've got."

"Okay, so whoever the killer is knows I wouldn't eat anything strange, but they could follow me home and push me onto the subway tracks, or—or—shoot me." Realizing how lame she sounded, she frowned. "You know what I mean."

"Where's all this paranoia coming from? Usually you're the one telling me you can take care of yourself." His lips twitched. "I never figured you for a wussy."

Great, now he was laughing at her. "Oh, all right," she muttered, hating that he knew her so well. "Let's just say it's not me I'm worried for. It's Lulu."

"The fuzzy hamster?"

"Yes, the fuzzy hamster. What if her win has changed the odds and the bookmakers are angry? Or another handler is pissed that she'll be up against their dog in the toy group?"

Sam ran a hand through his hair. "For the love of—" Heaving a sigh, he looked at her as if she

131

belonged in a padded cell. "Okay, let's say the killer is after the dog. If that's the case, we should be more worried about Mrs. Steinman. The hamster's going home with her, not you."

Ellie's heart skipped a beat. She'd been totally self-absorbed. Flora needed a bodyguard, an escort . . . someone to keep an eye on her until the show was over. "You're right. I've been selfish, worrying about myself when Flora and Lulu are the ones at risk." She stood. "I have to warn them—er—her."

"Take it easy. I was only joking." He grasped her elbow. "I can't believe she or her mutt is in danger."

"Lulu's not a mutt."

"I know, I know." He opened the office door and led her back into the hall. "Have dinner with me and we'll talk about it. I have a couple of things to take care of here, then I'll call Dr. Bridges and see if anything else popped up in the autopsy. After that, I should be able to slip away for a quick bite."

"No, thanks. Rudy and I are spending the night with Flora."

"I'm sleepin' with Lulu. I'm sleepin' with Lulu." Rudy paced alongside the bed. His singsong voice had been going nonstop for the past ten minutes. *"How about you spritz me with a little cologne? Maybe give me a swig of your mouthwash?"*

Ellie bit the inside of her cheek to keep a straight face. Her boy was gaga, completely silly, over the moon with happiness, all because he was spending the night at Flora's. She slipped a clean sweater into her roller bag and added a sleep shirt and robe. Walking to the closet, she stared at the offerings. "You don't need cologne or mouthwash. Now help me out here. What should I wear for the next big event?"

At her request for a fashion consultation, the yorkiepoo came to attention. *"How about the suit that matches that disgusting vegetable you made me taste last week. The purple one. Egg something or other."*

"Hmm. Maybe I should ask Viv. She might even have something I can squeeze into that's perfect for television."

"Why ask me if you weren't going to listen?"

Ellie sat on the bed and grinned. "Because Viv's not color-blind and she actually keeps up with fashion trends."

"Hey, I watch Tim Gunn whenever you do. The man's a genius on style."

Before Ellie could comment, there was a knock on her door. "That's probably Viv. She's left a couple dozen messages on my cell, and I haven't had time to call her back. You and I can talk while we walk to Flora's."

Arriving in the foyer, she peeked through the peephole, then unlocked and opened the door.

"You're harder to track than a polar bear in a snowstorm," Viv declared as she barged inside. "What the hell is going on? And please don't tell me you're the one they were talking about in that newspaper article."

Ellie led her best friend into the kitchen and went to the fridge, where she pulled two containers of their favorite ice cream from the freezer. "Sit," she commanded, plunking their leftover pints of Häagen-Dazs Caramel Cone on the table. She removed spoons from a drawer and handed one to Viv. "This might take a while."

Viv snapped off the lid and did as commanded. After downing a huge spoonful, she heaved a contented sigh. "Okay, I'm ready. Shoot."

The gooey caramel and chocolate melted on Ellie's tongue before she spoke. Fifteen minutes later, Viv scraped the last of her ice cream from the pint and licked the spoon clean. "Good Lord, girl, if I was superstitious, which I'm not, I'd say there's a huge black cloud hanging over your head."

"Seems like, doesn't it?" Ellie capped her container. "I'm surprised I have any clients left at all, considering how many murders I've been involved in over the past year."

"And Sam is the lead detective again? What are the odds?"

Standing, Ellie tossed Viv's empty into the trash and returned her carton to the freezer.

"Trust me, the good detective isn't happy about it either."

"I'll bet." Viv grinned. "Not to change the subject, but what are you going to wear?"

"Just jeans and a sweater. Flora's not formal or anything."

Viv tsked. "I'm not talking about tonight. What are you wearing for the show's televised segments?"

"Beats me. Rudy and I were going over my wardrobe choices when you knocked."

"I'll bet he had a couple of good suggestions," Viv said jokingly. "Doggie drab? Puppy puce or maybe canine coral?"

"Very funny. Come on, give me a hand."

Viv followed her to the bedroom and plopped on the bed. "You're not packing for tomorrow now, are you?"

"Nope, just planning. I'll have breakfast with Mrs. Steinman, do morning rounds, check in with Joy, and come back here to drop off Rudy and change. Flora's picking me up in her chauffeured limo at one thirty."

"Wow, talk about star treatment."

"I know. Except for Sam's old Chevy and the city's yellow cabs, it's been years since I've been driven anywhere."

"Hah! You were lucky the D took you in a taxi. Good thing he was out to impress his clients or he would have made you ride the subway to the theater."

Afraid thoughts of her ex-husband might ruin her night, Ellie pulled the plum-colored pantsuit from her closet and held it to her chest. "What do you think?"

"Hmm. What color top?"

Laying the suit across the bed, she returned to the closet and scanned the shelves. "I have black and . . ." She flipped through her blouses and sweaters. "Black. Or white. How about this cashmere sweater?"

"Still black, but not too shabby."

Ellie sighed. "If I had time, I'd go to Saks, but I don't think I can squeeze it in. This will have to do."

"What about something bold yet tasteful to break up the single shade? Like a scarf?"

"Don't have one of those," Ellie said.

"But I do. Come down and take a look."

"Okay, sure."

Rudy yawned and began licking his privates. Viv took one look at him and bounded toward the bedroom door. "You really need to do something about your dog."

"Hey, my owner's not giving me a bath," Rudy complained. *"I gotta do something to tidy up."*

"Just don't mess the coverlet," Ellie warned him, picking up the suit. "I'll be back in a couple of minutes and we can leave."

A few moments later, she sat on Viv's king-size bed and participated in an accessory show. Vivian tossed designer scarves from a drawer like a magician tugging hankies from his sleeve, then held up a silky swath of cloth in shades of gold and cream and laid it across Ellie's suit. "What do you think?"

"Fine. But I'll probably bring it to the show and have Flora tie it. I'm all thumbs when it comes to stuff like that."

"Whatever." Viv sat beside her on the mattress. "Speaking of Flora, how is she holding up?"

"So far she's put on a brave front." Ellie folded the scarf and tucked it in one of the suit's pockets. "But I can tell she's miserable inside. I'm afraid that at her age the stress of this competition and the loss of a sweetheart might do her in."

"What did Sam say about it? Does he see it your way?"

"So far, he's been too busy lecturing me to show any concern for Flora."

"Are you still angry with him for issuing that ultimatum?"

Ellie shrugged. "Now that I've had time to think about it, I guess not."

"Because he said the two of you are a couple?"

"Not exactly, but it did get me going for a while. I vowed I'd never be the better half of a couple again, and—"

"Does that mean you've forgiven him for what he did in April, and he thinks you'll sleep with him?"

"He's been angling to get back in my bed for

the last few months, but I'm still on the fence. I doubt he'll give it a thought now that this case fell in his lap."

"He's a man, kiddo. Sex is the one thing they always think about, job or no job. And why are you still unsure?"

Standing up, Ellie told herself she should have left before Viv had the chance to dissect her love life. "I have to run."

"Come on, let me in on what you're going to do about Detective Dreamy." Viv followed her to the door. "If you do, I'll tell you about me and Dr. Dave."

Ellie turned at the front door. "What about you and the adorable vet?"

"Uh-uh." Viv propped herself against the foyer wall. "You go first."

"Right now all I can say is sex is the farthest thing from my mind. I can't think about going to bed with Sam until this entire episode is over."

"Are you confident Lulu will win tomorrow?" Mr. T wandered into the hall and sat at his mistress's feet, where Viv picked him up. "I bet if my little man was entered, he'd win. Wouldn't you, sweetheart?"

The Jack Russell gave Viv's cheek a lick, then gazed at Ellie. *"I got her wrapped around my left paw."*

"I'm sure he would, if the judge was blind," Ellie answered, shaking her head.

138

"Hey, fool, I'm a purebred just like Ms. Pickypants."

"I have Twinks's papers. Maybe I should start showing him." Viv's brown eyes brightened. "Hey, now that you have the experience you could be his—"

"Oh, no. Find someone else to wield a whip and chair to keep him in line." Ellie gazed at her naked wrist. "Good golly, look at the time. I've got to run." She opened the door and slipped into the hall, but she heard Twink grumble all the same.

"Wait until next time, Triple E. Nobody talks like that about Mr. T."

Chapter 8

Ellie and her fuzzy buddy spent a pleasant night in Mrs. Steinman's large, airy, and—what else—pale pink guest bedroom complete with private bath, brass towel warmer, and Jacuzzi. Rudy considered the sleepover a rousing success because sometime before dawn Lulu sneaked into the room and snuggled with him in the doggie bed Flora had provided. Even though the canines whispered greetings when they met, Ellie heard every word, and once awakened, she wasn't able to fall back to sleep.

After eating Nelda's expertly prepared breakfast of bacon, pecan waffles, and fresh fruit, she and Rudy set out on their morning rounds and finished the walks without a hitch. On their way home, she decided to call her assistant and make sure all was in order for the dogs that needed a second outing later in the day.

"Hey, Joy," Ellie said when the girl answered. "Are you set for this afternoon?"

"Um . . . sure." There was a long silence, then, "I guess."

Ellie's brain jumped into uh-oh mode. "Is something wrong?"

"Not exactly. It's just that . . . would you mind if I ask my pal Marilee to take over for me?"

Who the heck is Marilee? "How good a friend is she? Have I met her?"

"I don't think you know her, but we're very close. In fact, we were roomies for a while, until she dropped out of college to go into . . . another line of work."

"Does she know anything about dogs?" Ellie asked, unhappy with the change in plans.

"She told me she had one when she was a kid."

Having a canine as a child and being responsible for walking a dozen in a couple of hours in one of the busiest sections of Manhattan were two completely different things, but Ellie kept that thought to herself. She didn't want to sound cranky when it was obvious that Joy had a problem.

"And Marilee is trustworthy? Giving her the

keys to those high-end apartments is a risk, you know." A risk she didn't want to take, but what else could she do?

"I'm well aware of that," Joy answered, her tone ruffled. "She's come with me on a few walks, so she knows the drill."

This was the first Ellie had heard of Joy bringing a companion along on the job. "And you'll give her the dogs' names, their apartment addresses, and the keys, correct?"

"Yep."

"And she'll return the keys to you by the end of the afternoon, say immediately after the last walk? That way I can meet you tomorrow at your morning stop and collect them."

"Definitely. Look, I'd never leave you in a bind if it wasn't important, but something came up and I—I gotta go."

Ellie slipped the phone in her tote bag when she heard the dial tone. Now what? Joy had her only extra set of keys, and there was no one else to call for help. If Marilee whoever did a bad job, Ellie would take the heat her offended clients were certain to dish out. Worse, if someone lodged a complaint about a theft or breakage, the bonding agency wouldn't honor the claim. They might even drop her completely.

"I say you run another ad," Rudy told her. *"That chick's as flaky as the Pillsbury Doughboy."*

"I thought you liked Joy."

"She was definitely better than the other nut jobs you tried out. I would have hired her on looks alone."

They crossed at the light on Park and Seventy-second. "That is such a sexist remark."

"I'm a guy. What can I say?"

Ellie ignored his comment, made a left onto Lexington and aimed for the nearest Joe to Go. She had a sudden thirst for coffee, but it had to be decaf. The last thing she needed was a drink that would add to her jitters. It was bad enough she had the MACC competition on her mind. Now she had to worry about a stranger taking over her afternoon run. Maybe she should take another look at the list of candidates she'd amassed, people who had answered her ad but for one reason or another didn't fit the bill. She'd thought Joy the best of the bunch. Now she wasn't so sure.

Rudy watered a trash can and she smiled. If only . . . "Sometimes I wish you were human. I know you'd never let me down or change plans like Joy just did."

"Trust me? To walk canines? You've got to be kidding."

Ellie skittered to a stop. "Hang on. Are you saying you wouldn't want to be a dog walker?"

"That's exactly what I'm saying."

"Why not?"

"Because besides scooping poop, the grousing and whining you put up with would drive me batty. If I have to listen to that dopey Poodle one more time—"

"Which dopey Poodle? We walk three."

"The new guy—Ranger. He's a hypochondriac, same as the diva who owns him."

"What do you know about his owner?"

"Just what he tells me. The woman sprays her throat with some special lemon and honey mix a dozen times a day. She wears a mask to block germs whenever she goes outside. And every time she gets a cough, Ranger gets one, too. Same with a headache or a sore pinkie toe."

"If I had Sunny Russo's golden voice, I'd be careful, too. The way I understand it, a woman with her mega-career can't afford to be under the weather. The Metropolitan Opera allows a star only so many sick days. If she's ill too often, she might not get another contract."

"Ranger says the same thing, but when he talks you'd think he was the one with the million-dollar recording deal."

"I haven't talked with her often, but I get the impression Sunny sees Ranger as more of a sympathetic friend than a pet. Her son doesn't come around very often, and if the tabloids are correct, there isn't a man in her life. She needs the little guy just like I need you."

"Please don't compare what you and I have to

anyone else. Unless, of course, you know of another human-canine couple who can do what we do."

"I have no idea if any other dogs and owners hold intelligent conversations, but that doesn't mean they're not out there. In fact, those that do are probably keeping quiet about it in case people hear them and think they're crazy. I didn't hear Ranger complain today."

"Oh, no? Well, guess what? The diva woke with a sour tummy, so she took a shot of Pepto and gave him one, too. He let everybody in the pack know, just in case he urped something up."

Her dogs were always "urping something up." She'd seen every color of the rainbow and every consistency in their upchuck, and she'd learned to take it in stride. "I thought it was odd when Sunny didn't come to the door to say hello this morning. Do you think she's really ill?"

"Ill—schmill." He gazed at her with a doggie glare. *"How about a lawyer joke to brighten the day?"*

"You haven't told me one of those in a while. Shoot."

He kept his focus on her as he walked. *"What's black and brown and looks good on a lawyer?"*

Ellie smiled. "What?"

"A pissed off Doberman Pinscher."

Rolling her eyes, she moaned. "That's terrible. Jokes like that give certain breeds a bad name.

Now answer my question. Do you think Ranger told the truth. Is Sunny ill?"

"I don't want to strain my brain on that neurotic pair for another second. Let's talk about the MACC. Did you and Flora plan strategy for today?"

"Not really. Flora said all I have to do is exactly what I did yesterday. Smile and give Lulu the lead. She'll take care of the rest."

"That's my girl."

"You and Lulu were very chummy before sunrise. If I'd had a camera, I would have snapped a picture of the two of you snuggling in that mink-lined doggie bed."

"I thought that fur smelled familiar."

"Familiar how? I don't own a mink coat."

"You don't, but Georgette does."

"I thought Mother had a silver fox."

"The woman has one of each. She also has a full-length Royal Crown Russian sable that goes for a hundred-fifty grand on sale."

Stunned by Rudy's statement, Ellie gasped as she led him into the coffee shop. Ever since this past summer, when she'd left him in front of the store and he'd been kidnapped, Joe had given her permission to bring the yorkiepoo inside. He promised that if someone reported him to the health department, he would say Rudy was a service dog, which allowed him in eating establishments.

When she scanned the counter and didn't see her college friend, she ordered a large decaf caramel bliss and stepped to the side to wait for her drink. As soon as she was certain no one cared about Rudy's presence, she squatted. "I couldn't tell the difference between Russian sable and a plastic rain slicker. How do you know Mother has one?"

"Don't you pay attention when she starts flapping her gums? Stanley gave it to her for Christmas."

"Christmas? But that's six—seven weeks away."

"I heard about it at Georgette's last 'brunch and brag.' She told a guest the judge gave her the coat early, so she wouldn't be cold for a single day this winter. Poor old Stanley has it bad."

Ellie had to agree. Her mother's sixth husband was totally besotted and spoiled his wife to the max. But the price Rudy quoted for a coat was outrageous. Stanley was wealthy, not stupid. "What makes you such an expert on the cost of luxury sable?"

"Your mother throws around designer names and prices like they were confetti. She name-dropped some guy named Zanotti and his seven-hundred-dollar shoes, then told the same guest about the coat, and the woman was so shocked she dropped her smoked salmon and caviar canapé. The treat practically fell into my lap. Needless to say, Georgette didn't appreciate my effort to clean her carpet."

Ellie stood, retrieved her coffee, and headed out the door. She had no time to discuss the many reasons Rudy didn't get along with her mother. Besides, once Georgette realized that her only child had neglected to inform her of her television appearance, Ellie would be sharing the doghouse with her fuzzy buddy.

But she couldn't chance screwing up this afternoon, and that's exactly what would happen if she thought her mother was watching the MACC and jotting down everything she did wrong. Knowing that Georgette would rather buy "off the rack" than turn on a dog show was the one thing that helped keep Ellie's sanity intact.

Firmly pushing Georgette out of her mind, she climbed the steps with Rudy to their apartment. She had to get ready for the event of a lifetime.

Two hours later, Peebles pulled up outside the Javits Center and scurried around to open the limo door. While Ellie climbed from the vehicle, she heard a confident Flora give her driver the afternoon off. The grinning chauffeur tipped his hat, jumped back in the car, and steered the white stretch Mercedes into traffic like he was late for lunch with a NASCAR driver.

"Flora, do you think that's wise?" Ellie asked as the vehicle disappeared. "If Lulu doesn't win Best in Group, you'll still need a ride home."

"I've taken cabs before, and Peebles will be

available after seven to drive us home. If my baby doesn't win the first competition, I plan on the two of us drowning our sorrows in a bottle or two of Roederer Cristal Rosé. After all we've been through, we'll deserve champagne."

"Champagne? Oh, but I don't think—"

"Of course, champagne. Mr. Steinman always used to say nothing cheered a body up like a five-hundred-dollar bottle of bubbly, and I agree."

Five hundred dollars? *A bottle!* Ellie almost swallowed her tongue. Besides her mother's wedding to Stanley, the only champagne she'd had since her own marriage was what Georgette offered at her brunches. Her mother was no slouch when it came to serving the best, but even she didn't buy wine that pricey.

Flora handed the Havanese to Ellie, wrapped her coat tightly around her, and headed into the Javits Center like a diminutive queen. If she'd had the nerve, Ellie would have asked Flora what type of fur she wore, but it didn't really matter. Fifteen years ago, when Georgette began her marry-for-money quest, Ellie decided that she herself never wanted the luxuries a couple of million would bring.

She enjoyed drinking beer and eating pretzels just as much as she liked Häagen-Dazs, filet mignon, and lobster tails, and someday she might want a bigger apartment, but that was it. She had a job she loved, good friends, and an exceptional dog by her side. What more could a girl ask for?

"Hey! Keep up. Flora's on the escalator," Lulu yipped.

She hurried to catch the matron, who was about halfway up the moving staircase by the time Ellie and her charge made it onto the steps. It was then that she spotted Edward Nelson standing beside Flora. When the man bent sideways and draped an arm around the senior's shoulder, she had to smile. "It looks as if your old handler is wishing your mistress good luck in today's competition. Maybe he's not such a bad guy after all."

"Hmmph," Lulu snorted. *"Don't believe it. This business is loaded with people who pat you on the back with one hand while twisting the knife with the other."*

"Jeez, lighten up," Ellie muttered. When the woman in front of her turned and glared, she added, "Uh, not you. I was talking to my dog."

The woman nodded as if she understood, which was no surprise. Every person at the MACC was a dog lover, and each of them had probably said the same thing to a four-footed friend at one time or another. Stepping off the escalator, she dodged spectators as she raced to catch up to Flora, who had stopped to speak to the dreaded Felicity Apgar.

"Do you think I should interfere?" Ellie asked Lulu.

"Give the old girl a chance to defend herself. She's a lot tougher than you think."

149

After a few moments of chitchat, Felicity bent forward and gave Flora a hug, which Flora returned with vigor. When the disagreeable woman walked away, Flora spotted Ellie. "I wondered when you would catch up. Come along. We don't want to be late."

Amazed by Flora's take-charge attitude, Ellie followed obediently. What had turned the sweet senior citizen with the charming personality into a drill sergeant?

When they reached the backstage holding area, she immediately noticed the change in atmosphere. Gone were the hundreds of wide-eyed visitors, bragging owners, and outgoing handlers. With fewer competitors and much more at stake, the smaller crowd was controlled . . . and very serious.

A steward greeted Flora and led them to Lulu's station. While Ellie got her charge settled, another steward stopped by with his clipboard raised, checked their names off a list, and handed Ellie her armband. Glancing at it, she saw that their competitive number was seven.

"Oh, good. They're keeping the names in breed order," Flora observed. "I love it when we're given such a lucky number."

Ellie straightened her suit jacket and let Flora help her with the armband, then pulled Vivian's scarf from her pocket and passed it over. "I'm all thumbs when it comes to tying one of these. Think you could do something special with it?"

"By all means. Just bend forward a bit."

Moments later, Ellie glanced down and found the gold-and-cream-colored scarf tied in a delicate knot and draped to hang just below the neckline of her black cashmere sweater.

"There." Flora brushed Ellie's jacket lapels. "You look lovely."

Before Ellie could thank her, a man hefting a huge camera on his shoulder and a woman holding a microphone approached. "Excuse me. I'm Carol Costello from Animal Planet," said the reporter. "Could we speak with you for a moment?"

Intent on staying out of the line of fire, Ellie stepped back and leaned against Lulu's table.

"What's wrong? Don't want to be interviewed?"

"Flora should handle the limelight. She's the one who tackled the work of getting you here."

"I beg your pardon?" the Havanese snipped. *"I got me here."*

"You know what I mean. Today belongs to Flora just as much as it belongs to you. She says you'll be retired after Westminster in February. Claims she's too old to keep up the pace of professional showings."

"That's why I plan to win here and at the big W. I intend to go out in a blaze of glory that will make her proud."

When the cameraman panned in their direction, Ellie turned her back, picked up a grooming brush, and fussed with the hair around Lulu's muzzle. After a few seconds, the dog sneezed. *"Enough already. They're gone. I'm surprised they didn't want to ask you about Arnie, you being his replacement and all."*

The incident reminded Ellie that she'd never asked Flora if she'd spoken to Arnie's children or knew anything about his funeral, but that really didn't matter. Once today was over, they'd have plenty of time to talk about things.

She glanced around the staging area, looking for Sam. It would have been nice to see him before going to the competition area, but he was probably on the floor keeping a lookout for anyone suspicious. She'd been meaning to ask him about the toxicology report on Arnie and the liver treats, but it had slipped her mind, as had most things since the MACC started. As soon as this contest was over, she'd make it a priority to catch up on Joy's problem, Arnie's funeral, everything.

She just had to survive the afternoon.

Sam scanned the show floor. The terrier group's competition was well under way. When the fanfare subsided and the ring cleared, the ankle biters were the next canines to take center stage. He'd meant to stop and check in with Mrs. Steinman and Ellie before their group lined up, but it was too late now.

Besides, his job was here in the thick of things. Vince had taken on the chore of assessing the backstage area, where he could listen to gossip, ask questions, and keep tabs on the handlers preparing to show their charges. Sam had to make sure that nothing unusual—make that deadly —happened out here. Especially to Ellie.

He trained his eyes on the competition ring, occupied by handlers, stewards, a judge, and about two dozen dogs that were parading around the perimeter like show ponies. Every so often he made certain his men were concentrating on the crowd, which consisted mostly of owners and their friends, seated immediately behind the action. Although he'd seen enough dogs in the past two days to give him a lifetime canine fix, he had to admit it was more interesting than watching a golf tournament or a spelling bee.

Minutes later, a hearty round of cheers signaled the end of the terrier competition. After the judge awarded the placement ribbons, the winning dog and handler accepted congratulations from the other competitors and circled the ring a final time. Then pictures of the canine were taken and reporters clamored for an interview with the honored pair. Finally, a voice on the loudspeaker announced that the toy group was ready to make its entrance.

He gave the arena floor another quick pass, then waited while the old group left and the smallest of the canines trotted in. Yep, there was his girl, her coppery curls shining under the barrage of lights as she led her dog into the ring. And she was competitor seven, a lucky number, too.

The entire herd rimmed the perimeter at a good clip, then stopped and stood next to signs identifying their breed. When Ellie squatted, ran a hand over her pup, and stood, it looked as if she was talking through her teeth, sort of like a novice ventriloquist.

Good thing most people were focused on the dog standing on the table, Sam decided, or they'd think she was off her rocker. Then again, with these nutso dog lovers, maybe no one would find it odd.

He alternated between watching the table and watching Ellie, nodding when she gave him a look he guessed was part panic over the situation and part relief that he was there. Knowing that he could be here for her was a nice feeling, he admitted, especially since she was always there for him.

Sometimes, when an investigation didn't go right or he reached a dead end on a case, she was the perfect person to talk to. Unlike Carolanne, his first wife, Ellie knew exactly what to say to ease his anger, convince him to find a fresh approach and, more importantly, make him smile. Being here, even if it was in an official capacity, was the least he could do for her.

Glancing at the lineup, he realized she'd be on in two more dogs. Next thing he knew, his fingers were crossed and he was holding his breath. She led her pocket pooch to the judging table and hoisted it up, where the tiny dog gave the same stellar performance she'd given a day earlier, including what Ellie referred to as a "perfect stack."

The judge, a stern-faced older guy who stood about five feet tall, asked her a question and she nodded. Then she set her dog on the floor, waited while Lulu did a bit of fancy prancing, and led the hairy hamster into and across the ring, where the dog gave her usual Academy Award–winning performance.

When she brought Lulu back to their place in line, she drew a breath so huge that Sam saw it from across the ring. Time seemed to slow as he gazed at her, hoping to catch her attention and give her a thumbs-up, but she was focused on her charge and the competition, nothing else.

Before he knew it, the judge walked down the row of contestants and pointed first at Ellie and her dog, then continued down the line, calling out others. Finally, a group of six canines stood in line. "Once more around the ring, please," the officious man ordered.

The handlers did as requested.

Sam blinked at what happened next, maybe from disbelief, maybe from surprise, but damn if it didn't occur.

"One," the judge said, thrusting a finger at Lulu.

Ellie stood like a statue, but her dog pulled her to the center of the floor as if it knew the time had come for a victory lap. When they finished their giddy march around the ring to the crowd's roaring applause, Ellie grabbed the pooch as it jumped into her arms.

Surrounded by photographers, the other competitors, and stewards, she scanned the area as if looking for someone special. Sam thought for sure it was Flora Steinman, until their gazes locked. Then, with glimmering tears in her eyes, she tossed him a brilliant smile.

Chapter 9

The Best in Group competition had finished an hour ago and Ellie was still shaking. Lulu had triumphed over the number-one-ranked Yorkshire Terrier in the United States, a champion Italian Greyhound, a high-ranked Pomeranian, even a world-class Maltese. When the judge had instructed her to bring the Havanese out as a finalist, she'd been elated. When he'd pointed at her dog and called out "One" she'd thought she might faint.

But Lulu had no intention of letting that happen. For an eight-pound pooch, she was strong as an ox and twice as stubborn. It was all

Ellie could do to rein her in before Lulu pranced into the audience and started giving pawprint autographs. After their victory lap, she practically had to wrestle the dog onto the podium for her championship photo. But once Lulu realized it was picture time, she stood in the stack position and gazed into the camera lens in an award-winning pose.

Now, as Ellie shared a quick bite with Sam in the Javits Center cafeteria, the knowledge that she still had one big—make that huge—hurdle to jump was just sinking in.

"Hey, you okay?" he asked.

"Hmm? Oh, yeah, I'm fine." Ellie hated getting caught in the middle of a daydream. "Sorry."

"There's nothing to be sorry about," he told her. "But I do think you should finish that pastrami on rye. You still have an important event ahead of you. You're going to need your strength to do it right."

She rolled her eyes. "That's one way to ruin a perfectly mediocre sandwich."

"Sorry, but it's the best advice I can give. I'm on deck for the big finish, just like you." He took a sip of his coffee. "I can't wait for this entire dog-athon to be over."

"Me, too," Ellie agreed. "But not for the same reason." She took a deep breath. "Having the best and the worst experiences of my life taking place on the same day has me edgy enough to

157

leap off the fifty-eighth floor of the Trump Tower."

"Don't even joke about that," he warned. "You looked like a pro out there. Maybe you should think about—"

"Ahh—no. Not a chance. I've done plenty of stupid things in my life, but becoming a professional dog handler will definitely not be making that list."

Sam grinned. "But count the pluses. No more heading out in hundred-degree temperatures or the freezing rain and snow to herd canines or scoop dog crap. Nor would you be required to walk ten miles a day. Your new job would be unusual, admired, even respected. Think of the party talk you'd inspire."

"I'm not into parties and the exercise is good for me." Those ten-plus miles she trekked every day took the place of a professional trainer's torturous workout agenda, something she'd dreaded doing when she'd been married. "The bad-weather trips aren't that terrible, either."

"How about all the free time you'd have?"

Ellie raised a brow. "Free time? According to the handlers I've talked to, I'd have to be gone three weekends out of four before I made any real money, and I don't have a place to keep and train the dogs I'd show, like most handlers have. Even more frustrating, I'd still need to deal with complaining hounds and griping owners, only they'd be snootier than the ones I care for now."

"I thought the owners complained, not the dogs."

"You know what I mean." She forged ahead, hoping to cover her slip. "Besides, I'd need a car to get to the show sites, which I don't have."

"You make a good living. You could buy one."

"After listening to you grouse about the parking problems in this city? Not a chance." She drank the last of her diet cola, thinking. Yes, she had a comfortable income now, but if she lost a few dogs or had to pay for a second assistant . . .

"Handlers only make money if they have clients, and those clients have to win. I wouldn't want to be in that competitive a position. Amassing enough canines to stay afloat in this town is tough enough."

Sam leaned back in his chair. "You could always branch out, become a regular small-business owner, hire people to walk the dogs you have now while you become a handler."

"Since when are you so concerned about my ability to support myself or the type of profession I've chosen?"

"Since I've seen how hard you work. You need another assistant, maybe two. I take it Joy is doing okay?"

Joy. She'd managed to put the girl out of her mind for today. Leave it to the discerning detective to bring up another of her worries. "Joy is . . .

having a problem. She's arranged for someone else to take her place this afternoon. Once I have the time to talk to her, we'll straighten it out."

"Is this 'someone' bonded and insured?"

Always a by-the-book cop, Ellie thought. "How about if we pretend you didn't ask that question and change the subject? Have you heard anything about Arnie's toxicology results?"

"Not much. That type of test result can take up to ten days to come through, but Bridges put a rush on it. She had to send the samples to Albany and some other lab she says handles difficult tests."

"Really? I'm impressed. But why?"

"That's something you don't need to know."

"Aw, come on, share a little."

"Let's just say it has to do with the suspects," Sam answered, frowning.

"Suspects?" Ellie downed a chunk of her sandwich. "Then you have more than one?"

"Never mind how many suspects I have."

"But why the rush?"

"Because one of them doesn't live in this city. If they're guilty, I'll have to wrap up the case before they leave for home, and that's going to be tough without a murder weapon."

"And which suspect might that be?" she asked in her best nonchalant tone.

"None of your business. This is my case, not yours."

"I'm just curious. Who are they?"

"Ellie," he said in that I'm-warning-you voice he used when he wanted her to stay out of things.

She grinned, hoping to tease him into cooperating. "Here's an idea. How about if I guess and you blink twice if I'm right?"

Sam gazed at her through narrowed eyes, then shook his head. "You are a trip."

"Please? Just this once."

He heaved a sigh. "Okay. Consider it your reward for leading that hairy hamster to a win and I'll do it this once."

She took a final bite of her pastrami and chewed, alphabetizing the suspects in her brain. "Felicity Apgar?" she asked after swallowing.

He groaned and slowly blinked—once—twice.

"The J boys."

When Sam just stared, she crossed her arms. "And why not the J boys?"

"For one thing, they live a couple hundred miles away. And whatever the killer used to lace that liver, if it was laced, was out of the ordinary—not something a twenty-two-year-old could get hold of easily."

"So it was poison? The ME is positive?"

"Not positive, but for some reason the old guy's blood pressure took a nosedive. Aside from poison, something caused that to happen. The only other thing that might have done it is the one we talked about that first day: sudden adult

161

death syndrome. Unfortunately, SADS is a long shot. Seems it almost always happens to adults under thirty, and Mr. Harris was way past that. Hence the idea of poison. If the ME can't identify the substance on the liver with this city's excellent forensic resources, it has to be unusual. Our data bank has a ton of toxins on file and none of them matched, so out it went."

"Best guess, what will she go for?"

"Bridges? She's never afraid to give a decision that will nab a bad guy, but she can't make things up. Without proof, probably SADS. She won't make a final statement until everything is in."

"And the killer will get a free ride. That sucks."

"I agree, but with no proof of foul play . . ."

"What would you need to prove foul play?"

"Something has to turn up in toxicology, for one thing. And a motive would be nice."

Right now, it sounded as if finding a motive would be easier than finding the cause of death. When he died, Arnie was leading a champion canine that any handler would be happy to call a client. If the killer took over, a blue ribbon here would have guaranteed him or her more jobs than could be manageable, which would lead to bigger fees and more bonuses. He'd also jump in his standing as a professional handler. Ellie filed the info away, planning to think on it later.

Sam finished his coffee and stood. "Are we done here?"

"Just one more name and then I'm through. Promise."

He mumbled something under his breath. "Fine. Last one."

"Edward Nelson."

She held her breath and waited. He finally gave two quick blinks, then looked at his watch. "There's less than an hour before the big event. I have to check with Vince, see if he's learned anything."

"And I have to call Viv and remind her to feed Rudy and bring him to her apartment so he can watch the show with her and Mr. T. Then I need to find Flora. She had dinner with a few friends, probably bragged up a storm. She's such a great lady."

"I can understand reminding your girlfriend to tune in, but your dog?" He grinned. "Isn't that overkill?"

Since there was no way to tell Sam that her best fuzzy friend loved watching Animal Planet, *DogTown*, *Dog Whisperer*, and anything else that had to do with canines, she gave a trumped-up response. "I've left Rudy home alone too often the past few days. He'll have fun spending time with Twink and Vivian. And it's possible he might recognize me on the screen, which could make up for my neglect."

"If you say so." He leaned forward and kissed her cheek. "Go get 'em, tiger."

"Yes, it's on now," Viv told her. "They started the segment by saying it was taped earlier, and they'll run the finals next. The terrier group just finished, and oh, my God, there you are, marching into the ring with Lulu and about twenty other dogs and handlers. How about giving me a clue." Her tone grew serious. "Did you win?"

"Just keep watching. You'll find out soon enough."

"Hang on. You must have won. Otherwise you'd be on your way home, no?"

"I don't want to ruin it for you, so I'm not saying."

"Well, crap. That is so not nice, making me wait."

"It's not going to take long, honest. We can talk until it's over."

"So what's up?"

"I just wanted to make sure you fed Rudy and gave him a walk."

"Of course I did. Then I brought him here to see you and Lulu triumph. Watching television seems to keep the boys too occupied to chew, bark, or lick their peckers, which is good enough for me. Now let me watch."

When Viv started to hum, Ellie said, "I can hang up if you want."

"Don't you dare. I want to—okay, you're on.

There you are, walking to the table . . . lifting Lulu up . . . now the judge is doing his thing . . . and now you're setting your girl on the floor. Oh, how cute. She's acting like she owns the place."

"I know. Isn't she great?"

"Uh-huh. Now you're walking down and back . . . stopping in front of the judge again . . . leading her to her place." Viv hissed out a breath. "I can't stand it. Tell me what happened."

"Nope, and it's time for me to hang up."

"Hang up and I'll call the ex-terminator," Viv threatened.

"Do that and I'll never speak to you again."

"I'd be happy to call Georgette and fill her in. You wouldn't even owe me a favor if I did."

Ellie sighed. "If you promise to take the call when Mother lectures me on my weight, my choice of dress, or how come I didn't tell her about the television show sooner, then sure."

"Do you think it'll be that bad?"

"Only if she finds out," said Ellie. "And I have my fingers crossed that it won't happen."

"Okay, but don't complain if you get a boatload of grief if she does hear about it."

"I figure she and the judge are eating dinner or watching *Wheel of Fortune* right about now, not flipping channels and looking for the latest in canine competitions."

"You are so naive. Georgette reads the newspapers, Judge Frye, too. That 'Death at the Dog

Show' story was on the front page of every rag in this city."

"But that doesn't mean she'll connect me to the murder. She has no idea I walk Lulu."

"The ex-terminator knows all and sees all," Viv joked in an exaggerated tone. "But it's your decision." Then she gasped. "This is it. The judge is walking down the line."

"Gotta run. 'Bye." Ellie snapped her phone closed and smiled. It wouldn't hurt to let Vivian watch Lulu's big moment alone. Besides, she was due at the Havanese's station in ten minutes. She stepped up her pace and arrived at her place with a minute to spare, where she found Flora cuddling Lulu and whispering endearments. "Sorry. I should have been here sooner, Mrs. Steinman. I hope you weren't worried."

Flora raised her gaze and gave a hesitant grin. "I knew you'd be here, dear. And I can't tell you again how grateful we are that you agreed to do this."

"I know you're grateful," Ellie said. "Just remember, it's only for this one show. You'll have to find a professional to take Lulu to Westminster."

"I understand." The older woman heaved a sigh and glanced at the waiting competitors. "No matter how often I've partaken in this experience, I still get goose bumps whenever my baby is about to perform. Watching her win is the only joy I have left in the world."

"Don't talk like that. There are plenty more fun things to come in your life," said Ellie, trying to sound positive.

She, too, inspected the backstage area. With only seven dogs in the final round, the noise level had dropped to a dim hum. Aside from the people clustered with the finalists, the area was now off limits to all but the main players: Owners, handlers and, in group order, an Irish Setter from the sporting group, a Beagle from the hound group, a Bedlington Terrier from the terrier group, Lulu from the toy group, an Akita from the working group, a Finnish Spitz from the non-sporting group, and a Belgian Tervuren from the herding group.

"Let me have Lulu, while you catch your breath and prepare yourself." Ellie held out her arms and collected the dog. Now was not the time to again confess that she was terrified of going into the ring, and doubly terrified of appearing live on national television. "I'll give her a final brushing while we wait for the announcer's call."

She set Lulu on the table and ran a grooming brush through her bangs. Lulu raised her muzzle to the ceiling and Ellie stroked her jaw. "Are you ready to win, little girl?"

"I'll be fine, as long as you remember the rules: Smile, hold the leash, and walk like you know what you're doing. I'll take care of the rest."

"Hang on while I fluff your ears," Ellie said, then dropped her voice to a whisper. "And stop telling me what to do."

"I know I've been demanding, dear," Flora interjected, sidling next to her. "If I've given too many orders, please accept my apology, because I certainly didn't mean to boss you around." She placed a hand on Ellie's arm. "I'd so appreciate it if you gave me a good going-over as well. I haven't been in front of a mirror in hours. I must look a fright."

Ellie sent Lulu a warning glare, then gazed fondly at the older woman. Though there was no doubt Flora was a member of AARP, she could easily pass for ten years under her true age. "You haven't been demanding, it's just me. I can't wait for it all to be over."

"For right now, just tell me if my lipstick is bright enough and I'm presentable," Flora pleaded. "We can discuss the competition when it's over."

"Your hair and makeup are perfect," Ellie replied. "How could anyone fault you for wearing those lovely pearls or that fabulous coat?"

Flora fingered the double strand of dime-sized gems at her throat. "These were a gift from my husband on our twenty-fifth wedding anniversary. He said they were the best Tiffany's had to offer."

Which meant they cost a fortune, thought Ellie, keeping the comment to herself. "And when did you get that coat?"

"This old thing?" Flora ran her hand down the chocolate brown lapel of her full-length fur. "Phillip gave it to me on our first Christmas together. We weren't married, just engaged, which means I've had it for fifty years this coming holiday."

"Wow, it looks brand-new," Ellie said, admiring the lustrous fur.

"With regular wear, proper storage, and good care, a mink will last a century. Would you like to try it on?" Flora made a move as if to take the coat off. "You could borrow it for New Year's Eve. I certainly won't be going anywhere, and it's a shame to have it sitting in a closet."

Flora was a size two, a four at the outside. Ellie wouldn't fit into the elegant garment if she used a shoehorn and a can of WD-40, and if for some bizarre reason she did manage to squeeze into the coat, she was sure to spill something on it that would ruin it. "No, no. I couldn't."

"You mean that nice detective isn't taking you somewhere fancy to celebrate the New Year?"

Sam hadn't asked her to go anywhere fancy or fun. Then again, she'd be just as happy staying home with him while they watched the traditional televised ball drop in Times Square. "Uh, not yet."

"Come now, you must be spending the holidays together. I can tell from his protective attitude that you're his one and only girl."

Protective? Try commanding—overbearing. Better still, downright dictatorial. "Sam will probably be on call." Georgette expected her for Thanksgiving, of course, but she and the judge were going to Barbados from the middle of December into the new year. "I think we're playing it by ear."

"If you find yourself at odds, you and Rudy can celebrate with Lulu and me. Arnie was supposed to join us, but after what's happened that's impossible. I'm afraid—" She sniffed and a huge tear rolled down her cheek. Searching in her Chanel bag, she pulled out a tissue. "Needless to say, we'll be alone."

Again reminded of Flora's kindness and bravery, Ellie took a step closer and embraced her friend. She couldn't imagine losing a man, losing anyone you were fond of, just weeks before the holidays. "It's so nice of you to ask us. I don't want you to be alone either. How about if you and Lulu come to my mother's for Thanksgiving? We'll talk about Christmas after that."

Once the words left her mouth, Ellie realized she should have checked with Georgette before issuing the invitation. But it was too late now. She smiled, ready to speak again, when a disembodied voice rang over the loudspeaker.

"Attention, competitors. Please line up and enter the arena in number order. Competition will begin in ten minutes."

Her heart began to pound like a jackhammer. Flora must have seen the terror in her eyes, because she reached up and patted Ellie's cheek. "Not to worry. You look fit as a fiddle and ready to win." She picked up Lulu and passed her over. "Now go out there and show my baby off."

Sam and Vince stood at the end of the competition ring farthest from the examination table, comparing notes about the investigation. "Damn," Sam said, frowning. "I can't believe there's no gossip behind the scenes. Like I've been saying all along, these dog people are not normal."

Vince exhaled a frustrated breath. "You got that right. Instead of talking about the guy who was snuffed and exchanging theories on who might have done it, all they do is complain about the lousy judging, inferior arena, and what terrible things their handler did with their mutt. Swear to God, I never heard a more single-minded group of nut jobs in my life."

"So we've got nothing," Sam said in disgust. "Which means we're no farther along than we were a day ago."

"I have the background checks we ran on Felicity Apgar and Nelson to go over later,"

Vince offered. He grinned. "Did you tell Ellie I said she was awesome?"

Sam shrugged. "Sort of."

"What does that mean?"

"It means I let her know what a great job she did. You can tell her she's awesome yourself."

"What the hell's gotten into you?" Vince demanded. Gazing at his partner, his grin grew smug. "Let me guess—Nancy Drew is at it again. She's got a couple dozen ideas on how to solve this case and expects you to follow her lead."

Sam ran a hand through his hair. "She's not letting it rest. We got a quick bite in the cafeteria, and she quizzed me about the investigation as if I were a rookie."

"And you told her . . ."

He hunched his shoulders. "As little as possible."

"Sure. Right. Tell me another story."

"Swear to God, she was born with a manipulation gene to rival my mother's. I tell her to stay out of my playing field, and the next thing I know, I'm trying to catch the half dozen fly balls she's lobbing my way."

"She's a woman. They all have that gene." Vince rocked back on his heels. "Especially when the man they're manipulating is in love with them."

Muttering, Sam stared at his shoes. "Mind your own business, pal."

"Hey, you are my business. Besides, I told you about Natalie, didn't I?"

"You told me about Natalie because you're a wuss. I don't want to ruin another relationship, like I did with Carolanne."

Vince crossed his arms and puffed out his chest. "You're an idiot. Ellie is ten times the woman Carolanne is, and she's perfect for you." When Sam returned his gaze to the crowd, Vince shoved his shoulder. "Don't blow it, *pal.*"

Before Sam could answer, a patrolman hustled over and held out a legal-sized white envelope with NYPD printed on the front in large block letters. "Earlier today, this envelope was found taped to a mirror in one of the men's washrooms. The guy who found it turned it in to a security guard, and he handed it to one of us. Smithers just brought it in from testing. It's been dog-checked and gone over with the bomb squad. Since you're the lead detective on this case, the captain said I should give it to you."

Sam stared at the item in question. "Thanks." Accepting the envelope, he offered it to Vince. "You want to do the honors?"

His partner held up his hands and retreated a step. "You heard the man. You're the lead on this case, not me."

Sam slit open the envelope, removed the single sheet of paper folded inside, and read the contents.

CHECK FLORA STEINMAN'S COAT.

He suspected that the message, all caps and typed, had been printed on a computer. Typical of this sort of note, there was no signature and nothing else in the envelope. He passed it to Vince, who read it, then said, "It's obvious, isn't it? Someone's setting the old gal up for a fall."

"I'd say so, but it can't be overlooked."

"Oo-kay. Now what?" Vince asked.

Sam returned the message to the envelope, stuck it in his inside breast pocket, and took stock of the competition area. The show ring entry point was about twenty feet to their right and would give them a good view of the proceedings.

"I doubt Mrs. Steinman is going anywhere until after this is over, so we can let it wait."

"What do you think they want us to find?"

"It can't be much. I doubt the lady is carrying."

"Hey," Vince said with a chortle. "These days, just about everybody owns a gun. If I were an old woman with her kind of money, I'd want a little self-protection, too."

"Maybe so, but if she does own a weapon, I'm sure she has a license and everything is on the up-and-up. She doesn't seem the type to break the law." The announcement signaling the beginning of the final competition rang out, and Sam said, "Too late now. It's showtime."

"Ease up on the leash," Lulu ordered. *"You're choking me."*

"Then slow down," Ellie answered, keeping her voice low. They'd just entered the arena for Best in Show. "We're not running a race."

The Havanese grumbled something, but did as she was told.

"That's better. Now take a couple of deep breaths," Ellie advised. "You need to act like a winner, the way you did a couple of hours ago."

"Hmmph. Look who's talking."

They took their opening lap around the ring with the other competitors and Ellie scanned the full house. Subdued by the cheering fans, she barely noticed passing Sam and Vince, who were standing at the far end of the oval. Staring straight ahead, she kept up her pace and carefully led Lulu to the correct spot on the sidelines. Then she focused on the judge, a tall, thin man she'd seen around the competition hall.

"Do you know the judge?"

Lulu sat and followed Ellie's gaze. *"I've never seen him before. Seems fishy to me."*

"Fishy?"

"Uh-huh. I thought I knew every judge on the East Coast circuit. He must be from the other side. Flora's going to have a fit if she thinks this gig is rigged."

Sure enough, a few seconds later the announcer

introduced the judge, a Mr. Donald Renfrew from San Francisco.

"Told you so," Lulu said, her voice a whine.

The first dog, the Irish Setter from the sporting group, headed toward Mr. Renfrew, and Ellie bent down and ran a hand over her charge's furry head. "There's nothing we can do about it. Just be on your best behavior, and things will be fine."

Instead of answering, the Havanese focused on the judge as if trying to read his thoughts. Ellie didn't want to break the pup's concentration, so she did the same. Fifteen minutes later, they were called to the table.

Chapter 10

Lulu snorted, her disdain clear. *"I told you that judge was a plant from the West Coast."*

"It had nothing to do with the judge," Ellie answered for the hundredth time. Talk about a sore loser. Since finishing the competition, the petite pooch had done nothing but complain, whine, or cry, sometimes all at once, when Ellie gave her opinion of the final segment of the MACC.

"Of course, it didn't, dear," Flora responded, assuming that Ellie was speaking to her. "O'Shea's Mighty Castle is a beautiful dog. Today was simply his day to win."

Ellie and Flora stood at their station, making sure they hadn't left anything of importance behind before they headed out of the Javits Center. The winner of the MACC, an Irish Setter known as Mighty, had come in first, while Lulu had taken third.

"I'll admit he was something to watch, striding around that ring as if he already knew he'd won," said Ellie. "I just wish it had been Lulu."

"Losing to that big boy wasn't as bad as ranking behind that smart-ass Finnish Spitz," the Havanese chimed.

"I wish my baby had taken first as well," Flora agreed. "But every dog that competed here is already a champion. When that's the case, you never know what a judge will decide."

"That is such a load of squirrel poop." Lulu raised her snout in the air. *"I love the old girl, but she really needs to get a grip."*

Ellie wasn't about to waste her breath on another lecture. The canine was carrying on as if she'd been fed a bowl of rancid dog food or given an exploding chew treat. She couldn't wait to get away from the spoiled pup and cuddle with her own four-legged buddy.

"Should I go up front and hail a cab while you say your good-byes?" she asked Flora.

"There's no need. Peebles should be there waiting. He'll drop us at my place so we can open that bottle of champagne I mentioned earlier."

Ellie grimaced internally. She'd completely forgotten about Flora's promise of an expensive bottle of bubbly, whether they won or lost the MACC. She was exhausted from the day's adventure and relieved that it was over. The last thing she wanted was a drink, no matter how excellent its quality. But how to tell Flora?

"I really should go home to Rudy. He's been alone quite a bit these last few days, and though he's with a friend right now, I'm sure he misses me."

"Bring him to our place. I need to talk to someone who understands where I'm coming from," Lulu whined.

"I understand where you're 'coming from' just as well as—" Oops! She smiled at Flora. "Sorry—what I meant to say was that Rudy always understands where I'm coming from and tries to make me feel better. Right now, he probably thinks I abandoned him."

"We could ask Peebles to stop by your friend's apartment so you can pick the little fellow up," Flora offered. "He's such a sweet boy, and Lulu loves spending time with him."

"Thank you for the invitation," Ellic began, still hoping to worm her way out of the situation. "But aren't you tired from all the activity? I sure am."

"I'm a bit weary, yes, but I promised you champagne if Lulu won Best in Group, which she did." Flora ran her fingers through her dog's fur. "I only hope a celebration will take my girl's mind off her defeat."

"Defeat! I was robbed!"

Ellie had heard enough. Gently wrapping her hand around Lulu's muzzle, she lifted the dog into her arms. "I'd be happy to come over tomorrow, but for tonight I'm too beat to do anything more than collect Rudy and hit the sack."

"Le'go'mm'mzl."

Flora tightened the lapels of her mink coat and heaved a sigh. "Lulu does seem agitated. Perhaps it's best I take your suggestion and we turn in early." Pushing the strap of her handbag over her shoulder, she gave a mischievous grin. "But I have a wonderful idea. What do you think of my hosting another party tomorrow night? I could invite the same people who came to your training session, and if you give me a list, I'll have Nelda phone all your clients and invite them, too. Imagine the fun we'll have toasting both you and my baby."

"No fun for me!" the Havanese all but shouted, forcing Ellie to again pull the muzzle trick.

"*All* my clients? I don't know . . ." She took a mental count. "I walk about thirty dogs a day. If most of them attend, we're talking close to sixty canines and people. Adding those who came to the training session, you might have a hundred guests."

"My apartment is huge. Nelda can rent extra

chairs, tables, linens—anything we might need."

Ellie opened her mouth to speak, but Flora plowed ahead.

"I'll have her phone a pet catering service for dog treats and chew toys." She tilted her head. "Oh, and I have a dear friend, maybe you've heard of her? Lorilee Echternach? She designs specialty clothing for canines. Her dog coats sell at some of the priciest boutiques in this city."

Ellie was familiar with the exclusive and very expensive canine outerwear. She'd thought about getting one of Lorilee's coats for Rudy, but when she made the suggestion, he'd put his paw down with an ear-shattering "No!"

"Winter is nipping at our heels. I'll purchase a new coat for every dog who visits and we'll hand them out as a thank-you for attending," Flora continued.

Great. It was bad enough she had to put rain boots and fancy jackets on most of the fuzzlets she walked. Dressing and undressing each one in a designer coat would double her time on the job. "But you need to know sizes, color preferences, that sort of thing," she said, encouraging Flora to see reason. "It would be a shame to spend the money and find out the coats don't fit or weren't wanted."

Flora tapped a finger on her chin, acting as if she hadn't heard a word. "You only walk dogs of fifteen pounds or less, correct? I'll simply ask

Lorilee to bring everything she has in the smaller sizes, and we can hold a canine fashion show or—" She focused over Ellie's shoulder. "Hello, gentlemen. What can we do for you?"

Ellie turned and found Sam and Vince waiting.

"Mrs. Steinman, we need to speak to you for a minute," said Vince. He smiled at Ellie. "Nice to see you again, Ms. Engleman. Great job today. Congratulations."

"Thanks." She kept her eyes on Vince, just in case Sam's all-business expression signaled trouble. "Can you make this quick? Mrs. Steinman and I are on our way out."

The detectives exchanged a look, then Vince said, "Mrs. Steinman, would you mind removing your coat? We need to check something. It should only take a minute."

"Her coat?" Ellie said. "Whatever for?"

"It doesn't matter. They're welcome to have a look." Flora slipped the mink from her shoulders and held it out to Sam.

"Hang on a second." Ellie blocked the exchange with a raised hand and glared at both detectives. "Don't you need a warrant or something before you search a person's belongings?"

Sam narrowed his gaze. "Mrs. Steinman has two choices. She can come to the station with us now and wait there until we get a warrant, or she can cooperate and all this will be over in a minute or so."

"It's fine, really." Flora waved a hand. "Go ahead, Detective. I have nothing to hide."

Sam held the coat up while Vince checked the lining. When he reached inside the left outer pocket, he raised a brow, drew out a sealed sandwich bag holding what appeared to be a blob of brown caramel, and sniffed the contents.

"Give her back the coat," he told Sam.

After Sam did as requested, Vince handed him the bag, which Sam inspected in the same manner. Then, ignoring Ellie, he said to Flora, "We'll have to take this downtown."

"I have no idea what that is or how it got into my coat, so please do." The woman wrinkled her nose. "It doesn't appear to be anything I'd want."

Sam stuck the bag in his jacket pocket while Vince scribbled in his notebook, tore out the sheet, and gave it to Flora. "This is your receipt. We'll let you know where and when you can retrieve your property."

"Thank you, but I can say for certain that is not my property," Flora replied, putting on her fur.

Without another word, the detectives took off. Watching them leave, Ellie's gut churned. She had a good idea what the men had found, but didn't want to alarm Flora unnecessarily. "Are you positive you don't know how that bag got into your pocket?"

Flora reseated her purse strap on her shoulder.

"Of course I'm positive. I may be old, but I'm not senile."

"I'd never imply such a thing," Ellie said by way of apology. She shifted Lulu to her other arm. "I'm all set. Are you ready to leave?"

"Certainly. I have a party to plan."

"You looked like you were born to the job. Honest. If I didn't know about your silly fear of performing in public, I would have thought you were a pro," said Vivian, ever the cheerleader. "I can't imagine the ex-terminator complaining about a single thing if she watched the show."

Vivian had been spouting positive reinforcement from the moment Ellie stepped in the door to retrieve Rudy. She appreciated her best friend's upbeat attitude, but felt positive that no matter how hard she tried to cover her tracks, her mother would find out about her daughter's momentary foray into television. "I can only hope." She snapped Rudy's leash to his collar. "I take it the boys were good while the MACC was running?"

"They were angels. Once the competition began, neither of them took their eyes off the screen, even during the commercials." Vivian gave a mock shudder. "Actually, it was sort of creepy."

"Wanted to see if Little Miss Pickypants blew her chance at stardom," groused Mr. T. *"She did."*

Rudy gave a low growl. *"Watch it, pal. That's my girl you're dissing."*

"She ain't nobody's girl, fool. Least of all yours."

"Oh, yeah? Well, how about we hear what Lulu has to say on the subject?" Rudy sassed.

"Hush." Ellie tugged the leash, jerking the yorkiepoo near. No way was she prepared to break up a canine wrestling match. Smiling at Vivian, she headed out of the living room. "Be prepared. You're probably going to get a phone call from Nelda."

"Mrs. Steinman's housekeeper?" asked Viv, following Ellie to the door. "Why?"

Ellie explained the reason for the party, ending with, "If you ask me, I think she's bummed about losing Arnie and Lulu's defeat, and needs something to take her mind off things." She opened the door. "Since Arnie died, that Havanese is all she has in her life."

"You think it would be okay if Dr. Dave joined us?"

"He's Lulu's vet, so why not?" Ellie propped a shoulder against the door jamb. "How are things going between the two of you, by the way?"

"Dr. D got called out on an emergency last night, so he didn't come back to my place. Other than that, things are moving along. What about you and Sam? Anything new in the investigation department?"

Ellie stepped into the hall. She didn't have the

strength to fill Viv in on all that was happening, including the Baggie the detectives had found in Flora's mink. "I'll tell you about it later. Right now, I just want to go to sleep."

"Are you walking Rudy first?"

"Yep. Then we're calling it a night."

"Hang on a second while I get shoes and a jacket, and T and I will join you."

"Why didn't you tell her we wanted to be alone?" Rudy grumped when Vivian left to collect her Jack Russell. *"T's been a royal pain all night. He did blow-by-blow commentary on that dog show as if he worked for ESPN."*

"Don't blame him for giving you a hard time. Lulu is a snooty know-it-all, so be prepared for the others to tease her the rest of the week." Ellie squatted and scratched under his chin. "I know you consider her your girl, but what will you do if Mrs. Steinman decides to breed her after Westminster?"

"Mind over matter," Rudy said with a snort. *"I'll keep telling myself she used a sperm bank until I believe it."*

"Pretending something didn't happen won't make it go away."

"Hey, it works for me."

"You say that now, but wait until it—"

"All set." Vivian walked into the hall with Mr. T, and shut and locked her door. "But let's make it fast."

On the street, the foursome headed west on Sixty-sixth and took their usual once-around-the-block evening route. Ellie didn't feel like talking, but that didn't stop Viv from asking questions or giving her opinion.

"Did the toxicology report come in?"

"Not yet," said Ellie.

"Any idea what it'll say?"

Ellie waited while Rudy watered a hydrant. "Nope. The ME told Sam they haven't been able to identify a poison through the regular channels and it's possible they'll never find it, even though they sent it to the state capital."

"So they do think poison is the cause of death?"

They made a left on Sixty-seventh. "It's either that or something called SADS. Ever hear of it?"

"Is that the condition people get in the winter? Depression from a lack of sunlight?"

"You're talking about seasonal affective disorder. This is different." Ellie filled her in as they continued around the block, telling Vivian the basics of sudden adult death syndrome while leaving out her suspicions about Edward Nelson and the Baggie in Flora's coat. She simply wasn't up to a lecture on how she should mind her own business and let the police do their job. Back in front of their building, they climbed the stairs to the outer foyer.

"So without a motive, weapon, or proof of

murder, the case will be closed." Vivian held open the door and they headed up the steps. "That sucks."

"Exactly what I told Sam. I keep thinking we're all missing something. A clue that's sitting right in front of us."

Vivian unlocked her apartment door. "We? Us? Don't let Detective Dreamy hear you say that."

"You know what I mean."

"Uh-huh, sure. I forgot to ask, has Joy called?"

Ellie rolled her eyes. "Thanks for reminding me. I completely forgot to phone her, and it's too late now. I hope she remembers to meet me first thing tomorrow morning so I can get those kcys."

"I hope so, too, because you have enough on your plate without worrying about your assistant. Let Sam take care of the investigation while you take care of your own business. Playing citizen sleuth twice is two times too many for any person." She and Mr. T stood in their doorway. "And get a good night's sleep. Tomorrow's going to be a busy day."

With her mind bouncing from point to point, Ellie let Rudy take the next flight of stairs ahead of her. Why were the police having such a hard time identifying the substance on that liver? What was Flora doing with a Baggie full of liver treats that looked suspiciously like what they thought might be the murder weapon? Could the glop in the Baggie really be tainted with the same poison? And what had made Sam and Vince decide to check Flora's coat in the first place?

Inside her apartment, Ellie unclipped Rudy's leash and followed him to the bedroom. Her buddy was bummed over Lulu's loss, but he'd get over it. Knowing him, she expected that he'd probably drown his sorrows by attempting to brighten the Havanese's spirits. She just hoped Lulu would appreciate his efforts.

Stripping off her suit, she set it aside to take to the cleaners. After putting on a sleep shirt, she turned on the electric blanket. Rudy jumped onto the bed and curled up at his usual bedtime starting point: the pillow next to hers.

She went to the bathroom, took care of her nightly routine, and returned to the bedroom, where she doused her light, pulled down the covers, and settled into bed. Snuggling Rudy in the crook of her arm, she said, "I know you're upset over Lulu, but I did show her to the best of my ability."

He wriggled around and gave her cheek a sloppy lick. *"You were great, Triple E. As good as those professional handlers."*

"So you're not angry with me because your girl didn't win?"

"I only wanted her to win because that's what Lulu wanted. She's gonna be miserable for the next couple of weeks."

"If anyone can cheer her up, it's you. And remember, we'll be celebrating her Best in Group win tomorrow night."

"I heard you talking to Viv about Arnie's murder. Do you still think the old handler did it?"

"Sam says there could be two suspects, and he may be right, but without more info on the rumor floating around about Felicity Apgar a couple of months back, I can't see it. In my book, Edward Nelson is the only one." She ruffled his ears. "Unfortunately, I have no proof that he had a motive or access to a poison, and that's what the cops need to bring the man to justice."

"Let me sleep on it. We'll find a way."

"Come on, hurry it up." Ellie half dragged Rudy to Lexington, where she planned to hail a cab. "We can't be late to meet Joy. I have to get my extra keys before she loses them."

She'd called her assistant first thing after waking to confirm their morning rendezvous. She and Rudy were running late because the yorkiepoo chose today to dawdle and grump about every little thing, even suggesting that he didn't want to accompany her on rounds. The temperature had dropped overnight, so she was certain that between the cold and facing Lulu after her defeat, he simply wasn't up to working through the day. When he realized she wasn't about to give in, he sulked, but he did cooperate.

Unfortunately, meeting with Joy at the opposite end of Fifth Avenue would force them to collect their customers in reverse order. It was no hardship for her and Rudy, but the difference in pickup time might just be enough to upset a few of her canine clients.

Climbing into the taxi, she noticed the driver was wearing a headset and bopping along to some barely recognizable rhythm. After giving him their destination address, she said to her boy, "Feeling better now that we're on our way?"

"Are you kidding? It's gotta be twenty below out here. I'd be freezin' my nuts off if I had any."

According to the morning news, the predicted high for the day was the mid-thirties, so Ellie had dressed in her down-filled parka, insulated gloves, and heaviest slacks and sweater. But Rudy refused to wear a coat of any kind, so it didn't surprise her that he was cold. Tonight would be soon enough to tackle the topic of outerwear.

"It should get warmer as the day progresses. If you can make it through the afternoon, Flora will have a surprise for you tonight."

"I hate surprises."

"Don't be such a grouch. It'll be good, I promise."

Ellie paid the cabbie when they pulled in front of the Cranston, Joy's pickup site, and led Rudy onto the sidewalk. Scanning the street, she didn't see her assistant, so she slipped into the building's entryway to get out of the cold. Across the street, the leafless trees of Central Park sparkled with a coating of ice. Bundled in heavy coats and colorful scarves and gloves, pedestrians stepped lively as they made their way to work, while the tailpipes of cars, cabs, and buses puffed clouds of white into the chilly air.

She stepped aside when Roxy, a dog walker she'd spoken to a few times, pushed through the door with her group of six very large canines.

The short, stocky girl grinned, her bright blue eyes a mirror image of the early-morning sky. "Hey, Ellie. Haven't seen you around this week. How're things going?"

"Nice to see you, Roxy." Ellie eyed the oversized cleanup bags hanging from the belt of the girl's coat. "I hired an assistant to walk the dogs in this building. You might have seen her around. Tall, pretty African-American?"

Roxy's grin froze on her face. "Joy somebody, right?"

"Yeah, that's her."

"She's not very friendly." Roxy's charges nosed the inside door, begging to be allowed entry to their homes. "Oops, sorry, gotta go." She brushed past Ellie calling a "We'll talk," over her shoulder.

"What do you suppose she meant by that?"

Ellie asked Rudy, though she didn't expect an answer. He was busy eyeing the black toy Poodle prancing in the door ahead of its owner.

"Cute pooch," she said, stepping back to give the woman and her dog room.

"Thanks." The gray-haired matron nodded, indicating that Ellie go inside first. "Your dog is a sweetie, too. Do you live here?"

"Me? No. I'm a dog walker, but Rudy is my boy."

"A dog walker? Really? I've seen them around and been meaning to talk to a couple, but I never seem to have the time. Can I ask you a few questions?"

Ellie spotted her assistant crossing Fifth Avenue with her pack and pulled a business card from her tote bag. She usually loved chatting with a possible client, but not today. "Sure, but I'm a little pressed for time right now. Here's my card. Call me when you get a minute and we can go over my services."

The Poodle and Rudy were nose to nose, making the woman smile. "Looks like my baby thinks your dog is a good one." She tucked the card into her Fendi shoulder bag and rang for the elevator. "I'll call you."

Joy walked into the building as the elevator door closed. Dressed in knee-high boots, a short skirt, and denim jacket, she reminded Ellie of a mocha Popsicle.

"Hi," the girl said as she approached.

"Joy. Uh, aren't you cold?"

Joy shrugged. "Yeah, but it's okay. I'll only be out a few more minutes. I plan to spend the rest of the morning in the library." When her charges, Millie, Dilbert, Sampson, and Edgar, clustered around Ellie's legs, clamoring for attention, she said, "Looks like the gang is happy to see you."

Ellie squatted and gave each one a cuddle, making her comments too innocent to be construed as personal conversation. "Hi, everybody. You all doing okay with this freezing weather?"

"Fine, fine, fine," Sampson, the world's fattest Pug, wheezed.

"When are you gonna walk us again?" asked Dilbert, a long-haired Chihuahua.

"Yeah. When? When?" the others clamored.

"I know Joy's taking good care of you," she said, not giving them a direct answer. Standing, she said to her assistant, "Do you have those keys?"

"Oh, uh, sure. Hang on a second." The girl passed Ellie the leashes and removed her backpack. After digging through the compartments, she found the key ring and handed it over. "Here you go."

Ellie dropped the keys in her tote pocket. "I've got some time. I'll take the gang up for you."

Joy's worried expression changed to one of relief. "Thanks. I'm in a rush and I—I think—maybe I'd better call you."

"Sure, fine," Ellie said, but she knew by Joy's hesitant tone there was trouble. More than likely, by the end of the week she was going to lose her fifth assistant.

Chapter 11

Ellie ate lunch at home and left Rudy to sleep for the afternoon. Her morning walks had gone well because most of her charges wore coats, and some even boots. But yorkiepoos, like many smaller canines, weren't meant to live in the great outdoors. Because he refused to wear any type of cover-up, Rudy had shivered the entire while, sometimes so badly she thought he was about to shake loose a couple of teeth. She didn't mind his complaints, but the idea of his small paws freezing to the sidewalk was a worry, as well as the possibility that he might catch a cold.

"I'll be back to change and we'll cab to the party," she told him as she headed for the foyer.

"You could drop me at the groomer. That guy over at Canine Styles on Lexington did a decent job last time I was there. Took a little too much off the top, but it grew back okay."

"Maybe I could give you a trim or—"

"Oh, no. I don't want you comin' near me with a pair of scissors ever again," he said with a snort.

"Hey, that was just a tiny snip on the tip of your

ear, and only because you moved. There was hardly any blood," Ellie said in self-defense. "Jeez, you have a memory like an elephant."

"I need it with you. Now about that groomer—"

"I agree, he did a great job, but you need an appointment, and there isn't time to make one. I have to run the afternoon walks, then come home and make myself beautiful so we can get to Lulu's party by seven o'clock on the dot."

"You always look good to me, Triple E. Even at five a.m., wearing bed head and your grumpy face."

She pulled on her down-filled parka and wrapped a red scarf around her neck. "That's very sweet, but the compliment won't get me home any sooner."

He stood on his hind legs and nosed her knee. *"I gotta make a good impression, knock Lulu off her feet."*

"How about if I give you a quick brushing and a spritz of rosewater? She should like that."

"Okay, fine, if you think that'll work. I just can't have some froufrou Poodle or one of them champion mutts horning in on my girl. She's worth the best."

Ellie squatted and gave him a cuddle. "You, my big man, are the best. And the most handsome dog in Manhattan—heck, the entire state of New York. Stop worrying. Lulu loves you for you, just like I do." She released him and tugged her gloves on. After pulling a black wool hat over her curls, she said, "Have a good nap, so you're rested for tonight."

"All right, but if my girl starts foolin' around with another canine while we're there, it'll be your fault." He walked to his rug in the corner of the kitchen, turned a couple of circles, and settled down. *"Hurry back."*

"I'll try to be fast. Now go to sleep."

Ellie skipped down the stairs, left her apartment, and set out on her second foray of the day. This time of year, it got dark early, so she power-walked to her first building, the Beaumont, and nodded at the second-shift doorman. Then she rode the elevator to the Fallgraves' penthouse, let herself in, dressed Cheech and Chong in matching lamb's wool–lined serapes, and headed for Flora's.

When she arrived at the Steinman apartment, the double doors were wide open so deliverymen carting folding tables could bring their trolleys safely inside. Men dressed in white uniforms carried shell pink and raspberry table linens into the dining room, while Flora's housekeeper stood in the middle of it all barking orders like an alpha female.

"Hey, Nelda. Looks like things are moving along."

"The party should come together by about six thirty." The tall woman pointed a worker toting table linens in the right direction. "And I have to tell you, Ms. Flora hasn't been this excited in years. Her and Lulu were as jumpy as tree frogs, so I sent them to the south wing to get them out of the way."

"Should I call for her majesty or find her myself?" Ellie asked, not wanting to make more work for the harried housekeeper.

"Just go straight through the living room and take a left in the back foyer. You can't miss their bedroom—done up like a fairy-tale hideaway it is."

Ellie and the Chihuahuas dodged a chair-laden trolley and headed into the living room. She'd been this way on the night she and Rudy slept over, but she hadn't seen Flora's private quarters. From Nelda's description, she could only imagine the appearance of the bedroom.

Turning left in the foyer, as directed, she met another set of double doors and gave a rapid knock. The answering yip told her that at least the Havanese had heard. She glanced at Cheech and Chong. "You boys be good."

As usual, they simply stared with their big buggy eyes. Maybe Rudy was right. There was a definite language barrier. She gave each of them a pat on the head, then stepped through the doors and saw that Nelda had been correct. The room could have belonged to a fairy-tale princess.

Besides the antique white furniture trimmed in

gold, pink was the dominant color throughout the massive room. Cream-colored wallpaper flocked with delicate pink, lavender, and green vines graced the walls. Deep pink thick-piled carpet covered the floor. A fluffy comforter that matched the paper was laid over the king-size bed, while fuzzy stuffed dogs in varying shades of pink decorated the pillows. Even the window treatments were a soft pink and rose, their flowery vines twining to the ceiling.

She glanced at the floor beside the bed and saw Lulu, grinning mischievously from her petal pink mink-lined doggie bed with a gathered top that resembled a circus tent. "You ready to go out, little girl?"

"It's about time! I almost got trampled by that crew bringing in the party supplies." Lulu scampered from her throne and skittered to a stop in front of Cheech and Chong. *"Hello, boys,"* she vamped in her best Mae West voice. *"Are ya happy to see me?"*

The Chihuahuas gazed at the saucy Havanese as if they hadn't a clue. "Lulu, stop that. If Rudy hears you teasing another canine, he'll pitch a fit."

Drying her hands on a fluffy pink towel, Flora took that moment to step into the room from what Ellie assumed was the dressing area. "Hello, dear. I thought I heard someone talking out here. I should have known it was you. I am so excited. Only three more hours until the party begins."

"I'm here to take Lulu on her afternoon walk."

"Stay for a minute, won't you, and help me decide which dress to wear tonight."

Ellie gazed at Lulu and shrugged. "I guess the pack can wait. Let's see your choices."

Flora waggled a finger and Ellie followed her, blinking when she entered a closet as big as her own bedroom. Elegant dresses, tailored skirts, and silk blouses hung on rods lining one entire wall. Another was lined with shelves holding boxes from Neiman Marcus, Saks, Yves St. Laurent, Chanel, and a few stores she'd never heard of. The third wall was covered top to bottom in shoe drawers, each one filled, she was certain, with the finest of footwear.

Two hangers mounted on the wall held almost identical dresses, one a deep peony pink, the other a pink as pale as cotton candy. "I brought these two out of storage," explained Flora. "Each one represents a special memory, so I thought I should wear one of them a final time before I . . . go to meet my husband."

"None of that talk," Ellie told her, eyeing the dresses carefully. "You'll have lots of chances to wear them, maybe when Lulu wins Best in Show at Madison Square Garden."

Inhaling a deep breath, Flora ran a hand down the peony pink dress. "This is a Hubert Givenchy original," she said, stating the designer's name in perfect French. "The darling man made it for me in 1957, when my husband and I were in Paris celebrating our third wedding anniversary."

Impressed at the beautiful yet simplistic style that would surely turn heads today, Ellie asked, "And the other dress?"

"This one," said Flora, removing the hanger from the wall, "was designed by Christian Lacroix the first year he opened his own house in, let's see, I think it was 1988." She hung the dress back in place and frowned. "No, no, it was 1987. We were in Paris for that anniversary as well."

Georgette had always lectured her on the beauty of designer originals, telling her they never grew outdated, but Ellie had a difficult time believing dresses that old could be in such perfect condition. "And you keep them here?"

"I have a specialty dry cleaner who hermetically seals the garments and guarantees them to be as fresh as the day they were designed if I store them with her. She delivered both of these this morning."

"I see." Ellie cringed inside. She owned very few outfits that went to her neighborhood dry cleaner. She bought ready-to-wear in natural fibers, because they were easier to care for in her line of work. "Well, I like the Givenchy best."

"Thank you, dear. I believe I'll take your suggestion. Mr. Steinman always loved this dress, and it does make me feel special." Flora led her back into the bedroom. "Now you just go about your business while I take my bath. Nelda will know what to do with Lulu when you return."

When Ellie and the dogs arrived in the front hall, the parade of furniture had slowed. Instead, deliverymen and -women were bringing in chafing dishes and stacks of glassware and china. "If you need help, I can be here early," she told the housekeeper.

Nelda shook her head. "Not to worry. The setup and serving crew is on their way."

"How many guests are you expecting?"

"Last count, the tally was sixty-six humans and twenty-seven dogs. The phone is still ringing with replies." As if on cue, the phone on Nelda's belt jangled a jaunty tune. "Ms. Steinman's residence," she said, giving Ellie a good-bye wave.

"I say we blow this joint, but I want my coat. It's freezing out there," griped Lulu.

Ellie walked to the entryway and reached behind a door, where Flora kept her baby's mink coat at the ready. Since Cheech and Chong wore serapes made by the famous Lorilee, why shouldn't a champion Havanese wear a fabulous fur by the same designer?

"Okay, let's make this quick," she told the trio as they headed toward the elevator. "I've got two more buildings to cover and I have to get ready for the big event myself."

Thirty minutes later she was on her way to the Davenport. Upon her arrival, she looked for Randall but found Kronk, the evening doorman, hovering behind the welcome counter, perusing his usual daily paper. Oh, well. It had been a while since she'd dealt with the nosy Russian. Now was as good a time as any to answer his pointed questions.

"*El-ee,* my friend. I hear your *pop* no make the *beeg* win at that dog *com-pee-tee-shun* yesterday." He shook his leonine head. "Boris is sad for you."

"We did our best." It took her a beat to ask, "How did you find out I was there showing a dog?"

"Randall, he tell me was one of your *pops* from the Beaumont. A *lee-til* girl, no?"

Making a mental note to remind Randall that her personal business was off limits to the interfering Kronk, she said, "The dog was a Havanese named Lulu. She didn't take the big prize, but she did win Best in Breed and Best in Group."

Kronk's shaggy white eyebrows rose to his hairline. "What kind of dog is this *'ave-en-eese'*? I have never heard of *eet.*"

"A breed from Havana—you know—in Cuba."

"Ah, I know. Is a good man, *Fee-dell.*"

"Uh, yeah, sure. I'm running behind, Kronk. See you on the way out, okay?" Not waiting for his answer, she slipped into the elevator and headed up to get Buckley, Sweetie Pie, and Bitsy. Unfortunately, the reluctant Buckley had no intention of cooperating.

"Stick that paw through the sleeve or you're going to be a pup-sicle in a couple of minutes, mister."

"You could carry me," the maltipoo whined. *"That's what Hazel does when the weather is lousy."*

"That's what Hazel does because you growl and snap at her when she tries to dress you. If I thought Cesar Millan would drive to New York, I'd write and ask him to come here and give you an attitude adjustment."

"Oh, yeah? Just let that dog whisperer try. We watch his show, so I'm wise to him and all that dominant and aggressive stuff he spouts."

"Enough. I will not carry you. Paw through sleeve. Now."

Buckley finally complied, but he griped all the way to Sweetie Pie's apartment, where the Westie was happy to don her sweater and boots before she took her walk.

From there they went to Bitsy's place. Ellie hadn't seen the tiny white dog's owner all week, so she had to ask, "Did Bobbi say anything about a party tonight?"

"I'll say. She's been primping all afternoon. Even canceled rehearsal so she could go to Lulu's house."

"Canceled a rehearsal?" Ellie had suspected the attractive blonde was a performer, but she hadn't been able to broach the subject with the elusive woman. Wrestling Bitsy into her hot pink sweater, she said, "What kind of show?"

"You know. Dancing and singing and all that stuff."

"Really?" said Ellie, thrilled to get a bit more info. "Does Bobbi sing or dance?"

"A little of both. But she's dressing different for tonight. Said she wanted people to see the real her, so she wasn't going to wear a bit of makeup."

Very interesting, thought Ellie. Of course, a woman as attractive as Bobbi didn't need cosmetics to look good. Still, on the few occasions she'd seen her, Bobbi had always been done up in full face paint.

Two down and one to go, she thought thirty minutes later as she walked toward the only building on her list that had no doorman and no name. Her first stop was the Gordon apartment to pick up a sweet-natured French Bulldog named Freud.

"I came home from my studio early just so Freud and I could attend the big party someone named Mrs. Steinman is throwing in your honor," said Esther Gordon when Ellie opened the door. "The woman who called said it had something to do with a celebration, and that you and Rudy would be there."

Ellie quickly filled Esther in on Lulu's triumph.

"You know, I thought that was you when I watched the competition, but my husband said I was hallucinating. I can't wait to tell Dr. G I was right."

"Is Dr. Gordon coming to the party with you and Freud?"

"Unfortunately, no. Tonight is one of his late-appointment evenings, when he schedules all the big-shot politicians and CEOs who are too busy to come in and whine during the day."

Ellie grinned at Esther's description of her psychiatrist husband's patients. Dr. Nathan Gordon was a shrink to the rich and famous, many of whom expected anonymity while being treated. He also consulted on several of the weekly television crime series filmed in Manhattan. Esther, a sculptor of some renown, never mentioned names, but every so often she would comment on the peculiarities and habits of her husband's clients.

"The man is always busy," Ellie said. "I don't think I've ever held a conversation with him longer than two sentences."

"He does all his talking to those poor misunderstood billionaires he retunes, sort of like a mechanic discussing the timing of an engine with a Jaguar or a Mercedes."

Ellie glanced at her watch. "This will be a short walk. I have to go home and get ready, too."

"I was told the dress was casual. Is that right?"

Ellie recalled the Givenchy Flora planned to wear. She had nothing as nice, but she'd look professional. "I'd wear whatever makes you comfortable. From the length of the guest list, I imagine there'll be all modes of dress."

Giving a wave, she headed out the door with her pack.

"Stop fidgeting," Ellie ordered Rudy, holding his grooming brush high in the air. "You said you wanted to look good, so let me do my thing."

The yorkiepoo jumped off the bed and shook himself, then glared up at her. *"I hate getting brushed, and the junk you sprayed on me stinks."*

She sniffed the air and smiled. "Rosewater does not stink. You smell mysterious—even sort of romantic."

"Romantic? Hah! Not to another dog, I won't."

She dropped the brush on the duvet and crossed her arms. "This was your idea, my friend. You said you wanted to smell good and look your best. I was just doing what you wanted."

"Okay, okay," he groused. *"But enough is enough. I'm a man's man . . . er . . . dog. No more sissy stuff. Let's get moving."*

"You'd better be sure, because I don't want to get to Flora's and have you pouting when Lulu talks to other dogs."

"She can talk. I just don't want her sniffin' butt. Makes a guy feel like he isn't good enough."

"You're good enough, but Miss Pickypants is a tease and you know it." Ellie walked to the mirror, where she ran her fingers through her curls and decided to forgo wearing a hat. They were taking a cab to Flora's and her hair looked good, so why mess it up? "I have an idea. How about if you play hard to get, just like Lulu does. It might make her think twice about paying attention to other males."

Rudy stood on his hind legs and rested his paws on her calf. *"You think that might work?"*

"It couldn't hurt to give her a taste of her own medicine." She went to her closet and gazed at her wardrobe. Everything she owned could be stored on one wall of Flora's humongous dressing area with room to spare. She had one fancy dress, a sparkling navy sheath she'd picked up on a fifty-percent-off rack, and that was it for designer duds. She glanced at her boy. "Now that you're ready, how about giving me a hand? I need a jacket to wear with this sweater and slacks."

Rudy took in her pale pink sweater and black pants. *"There's not much choice, far as I can see. Your black wool blazer is it. But are you sure about that sweater?"*

"I know redheads shouldn't wear pink, but the shade is soft, and I'll be color-coordinated with Flora . . . sort of."

Ellie slid her feet into black flats, took the

jacket off its hanger, and shrugged it on. When she slipped her hands in the pockets, she gasped.

"What? What?"

Sitting on the bed, she stared at the tissue-wrapped blob of brown goo. "Oh, my gosh. I forgot I had this."

Rudy gave the tissue a sniff. *"Yetch, what is that glop?"*

Ellie peeled open the packet. "It's a dog treat."

"No way," he answered, his eyes fixed on the liver. *"That's nothing I'd ever eat."*

"But it's supposed to be irresistible to canines. Here, take a good sniff." She held Arnie's treat under his nose. "What do you think?"

Rudy reared back, his muzzle clenched in a grimace. *"Nasty is what I think, and I can't imagine any* dog *taking a taste."* He narrowed his eyes. *"What genius gave you that poor excuse for squirrel poop?"*

"Arnie Harris. He said—" It took a couple of seconds for her to connect the dots. Rewrapping the liver, she stood and tossed it on her dresser, ready to kick herself for being so stupid. If she'd come home and given her boy that treat . . . She took a calming breath. Nothing would have happened because Rudy was too smart to have eaten it, but still . . .

"Don't touch it. Don't even look at it."

"Not that I'd want to. That stuff is poison."

"Poison? But how—what—how do you know?"

He stretched his front legs and raised his rear in the air. *" 'Cause I'm a dog. The nose knows and all that."*

Ellie plopped back on the bed. She was an idiot. How could she have forgotten the treat? Arnie had given it to her right before he took Lulu into the ring. It had come from the same bag he'd pulled Lulu's liver from before he died.

"I don't like the look on your face, Triple E. Care to tell me what you're thinking?"

"I'm thinking I have an exact copy of the murder weapon that killed Arnie. Only he gave it to me himself—for you. Which only proves my theory."

"Proves what theory? That he was into poisoning innocent canines and the stunt backfired?"

"Of course not. Flora trusted the man implicitly and I thought he was trustworthy too. Arnie loved dogs. There'd be no reason for him to give me something that would kill mine." She rose to her feet and began to pace. "Someone must have exchanged the bag in his pocket for one filled with poison liver before he got to Lulu's stall."

"Maybe so, but why? And who?"

"Darned if I know." She ran a hand through her hair, trying to remember that morning. She'd been excited about the show, taking in all the sights, sounds, and smells of the canine elite. The preparation area had been swamped with people brushing against each other, invading private space, practically breathing down other attendees' necks. "It was so crowded I remember thinking the backstage area was a pickpocket's dream. Anyone could have done a switch, removed something from another person's pocket and added something else, and they never would have felt it."

"You think that's how it happened? The killer exchanged bags with Arnie and he was too focused on Lulu to notice?"

"That has to be what happened." She dropped onto the mattress again. "It's the only explanation that makes sense."

"But what was the point? Arnie was already showing Lulu. Why kill him on the floor?"

Ellie heaved a sigh when a single answer popped into her brain. "Arnie told me himself he'd just started baiting Lulu that week in hopes that she'd perform better. Whoever it was didn't know he'd changed the way he handled her. They thought Lulu would be the one to get the treat. They weren't out to kill Arnie. They wanted to kill your girl."

Chapter 12

Ellie racked her brains on the cab ride to the Beaumont, mulling over everything she knew about Arnie Harris's death. With Rudy focused on impressing Lulu, he was in no mood to talk about a suspected murderer. He'd been miffed, of course, when she announced that she thought the Havanese had been the intended victim instead of Arnie. He'd even given his opinion in his usual candid manner. *"Just let somebody try to get my girl while I'm around. I'll bite his nuts off, and we'll see who laughs last."*

Rudy's bravado was well meant, but it wouldn't help her catch the killer, whether it was Lulu's old handler or anyone else.

Her mind kept returning to the first time she'd met Arnie at the MACC. He'd threaded his way through that opening-day mob like a salmon swimming upstream along with a couple of hundred other people. Any one of them could have picked his pocket and exchanged his treat bag for the bag that held poisoned liver. Though he'd chatted with Edward Nelson for a few minutes before reaching Lulu's stall, there was no proof that the ex-handler was the one who had made the switch.

Still considering possible suspects and exchange scenarios, she didn't notice that they'd arrived at the Beaumont until the taxi driver announced in a loud voice, "Lady, I said that would be eight seventy-five."

"Oh, sorry." She dug her wallet from her tote, pulled out a ten, and passed it over the seat.

He answered with a nod, and she and Rudy exited the cab. Just then another taxi pulled up.

She thought it might be someone she knew on their way to the party, so she stepped into the entry foyer to wait.

The cab door opened and a tiny white dog in a hot pink sweater jumped onto the sidewalk. Positive that it was Bitsy, she readied herself to meet Bobbi in her "normal dress" regalia. When a tall man wearing a tan topcoat and leather gloves stepped out holding Bitsy's leash, she figured that Bobbi had brought a date to the party.

"Oh, boy," muttered Rudy, peering through the glass door. *"I knew you'd find out about this one way or another."*

"Find out about what?" she asked, still gazing at the pair. Surprised when the cab pulled away, she said, "I thought that was Bitsy, but Bobbi's nowhere in sight, so it can't be her."

"Uh, Ellie. That is Bitsy, and Bobbi's holding her leash."

Ellie studied the duo heading toward the Beaumont. "I don't think so. That's a man holding the leash, and Bobbi would never send her baby here without her, even if the guy was a friend."

After the doorman tipped his hat and opened the lobby door, the tiny white pooch lunged for Rudy. *"Hey, big guy. We're here! We're here!"*

She stared at the handsome man holding Bitsy's leash. About six feet tall with neatly trimmed blond hair, a perfectly sculpted nose, a sexy mouth, and a twinkle in his bright blue eyes, he was a heartbreaker for sure.

"Hi, Ellie. Long time no see," he said, smiling.

Though his voice didn't have a deeply masculine tone, it wasn't light and delicate either, but it did sound familiar. Too familiar. She opened and closed her mouth. "Hi . . . er . . . hello."

The man held out his hands, as if modeling his clothes. "What do you think of the duds? I love Armani."

Ellie swallowed her answer. She had never given Bobbi's theatrical clothing and makeup a second thought—until now. If this guy was who she thought he was, it would be one more reason for Sam and Vivian to tease her about her babe-in-the-woods attitude.

Squatting to Bitsy's level, she scratched the dog's ears. "Is there something you want to tell me, missy?"

"Nuh-uh. Not me. Rudy swore me to secrecy. Said you'd find out when the time was right. I guess that's now."

Great. She'd been played for a fool by Bitsy, Bobbi, and her own fuzzy pal. Ellie glared at her yorkiepoo, and he answered with a doggie shrug. Heat rose from her chest to her collarbone. Heaving a sigh, she stood and tossed the man what she hoped was a smile. "Clue me in. Are you Bobbi tonight, or should I call you Bob?"

"I prefer Rob. Bobbi's just my stage name," he said, still grinning.

Ellie swallowed hard, again at a loss for words. At least she'd been correct in thinking she . . . er . . . he was in show business. This time Rob got the message.

"Oh, gee. You didn't know, did you?" he asked as they walked to the elevator.

The heat surged from her collarbone to her jaw-line and raced to her cheeks like a flash fire in July. "Uh, sure, I mean, no. I mean know what?"

The elevator door opened and they stepped inside. "That I'm a cross-dresser. I play a drag queen onstage."

A drag queen? She pushed the button for the correct floor, still unable to compose herself.

"I'm sorry. I thought you knew what I did for a living."

"Bobbi . . . er . . . Rob, how could I know? We just talked that one time when you hired me to walk Bitsy, and you were dressed like a femme fatale. I've only seen you maybe once a week since then, and you always seemed to be in . . . in . . ."

"Full battle uniform?" He grinned again. "I thought Randall might have said something, or that other guy—Kronkovitz. He's seen me going to rehearsals dressed like I am now and returning in drag around midnight enough times to have figured it out."

"Kronk is an idiot. And Randall probably thought he was being cute, pulling my leg because he knew I was . . . that I don't . . ."

"You don't approve?"

"Who am I to disapprove? It's your life and you're free to live it as you choose." How could she tell him she was so naive that she'd never even considered he was a cross-dresser? She raised her nose in the air. "I'll be sure to let Randall know how much I appreciate his joke on Monday morning."

The elevator stopped, and Mr. and Mrs. Best, along with Bruiser, the Pomeranian Ellie walked every morning, stepped inside. Bruiser stood next to Rudy and began a conversation, but she couldn't hear what they were saying because Mrs. Best was talking to her.

"Ellie, hi. We heard about your big win at the MACC. Congratulations."

"Don't congratulate me. It was all Lulu's doing," she said, happy that the topic had changed. "And Flora Steinman's, of course. She's gone above and beyond to see to it her Havanese got championship validation."

"Bruiser has papers, too," Mrs. Best said. "In fact, we've been thinking about showing him. I heard there's a man named Nelson in this building who shows high-caliber dogs. I was thinking of calling him."

Rudy and Bruiser broke from their huddle and

the yorkiepoo gazed up at her. *"Bruiser says he's not about to prance around a show ring like a horse on parade. Said he wants you to tell the Bests how he feels."*

Ellie held back an eye roll and concentrated on Mrs. Best. "Um, you might want to bring Bruiser to a show before you decide. The way I hear it, not all dogs are comfortable in the conformation ring. And if you want to know about Edward Nelson, I'd talk to Mrs. Steinman before I phoned him."

"You have a cute little girl," Mrs. Best said to Rob. "Wouldn't you want her to be crowned a champion?"

Rob gazed at the Poodle-Chihuahua mix that Ellie laughingly considered a poohuahua with love in his eyes. "Bitsy isn't a purebred, so that will never happen. And even if she were, she's already a champ in my book. I don't need anything else."

He and the Bests exchanged a few more pleasantries, then the elevator doors opened. Mr. Best let the others step out, then he and his wife pulled ahead, leading the way to Flora's apartment.

"We should talk sometime," Rob said to Ellie as they followed the happy couple. "I can tell you're upset."

"Don't worry about it. I have a lot more on my mind than having a drag queen for a client."

"But I'm not . . . I mean . . ."

Ellie walked through the wide-open double doors. She didn't have time for excuses, and Bobbi . . . er . . . Rob didn't owe her an explanation. Right now, she was on the hunt for a killer.

As soon as she and Rudy entered the premises, a woman dressed in a maid's uniform shuttled Rudy, Bitsy, Bruiser, and a few other dogs into a back room that, according to Nelda, had been turned into a puppy playground.

Ellie had peeked inside once and seen her boy and Lulu crouched side by side munching on treats, while a couple dozen more dogs spaced around the room were doing the same. In a far corner, three pups were chasing a ball. Bitsy was playing tug-of-war with Jett in the center of the room while Sweetie Pie tried to join in the fun. So far, there was no sign of Cheech and Chong, but it was possible both Fallgrave sisters were out of town.

An hour later, Ellie found herself in the living room still waiting for Edward Nelson to show. Sitting on the pink silk-covered couch, she watched Bobbi . . . er . . . Rob flirt with several women. He appeared to be in his element, because the women laughed out loud at almost everything he said. She thought about their last few words as they left the elevator. She'd been rude, when in fact she was embarrassed. She was a grown-up. She knew there were cross-dressers in the world—and drag queens. But she'd never met either one in person before, so how was she supposed to know Bobbi was a Rob? Besides, what Rob did for a living was none of her business. It was clear that Bitsy was well loved and cared for, and that was all that mattered.

Putting her inappropriate conduct on the back burner, she made small talk with a man and woman about Lulu's Best in Group win. As time passed, she cuddled a few dogs she'd never met before. Then Flora introduced her to Lorilee Echternach, the maven of doggie design, and they had a conversation about the fashion show she had planned to wind up the evening.

When Lorilee and Flora left to talk with other guests, Ellie realized it was time to take a walk, so she headed into the foyer for a drink. It couldn't hurt to knock back a glass of white wine while waiting for the ex-handler. If Edward was a no-show tonight, people would think him a sore loser, and she couldn't imagine the pompous man wanting that unpleasant title hanging over his head.

She ordered a Pinot Grigio and accepted the glass the bartender handed her. When she heard a girlish giggle, she turned to see Flora welcoming Edward into her home. Mitzi, the woman she'd met the night of her training session, was standing at his side dressed in what Ellie thought was a Michael Kors original. Georgette owned a few of his designs, and she recognized his style.

Ooo-kay. Now things would start to happen. She'd wait until the Nelsons greeted acquaintances and relaxed a bit. When they separated, she would do a little sleuthing. She turned her back as the couple approached the bar and feigned interest in the lovely Monet displayed nearby. Gazing at the priceless painting, she saw that it hung above a sculpture situated on a three-legged Hepplewhite table. Looking down, she read the name of the artist who had created the beautiful reclining woman carved in pink marble. The statue was a signed Esther Gordon. Since Ellie was sure that Flora was no slouch in the art department, she now knew for certain that Esther was tops in her field.

Glancing to her left, she glimpsed Mitzi going into the living room while Edward ambled toward the dining room. She was about to follow him when Vivian, Dr. Dave, and Mr. T appeared in the doorway. Ellie caught Viv's attention, and the trio headed her way.

"Sorry we're late," said Viv. "Dave had an emergency."

"One of my patients swallowed a penny, or so his owner thought," the vet said, shaking his head. "Had to bring the little guy in for an X-ray and exam, but I didn't see anything. So either the penny is on the way out or he didn't swallow it. They should know for sure in the next twenty-four hours."

"Ee-uww," said Viv.

Dave just smiled as if he enjoyed Vivian's outlandish comments and asked, "You want a glass of Merlot, babe, or something stronger?"

"Merlot is fine." Viv waited until he moved to the bar before saying, "Honest to God, the things that man does for his dogs. Last week he had to unplug a St. Bernard that had eaten an entire pound of cheddar cheese with a peanut butter chaser. Can you imagine?"

The attendant that had met Ellie and Rudy earlier sidled over and spoke to Vivian. "Ma'am, there's a room with treats and toys set up in the back. I've been instructed to invite all the canine guests there to play."

"I ain't goin' nowhere with you, fool."

Ellie grinned when Viv passed the woman T's lead. The Jack Russell could be a handful on his best day, and from the sound of his grousing, this was not a good day.

"Be a sweet boy and find Rudy and a few of your pals," Viv told him when he growled. "You'll have fun without me."

"I said I ain't goin'," Mr. T howled.

Vivian waved her fingers at the dog. "Go on now. You'll like it when you get there."

T parked his butt on the floor and tossed his mistress a look of disdain.

"Maybe you should carry him," Ellie suggested, knowing her friend would do no such thing.

"You've got to be kidding."

"Well it doesn't look like he's going to get there under his own power, now does it?"

The attendant heaved a sigh. "If you promise me he won't bite, I can carry him."

Viv grabbed the leash and tugged, dragging T about three inches forward.

"Ow! Ow! Ow! That's canine brutality. I'm callin' those suckers at the SPCA when I get home."

Ellie passed her wine to the waiting woman, dropped to her knees, held T's muzzle, and gazed into his brown eyes. "Be a big boy and go with the nice lady. Rudy's in the puppy playground and so is Lulu, along with Jett and Sweetie Pie and a bunch of other dogs. It's nice to make new friends."

"I ain't about to make friends with uptight champion wannabes livin' to flaunt their AKC papers."

"No one is asking you to, and not all the dogs are champions. Just nose around for a while, enjoy yourself. I saw a guy passing out treats in there."

"I don't like them Nylabones, and I won't eat anything with wheat gluten or preservatives," he stated, sounding like a canine dietary consultant.

"Since when?"

"Since I been watchin' Rachael Ray's commercials on Animal Planet. Her Pit Bull gets

gourmet eats. If it's good enough for a Pit Bull, it's good enough for me."

"What if I escort you inside and check things out? I might as well see how Rudy's doing while I'm there." Standing, Ellie took his lead from Vivian and turned to the waiting attendant, accepting her wine. "A couple more guests with dogs have arrived. Why don't you take care of them while I handle this big boy?"

"Ellie, really. People smiled when they heard what you were saying," Vivian lectured. "But I could tell by the look in their eyes that they thought you might have a couple of screws loose."

Dr. Dave appeared and handed Viv her Merlot, and Ellie ignored her friend's warning. Any owner who truly loved their dog talked to them. She didn't care one biscuit for those who didn't, nor did she care what they thought of her. Smiling at Dave, she said, "How about coming with us? You have to see what Mrs. Steinman set up for our four-legged friends."

When they arrived at the pooch playpen, the vet stepped over the protective gate and glanced around the room, now holding about twenty-five canines. Ellie passed Mr. T over and he and Dr. Dave took off, ready to play ball, check out the treats, and say hello to the other dogs.

"Some friend you are," said Viv after sipping her wine. "He'll be in there for the rest of the night."

"Are you referring to the two-legged or the four-legged he?"

"Both, I guess. T seems to have taken a shine to Dave, obeys him more than he does me."

"Then let them have some fun together, because I have something that will keep you busy." Ellie crooked a finger, motioning for Viv to follow her into the living room. "Are you game for a bit of sleuth duty?"

"Sleuth duty?" Vivian blinked. "Does Sam know?" She raised a hand. "Forget I asked that. Of course he doesn't know. If he did, you'd be out of here faster than a barnyard cat, and if he knew I had a hand in it—"

"You don't have to do anything more than keep a guest busy while I find my number one suspect." Ellie finished her wine in one gulp and set it on a side table. "You'll like this job. I guessed two eye lifts, a nose job, Botox, and a chemical peel the first time I met her. Maybe you can beat my record."

"Holy cannoli. Two eye lifts? How old is this woman?"

"No more than fifty would be my guess. Maybe you could find that out too, just for the record."

"Hang on a second. Let's see if I can pick her out." Viv scanned the guests scattered around the living room. "How about the lady in red over by the windows?"

"That's not her."

Viv continued her inspection. "The woman in blue chatting with Mrs. Steinman?"

"Nope."

"But she's in this room?"

"Yes."

"There are at least twenty people in our viewing area. How about a little hint. Just say 'near the windows' or 'around the sofa' or maybe 'in front of the bookcases.'"

"Check out the couch."

Viv zeroed in on the dozen or so guests sitting on the barge-sized sofa or standing behind it. In a moment, she smiled. "The woman with the dangling diamond earrings, wearing Michael Kors. Not that I think any less of her. The suit will stay in style for a few more years."

"Okay, killer. Keep her talking for at least thirty minutes, more if possible."

Ellie left Vivian to do her thing, crossed the foyer, and sauntered into the dining room. Scouring the crowd, she spotted Edward at the buffet table selecting delicacies from the elegant spread. Hefting a snow-white dinner plate, she stood across from him, planning to meet him when he rounded the end of the fifteen-foot table. She kept her eyes on the food, choosing carefully. Lobster salad, bits of steak skewered between mushrooms, a warm salad of string beans and snow peas with a horseradish and honey glaze, a double-baked potato smothered in blue cheese . . .

Head down, she raised her eyes and saw Edward nearing her intended destination. Passing the dinner rolls and garlic bread, she took a step sideways, gently bumping her quarry's arm.

"Excuse me—I—" She gazed at Edward with a look of complete innocence. "Oh, Mr. Nelson. I'm so sorry. I didn't see you there."

"Not a problem, little lady." He moved to one of the round tables set for four that a maid had just cleared and sat down.

Ellie pasted a smile on her face, followed him, and took the plunge. "Would you mind if I joined you?"

He downed his scotch, then gazed at her through narrowed eyes. "Sure. Sit and take the load off."

She dropped into a chair, opened her napkin, and gracefully laid it on her lap. "How have you been since the MACC?"

"Me? I've been fine." He exchanged his empty glass of scotch for a flute of champagne from a passing waiter. "Why do you ask?"

"No reason, really. I just thought—never mind."

He took a drink of the bubbly, then raised a brow. "You're wondering how I feel about losing Lulu first to Harris and then to you?"

"No, I mean, yes, I mean, well, I won't be showing Lulu again, so it doesn't really matter."

"Not showing her again? Not even at Westminster in February?"

"Nope."

"That means Flora needs a handler again."

"She does, and she's had plenty of offers. Do you know a woman named Felicity Apgar?"

"We've run into each other a couple of times. She lives in Connecticut and she—hang on, are you saying Felicity is trying to cut a deal with Flora?"

"I don't know much about 'cutting a deal,' but I do know she's been pestering Flora about Lulu. It seems she didn't approve of me, a novice, taking a champion into the ring at such an important event."

"She came out and said that?"

"She implied it, and it ticked Flora off. But they called a truce on the day of the finals."

"If I know Flora, she turned Felicity down for another reason besides her being pushy."

Ellie took a bite of her lobster salad, savoring the mayonnaise dressing with a hint of mustard mellowing in the background. Was it possible Edward would give her some info on that rumor no one wanted to discuss? "Really? Funny, she never mentioned anything to me. Maybe you could fill me in?"

"Felicity got a little too big for her britches about six months back. Scheduled more dogs than she could walk, a couple who were ready for

Best in Show." He swallowed another round of champagne. "People thought she purposely tanked two of the canines during breed competition and did a dynamite job with her favorite."

Ellie had hoped there was more to it than that, but maybe Felicity had decided there was another way to fix the competition. "Was she disciplined or sanctioned by the Professional Handlers' Association?"

"Nope, but Arnie Harris was at the show, and he brought it to the officials. When push came to shove, neither owner was willing to lodge a formal complaint, so the incident was dropped."

Ellie finished the last of her lobster. Was Felicity vindictive enough to try and kill Arnie? She vowed to run the theory by Sam and hear what he had to say. "This food is wonderful. Flora has excellent taste. Don't you agree?"

"It's easy to have good taste when you're loaded," Edward said in a slightly annoyed tone.

"I got the impression everyone in the conformation world was loaded. Traveling from show to show, paying trainers, groomers, handlers, entry fees—it must add up."

"More than you'd imagine." He downed his champagne and accepted another glass from the same waiter. "Care to tell me why you don't want to handle Lulu? You could make a pretty penny, more if you repeated your MACC performance at Madison Square Garden."

Ellie screwed her face into an expression of misery. "The job is too stressful. I hate putting myself on display, which is what you have to do when you take a dog around the ring. I'm also afraid I'd be a liability to Lulu. There are a lot of politics in that business, and I don't play the game very well. My tongue starts talking before my brain goes into gear and—well, you can see what I mean."

Edward nodded, finished his second glass of champagne, and grabbed two more from the next passing waiter.

Ellie hoped she was pushing him in the right direction, getting him to consider her a friend, not an adversary. If she got on his good side, he might let something slip about his own feelings. Especially after a double shot of premium scotch and a bottle of high-dollar bubbly.

"So, would you be up to talking with Flora, say, sometime this week? I'd be happy to set it up for you."

"You'd do that for me?" He drained the first of the newest glasses of champagne. "What's in it for you?"

"Me? Why, nothing. My only concern is Lulu. She deserves the best, and from what I've heard that's you," she told him, piling on the compliments.

Glass number four was upended and emptied before he said, "Monday might be okay. Our apartment's being painted and I've been ordered to vacate for the day, so I'd have time to stop by her place. Of course, I'd only be doing this as a favor to the old gal."

Yes! Ellie wanted to high-five the air. "Let me talk to her. If she can make Monday, I'll call and let you know. Do you have a card?"

He dug a card from his inside breast pocket as Nelda raced into the room. "Ms. Engleman, please, come into the foyer. There's trouble brewing and you're the only one who can help."

After tossing her napkin on the table, Ellie dropped the card into her tote and raced after the housekeeper, her mind awhirl with disasters. Had Rudy gotten into a fight because Lulu decided to vamp some hotshot Poodle? Maybe Mr. T had knocked down the gate on his way out of the playground and was running wild looking for Vivian. Entering the foyer, she skidded to a stop.

Sam hadn't said a word about being invited here, yet there he was in the doorway wearing his usual I-mean-business scowl. Vince stood beside him and there were two uniformed officers at their back.

Then she spotted Flora, practically cowering in front of them, and her gut clenched. Shouldering her way through the gathering crowd, she walked to the older woman's side. "Flora, is everything all right?"

"Stay out of this, Ms. Engleman," Sam warned in a no-nonsense tone.

Like she'd listen to him when he was being a bully. "Why are you here, and why is Mrs. Steinman upset?"

"People who are upset usually have something to hide."

Ellie straightened her spine. "Does Mrs. Steinman need her lawyer?"

"That all depends. Does Mrs. Steinman have something she wants to tell us?"

"They've asked me to come downtown for questioning, dear. I have no idea why, but I don't want to go alone." Flora clutched Ellie's hand. "I'll go if you come with me."

Sam huffed out a breath. "An attorney might be better, ma'am. Someone who knows the law and criminal rights."

"Criminal rights?" Ellie took a step forward, invading his space. "Are you saying Mrs. Steinman is a criminal?"

Sam ran a hand through his hair. Picking up on his partner's frustration, Vince said, "Maybe we can take this outside?" Standing back, he indicated that Ellie and Flora should leave the apartment.

After shutting the door, the group clustered in the hallway. Furious that Sam hadn't clued her in on whatever this was about, she put a protective arm around Flora's trembling shoulders. "Please explain the reason you're here, and why Mrs. Steinman needs to go in for questioning."

Sam opened his mouth to speak, but Vince seized the moment. "We have new evidence in the Arnie Harris murder that directly affects Mrs. Steinman. All I can say is she has the right to call an attorney and have him meet us at Midtown."

Chapter 13

Pacing the hall outside the interrogation room that held Flora, Sam, Vince, and Flora's attorney, Ellie recalled leaving the Beaumont in a rush. She'd tugged her coat on while she talked to Vivian, telling her, "This could take a while. Can you bring Rudy home when you leave here, and settle him into bed? Make sure he's calm without me, that sort of thing?"

"No problem," Viv had said. "But where are the cops taking you and Flora?"

With dozens of guests milling in the foyer, Ellie had lowered her voice. "The Midtown Precinct. It seems Detective Ryder wants to have some private time with her and she doesn't want to go alone."

"I don't blame her. Is this about that handler's death?"

Before Ellie could answer, Flora had tottered toward them, pale as paste and wrapped in her mink, and Ellie had taken her arm, then said to Vivian, "I'll tell you about it later. Just take care of my boy, okay?"

Though she had no positive idea what the cops wanted, her mind kept returning to that Baggie Sam and Vince had pulled from Flora's coat just a day earlier.

The stuff in that bag had to be their "new evidence." What else could they have on a seventy-year-old woman who was sweet, kind, and innocent? And how long before they allowed her inside that room so she could hear what they were discussing?

Her cell phone rang and she checked the number. Seeing that it was Viv, she answered the call. "Hi. Are you home?"

"I am. I used my key to drop Rudy off about ten minutes ago. Flora's housekeeper did a good job of handling things after you left. Lorilee saw to it that her fashion show became the focus of the evening, and everyone was thrilled that their dog got a brand-new coat as a memento of Lulu's big win."

"I'll tell Flora that things went well. I'm sure it's been on her mind."

"So, what's going on?"

Ellie gazed at the drab corridor filled with cops rushing from place to place, some leading men in handcuffs, others scribbling on clipboards. "Not much. They put us in a room almost two hours ago, and neither Sam nor Vince stopped by. When Flora's lawyer showed, a detective came in with him and the attorney asked me to leave. I don't have a clue what's going on."

"Who's the old girl's rep?" Vivian asked. "Somebody famous, say a Mark Geragos type?"

"Not so you'd notice. Merlin LeRoy looks more like a soup kitchen chaplain than a lawyer. My guess is he's into estate planning and corporate stuff, not criminal law. If things don't go well, I'm sure he'll recommend someone better acquainted with the justice system to help his client."

"Jeez, I hope so. I can't imagine a woman like Flora Steinman spending a night in the slammer, can you?"

Ellie had to admit it would be ludicrous. She also hoped that the short, rotund man had enough smarts to know if Flora was in real trouble. "Not in my lifetime."

"Want to hear about the fashion show? It might help pass the time."

Dropping into a molded plastic chair, Ellie glanced up and down the hallway. She was getting so used to the police precincts in town that she barely noticed the lack of ambience. "Sure, go ahead. Anything is better than standing around in this depressing place."

"Lorilee does fabulous work. Every canine left with a custom-fitted coat—and not just any coat, but the perfect coat for that pooch. Even Mr. T and Rudy."

"Hang on. Did you say my boy left with a coat?"

"He sure did. It's adorable, too. Black-and-red plaid wool. Lorilee even brought a couple of seamstresses, and one of them had a fancy embroidering thingamabob attached to her sewing machine. The woman embroidered Rudy's name on the back end, cute as could be."

"Good grief. He fights me tooth and nail when I try to get him into outerwear. How the heck did it happen?"

"Beats me. Since you weren't there, Dr. Dave went into the dressing area with him. Dave says they had a man-to-man talk and Rudy cooperated."

Ellie rolled her eyes. "Good Lord, I still don't believe it. And Rudy wore it all the way home?"

"Sure did. I took it off him and set it on your kitchen table. You'll see it when you get here."

"How about Twink? What did he end up with?"

"The only coat he let them put on, and it's the most flamboyant thing you could imagine. I swear, it could belong to one of those over-the-top television pimps from *Miami Vice*. Purple, yellow, and white knit, with feathers on the shoulders and gold chains hanging around the neckline. Twink took one look at the thing and practically nosed himself into it."

The Jack Russell had been a pistol ever since he'd taken on his Mr. T persona. He would never act like a normal dog wearing that type of coat. Shaking her head, Ellie changed the subject. "I have to ask, was the gossip bad?"

"You mean about Flora?"

"Well, yeah."

"Not really. People were so enamored with the four-legged fashion show, they didn't say word one about Mrs. Steinman. Of course, Lorilee had a lot to do with it. She took charge and kept the audience grounded."

"Good. Now I have another question."

"Shoot."

"What did you learn in your talk with Mitzi Nelson?"

Vivian snorted. "That is one self-centered woman. Doesn't care about dogs, cats, even thinks what her husband does for a living is boring and useless. It also sounded to me like she had all the money in the family. It seems that in Mitzi's eyes Edward never amounted to much. He taught at some college when they first met, but nothing ever came of it, so he went back to handling dogs, something he started doing when he was thirteen."

"But there's supposed to be good money in the dog-handling business if you're successful. At least that's the impression I got this week."

"Maybe so, but I don't think the money is enough for darling Mitzi. Best guess, her diamond drop earrings cost five big ones, and when I complimented her on them she said she bought them for herself. Apparently Edward isn't into giving his wife gifts with that kind of price tag."

"Did you see Mitzi and Edward interact?"

"For a couple of minutes, but they left before the fashion show started. Of course, once Edward made a joke about his 'pets,' I didn't blame them. I doubt anyone's ever made a coat for a frog."

"A what?"

"F-R-O-G. Frog. As in *ribit, ribit*."

"Good grief. I didn't think they owned any animal," said Ellie, recalling the last conversation she'd had with Mitzi.

"I'm positive that's what Edward said, though Mitzi gave him the hairy eyeball when he did. Then she latched onto his arm and practically dragged him out. Personally, I think he was drunk."

After a couple tumblers of scotch and several glasses of high-priced champagne, that made sense. "You're sure the word was 'frogs'?"

"Yep. Frogs. As in amphibians."

"And they own them as—as pets?"

"So said Edward."

Ellie was an animal lover, but she couldn't imagine anyone transitioning from dogs to frogs.

"You still there?" Viv called into the phone. "Did I do good?"

"You did great, like Hercule Poirot, Miss Marple, and Sherlock Holmes all rolled into one. Maybe you should get a job with the police as an interrogator."

"Thanks. But you haven't asked. Want to know what kind of business Mitzi runs?"

Ellie was afraid to ask, but she did. "What?"

"She's a regular Joan Rivers when it comes to facial restructuring. She owns a company that specializes in all types of cosmetic surgery, and from the sound of it she has so many famous clients her cash register is ringing like crazy. She has a motto: "Your face is your billboard—""

"Catchy," Ellie interjected.

"She even said she had something new in the works. Something that would revolutionize the face-lift world. Then she went on and on about her biggest seller, an injectable product called Juvariva. It's a secret formula her company came up with. Told me if I came to her shop, she'd let me try it for free."

"Vivian, your skin is flawless. Why would you mess around with chemicals?"

"Hey, I have no idea when I might start to show my age. Forewarned is forearmed, or however that saying goes."

"I'll need it before you do, and even then I'd think twice before I let someone inject anything into me—anywhere."

"Your mother gets stuff done."

"That's because Georgette is always on the hunt for another husband. But since she married Stanley—" Just then the interrogation room door opened and Vince waved her over. "I've got to run. We'll talk about this later."

Steeling herself, Ellie rose and headed toward Vince, who gave her a grin. Maybe things wouldn't be so bad after all.

Ellie and Flora sat in the back of Flora's limo on the ride home from the precinct. She hated to see her friend upset, but there was little she could do besides offer comfort as she listened patiently to the older woman's replay of the police inquiry.

"They were quite pleasant," Flora repeated. "But Detective Fugazzo did seem to have a one-track mind. He kept repeating the same questions, though each sentence was constructed a bit differently."

"What do you mean?"

"Oh, you know. First he'd ask me where I got the Baggie. When I said I had no idea, he'd ask if I ever saw it before. When I said 'no' to that, he asked me if I knew where it might have come from. When I said 'no' again, he wanted to know how it got in my coat pocket."

Thanks to all the times she'd been interrogated by the cops, Ellie knew the drill. Repetitive questions were a police tactic used to trip up the suspected criminal, a way to make the person answer an almost identical question in a different manner, so the cops could accuse the suspect they were grilling of lying.

"As long as you answered each of their questions truthfully, I doubt there'll be a problem," she told Flora. "It's when you lie that things get dicey."

"I would never lie to the police. They're just doing their job. Besides, if anything I said helps them catch Arnie's murderer, I don't mind."

"I'm sure it's going to be all right. Didn't Mr. LeRoy say there was a man in his firm who was a top-notch criminal attorney, and he'd be at your disposal the next time the detectives wanted to question you?"

Heaving a sigh, Flora patted Ellie's hand. "Whoever he is, he's going to be at your disposal, too, dear. I'll see to it."

My disposal? "Um . . . why would I need a criminal attorney?"

"Well, some of the questions revolved around you being hired to take Arnie's place. I told them you wouldn't accept money for showing Lulu and that I had to practically force you into the job, but that didn't seem to matter."

Ellie swallowed her anger. How dare Sam try to implicate her! He knew she had refused the task of handling the Havanese. She'd told him so a dozen times. What the heck was going on?

She squeezed Flora's fingers. "I don't think either one of us is in real trouble. Tell me again what they said about the liver in that Baggie."

Flora heaved a sigh, "Detective Fugazzo

seemed most interested. In fact, he led the questioning. He didn't come right out and say so, but he intimated that the liver they found in my coat pocket was soaked in the same unknown substance as the treat Arnie had put in his mouth."

"And they didn't say what this substance was?"

"Not a word." The limo pulled in front of Ellie's apartment, and Peebles hopped out to open her door. "I might remember more after I get a good night's sleep," Flora said. "Stop in tomorrow if you get some free time, and we'll talk. Nelda can fill us in on more of what happened at the party after we left."

Ellie hadn't gone very far into the details of the fashion show, because she was more interested in the actual questioning by the cops. "I'll be happy to pay you and Lulu a visit, if it won't inconvenience you or your housekeeper. I'll call first." She stepped onto the sidewalk. "Get a good night's rest and don't worry. Things are going to work out."

She climbed the porch steps and turned in time to see the white stretch glide into traffic. Then she checked her watch. It was past midnight, too late for her to wake Vivian or do much of anything else, but she needed something to calm her down.

After taking the stairs to the third floor, she entered her condo, removed her coat, hat, and gloves, and hung everything in the closet. Then she walked into the kitchen and turned on the light. Maybe a cup of tea would help her fall asleep faster.

Smiling when she saw Rudy's new coat on the table, she picked it up and examined the stitching, the warm lining, and the way the plaid matched perfectly at the seams. No doubt about it, the item was top of the line. Smoothing the coat, she set it down and went to the counter, where she filled a cup with water and placed it in the microwave.

Just then her buzzer rang. Thinking it was Peebles returning to tell her about something Mrs. Steinman had forgotten to convey, she simply pressed the entry buzzer, then walked to the door and waited. When she heard a soft knock, she peered out the peephole and gasped.

There stood Sam, wearing a scowl and pacing in a circle.

She opened the door, and Sam brushed past her and stomped into the kitchen. He took a mug from her cupboard and set it next to hers in the microwave. Then he hit the timer and started the oven cooking.

She didn't say one word, just went to her pantry, brought out two bags of herbal tea, and put them on the counter. If the dastardly detective wanted to talk, he could make their drinks. She was so angry, there was a chance she'd bean him on his self-inflated head if he gave her a chance to touch a mug.

She took her usual seat at the table and waited. The timer rang and he removed the cups, added the tea bags, and opened a drawer to get spoons. Then he brought everything to the table, set the drink and a spoon down, and pulled up a chair.

Continuing to ignore him, Ellie fiddled with her tea bag, sloshing it up and down, then squeezing out the drippings. Taking a napkin from the holder, she used it to drain the bag. When she raised her eyes, she saw that he was watching her.

"Ellie, I—"

She stood and went to the pantry, where she found a box of chocolate chip cookies. After removing one for herself, she placed the package on the table.

"Look, Ellie, I—"

"Excuse me, did you say something?" She sipped her tea, hoping not to choke as she swallowed.

"Yes, I did. I'm trying to—"

"To what? Kick me when I'm down? Or maybe you think it's more fun to kick a senior citizen."

He blew out a breath. "I'm trying to apologize."

She bit back a sassy retort. It wasn't often Detective Demento apologized, so she decided to let him talk.

"Are you going to listen?"

She shrugged as if she had nothing better to do, and took a bite of the cookie.

"It wasn't my idea to bring Flora Steinman in for questioning."

"Really? I thought you were the lead on this case."

"I was." He took a swallow of his tea.

"'Was'? What do you mean 'was'?"

"Vince is the lead detective now. I was asked to step back and do the legwork."

Ellie blinked. "Step back? But why?"

"Don't take this the wrong way, but it's because of you." He reached across the table and clasped her hand. "Someone at the top heard you were involved in this mess, and they told Vince that he should take the point position. They didn't want it to look like we were going easy on you or Flora because you and I are dating."

She stiffened in her chair. Okay, so she'd been involved in a couple of murder investigations. So what? The real culprit had been found in each case, both times with her help, so how could the cops at the top think her a liability? And how dare they view Sam Ryder, one of the most trustworthy and honest men she knew, as a guy who would put personal involvement before his job?

"That's the dumbest thing I ever heard," she said, entwining their fingers. "You would never let anyone get away with murder, even the woman you . . . you're . . . seeing."

"I'm happy you feel that way, but you don't run things at headquarters. Captain Carmody said it wouldn't hurt my chances of a promotion or any-thing, and it wasn't a slur against my work ethic. He just thought it might be better if Vince took charge."

"And Vince is okay with this?"

Sam grinned. "Yeah, sort of. He likes things that are a bit more meaty. Thinks the whole idea of someone killing to win a dog show is baloney. Carmody tended to agree. Said if we don't get proof positive that a crime was committed, we had to let it go."

"Let it go? But that means Arnie's murderer will get away." She drew back her hand. "I can't believe you'd let that happen."

"First off, it's no longer my call. Carmody's right—without something concrete we don't even have a case." Sam took another swallow of tea. Then he set the mug down and heaved a sigh. "Use your head. We have no evidence of foul play. Hell, we don't even have a murder weapon. All we have is conjecture. Nothing more."

"I spent some time with Edward Nelson tonight. Did you know that Arnie Harris tried to get Felicity Apgar involved in a disciplinary action?"

"We heard. We also know that it didn't go any-where." Sam frowned. "Stop talking to Mr. Nelson about this case. It won't do you any good."

Ellie ignored his comment and pushed on. "So

the ME will just go along with the SADS theory and let the case go?"

"What else can Dr. Bridges do?" Standing, he brought his cup to the sink, rinsed it out, and placed it in the dish drainer. Then he turned to face her. "I understand you have a strong suspicion that something was odd about the way the man died. I do too. But without proof—"

"What about the toxicology report on the dog treat Arnie put in his mouth? Isn't that why you brought Flora in tonight? Because she had a bag of liver with the same substance on it?"

"You got it."

"What made you search her coat?"

"I can't say."

Ellie finished her tea, walked to his side, and put her cup in the sink. "You can't say because it's none of my business or—"

"Not just because it's none of your business. Because I don't want you involved any more than you already are." Sam grabbed her upper arms and pulled her close. "I don't want to see you hurt—in any way. Since we've met, you've been in a couple of situations that were downright terrifying. Carmody was right about one thing, which is why I didn't argue. I can't do my job if I'm worried about you."

She opened her mouth to protest and he bent forward, brushing her lips with his. "Shh. Don't talk. Just listen." He pulled her near, and she rested her head on his chest. "I don't want anything to happen to you. You're not just another citizen of this city, you're my girl. And I protect what's mine. It would be a lot easier to do that if you kept your nose clean."

Ellie stared up at him. "Why, Detective Ryder, it sounds like you care."

Instead of answering, he leaned forward and captured her mouth in a kiss that was both sweet and filled with passion. She melted when he molded his body to hers. The kiss lasted forever, and Ellie lost herself in desire until slowly, almost reluctantly, Sam drew back.

"When this is over, I want a date night."

A blush heated her cheeks. Though Sam's eyes darkened to the color of rich coffee, telegraphing the true meaning of his request, she had to be sure. "You've had a couple of dozen date nights in the past several months."

He grinned. "You know what I mean."

"Oh."

He stared at her as if she was a life preserver on the *Titanic* and he was a drowning man. "Yes, 'oh.' I want to spend the night in your bed."

Weak-kneed, she nodded. He gave her another quick kiss, then stepped aside. "I've got to run. I doubt I'll be able to break free this weekend, but I'll try. Lock the door behind me."

He sauntered out of the room and it took her thirty seconds to gather her senses and do what he'd told her to do. After locking the door, she turned and found Rudy at her feet.

"What did Detective Doofus want?"

"What are you doing up?" She walked to the kitchen, flicked off the light, and headed down the hall.

"The diphead dick woke me. I'd know his voice anywhere. And that means trouble."

She went into her bedroom and stripped off her jacket and slacks. "You know he only wants what's best for me." She grabbed her sleep shirt from the foot of the bed. "I'll be back in a minute."

After taking care of business in the bathroom, she returned to the bedroom, where Rudy was already curled up on the pillow next to hers. "I see you got your present from Flora tonight."

"I had to accept it. Dr. Dave told me so."

Ellie plopped on the mattress. "Wait a minute. You'll listen to your veterinarian but not to me? What kind of a deal is that?"

"Lulu picked it out, so I had to say yes."

"What do you mean, 'Lulu picked it out'?"

"She followed me and Dr. Dave into the dressing room. Told me the red plaid would look good with my coloring. I didn't want to hurt her feelings, so I said okay and tried it on."

"And . . . ?"

"And it looked okay. It isn't knit, so you don't have to pull it on over my head, and it doesn't itch. That was the big selling point."

"Why didn't you tell me that was the problem with the other coats? I could have found you one that didn't go on over your head and didn't itch." She scratched his ears. "You know I'd give you anything you wanted. Within reason, of course."

"I know, it's just that—"

"I'm not Lulu."

"Hey, you're my number one girl, but just like you tell me about Sam and you, well, it's the same for Lulu and me." He snuggled under her stroking fingers and raised his chin to show his favorite scratch spot. *"We're canines and you're humans, and the twain can never meet."*

"Fine. Let's just leave it at that." She stood and went to her dresser to brush her hair. It was then she spotted the piece of liver she'd found in her blazer pocket earlier. "Oh, Lord. I forgot to tell Sam about this."

"So what? We don't need him to figure it out."

"Figure what out?"

"Who murdered Arnie Harris."

"Sam just made a point of asking me to stay out of things."

"Since when has that stopped you?"

"Since now. Besides, it doesn't look like we'll find any proof that a crime was committed, and if I keep nosing around I could be arrested for hindering an ongoing investigation. The last thing I want is to be represented by a criminal attorney for butting in where I don't belong."

"Are you involved with another attorney?"

"Not like I was with Kevin McGowan," she said, since he'd brought up the louse who'd used her to scam a friend. "Flora's lawyer would help me out."

"Guess it's time for another joke, then."

"Ugh! I want to go to sleep, not be regaled with dopey lawyer jokes." She climbed into bed and pulled up the covers. Seeing the yorkiepoo's sad expression, she said, "Okay, but only one, and it had better be good."

Rudy circled the pillow and gave a yawn. *"What do you say when you see a lawyer buried up to his neck in the sand?"*

Ellie turned off the bedside light, then drew him into the crook of her arm. "I have no idea."

"That's easy. There's not enough sand!"

Chapter 14

Yawning, Ellie stood at the sink and filled the carafe with water. After grinding beans and measuring the coffee into the coffeemaker, she clicked the machine on, sat at the kitchen table, and rested her head in her hands. Still in a daze from her night of hellish dreams, she tried to make sense of it all.

The nightmares were crazy, off the wall, frightening. The strange scenes had rolled from one reel to the next, as if a dozen movies were playing one right after the other on the screen. Between the poisoned flies that Sam had eaten while she shouted out warnings and the frogs parading around the ring on leashes held by dogs walking on their hind legs, she wasn't sure which had terrified her more.

But the most bizarre scene had to be the one where Mitzi Nelson was judging frogs on a table in a darkened room. It made sense that Edward handled every frog, but when he killed each one after it hopped to its place on the show ring floor, well, it was downright disgusting. At one point, probably when the winning frog had danced across the ring to a funeral dirge, she'd actually started to cry. It was then that she'd grabbed Rudy in a choke hold and squeezed him so tight he'd howled, waking her up as she screamed.

She managed to fall into a restless sleep sometime around dawn and had awakened less than an hour ago. The quick shower she'd taken hadn't cleared her brain, nor had her morning walk with Rudy, so her next lifeline was a cup of coffee laced with caramel sauce and a dollop of whipping cream.

If that didn't help, she'd try to get an appointment at a spa that specialized in massages—painful, muscle-drilling, potato-mashing massages. It was all she could think of to bring her out of her haze and back to the land of the living.

The coffeemaker buzzed and she walked to the refrigerator, where she pulled out the can of whipping cream and the container of homemade caramel sauce. She loved the thick, rich goo so much that she'd learned to make it herself a few months ago. It was loaded with sugar and heavy cream, but she figured she walked enough each day to burn off the extra calories. Besides, on mornings like this, she deserved something special to mellow her out and bring a sense of well-being to her soul.

She smiled at the sound of Rudy's nails clipping on the tile floor. Her boy was usually able to mellow her out, too, on a normal morning, but after her creepy dreams, this morning was far from normal.

After adding a scoop of caramel to her cup and pouring in the dark, strong coffee, she added a squirt of cream, inhaled a gulp, and turned. "Hey, big guy. Sorry about last night."

"It was morning when you got me in that death grip, Triple E. What the heck was going on?"

"Nightmares. Very bad nightmares." She sat down and took another sip of coffee. "You ever have one?"

Rudy meandered to his food dish and nosed his morning nibble. Plunking his bottom down, he gave her a pointed look. *"Sure. Sometimes I dream my dinner doesn't show. I follow you around, but you ignore me, make your own supper, and don't even share. Other times, I dream that Lulu has the hots for some big-time show dog with a pigheaded pedigree and a pompous attitude to match. The canine's name is usually Pierre, but I have no idea why."*

"Pierre, huh? Interesting."

"I get day-mares too, but that's usually when I'm catchin' a little shut-eye sitting with you."

"You mean when you whine and twitch on the sofa while we watch television."

"Exactly. But those aren't too scary. They usually revolve around chasing the furry-tailed rodents that roam Central Park, but mostly they're about food."

"I know the feeling. I dreamed about good food the entire time I was married to the dickhead. Always being on a diet will do that to a girl." She swallowed another gulp of coffee, letting the sweet, hot brew warm her insides and clear her mind. "So what's the worst nightmare you've ever had?"

"Trust me, you don't want to know." Standing up, he nosed his kibble, then took a bite and chewed.

"Aw, come on. Is it something else involving Lulu? Mr. T? How about Cheech and Chong? The way you carry on about those Chihuahuas, I can only imagine the dreams you have about them."

Rudy finished his breakfast and took a long

drink of water. Walking to her, he put both paws on her thigh. "It's not about those two bean-eaters, or any other dogs."

"Really? What, then?"

"Okay, but don't say I didn't warn you." Laying his head on her knee, he sighed. *"I sometimes dream we've lost each other again. I'm in a dark tunnel and I'm callin' and callin' your name, and you don't answer."*

Tears sprang to Ellie's eyes. Rudy was right. This was one story she didn't want to hear. She knew dogs rarely outlived their owners, and she recalled how difficult it had been returning from her honeymoon and getting his ashes from Georgette. In a way, she was glad the dickhead had stopped her from adopting another dog after that, because if she had she might never have found Rudy again.

Reaching down, she hoisted the yorkiepoo onto her lap and nuzzled her nose in his neck. "That dream would upset me, too. I can't imagine what I'd do without you—where I'd be—how my life would turn out." She sniffed. "I love you."

He licked her jaw. *"But you'd have Detective Dipstick to keep you warm at night if I left. You don't need me."*

"You mean the world to me. If you told me a man was a 'no-go' and had a good reason for it, I'd listen."

"Then let's talk about the demonic detective."

"We've discussed Sam a hundred times, and you've never given me a single concrete reason to ditch him. Aside from that one dumb thing he did last April, he's been a gentleman."

"Maybe so, but that could change at any moment." He gave her another lick, then jumped down. *"I guess I have to accept the fact that you really like him, huh?"*

"Afraid so. Even if I'm not sure how he feels about me."

"Hah! He's hot for your bod, of course. What human male in his right mind wouldn't be?"

She glanced down at her C-cup boobs, which she figured were a plus. Then she rubbed the annoying roll sitting above the waistband of her jeans. Her body was generously shaped, her legs well defined because of her profession, but she would never be the size of a Hollywood starlet or fashion model.

"Most males like women who are built like Vivian, and many of them want a woman who puts them first, even if they're slobs who drop clothes wherever they go, leave the toilet seat up, or fart and belch for the fun of it." Ellie walked to the treat cupboard, took a Dingo bone from a package, and tossed him the chew. "There are a lot of men like the dickhead I once called a husband. They think women were born to do their bidding."

"Yeah, but you got wise and dumped the asinine airbag."

"And now I have you . . . and Sam. I just hope the two of you can resolve your differences. Then everything in my life would be—" A knock at the door stopped her cold. "Hang on. That's probably Viv wanting to hear about my night at the precinct."

She rushed to the door and checked the peephole. Sure enough, there stood Vivian holding what looked to be a bag of booty from Monsieur Bagel. Ellie swung the door open and bowed. "Enter, oh dear best friend who brings gifts covered with lox and a schmear."

"Sounds to me like you have yet to eat breakfast." With Mr. T walking beside her, the dark-haired investment banker strode in and headed for the kitchen. "I thought about buying coffee, too, but I figured you had a pot brewing." After setting the bag on the table, she dropped a huge glop of caramel into a mug and poured coffee in. "Got any cream?"

"Just the kind in a can." Ellie plucked a Dingo bone from the cupboard and tossed it to Mr. T, who caught it midair and disappeared into the hall.

"Guess it'll have to do." Viv sprayed a mound of the white frothy stuff into her cup and took a seat. She started to blow on the coffee, but all that got her was a nose dotted with cream. "Oops." She wiped the spot with a napkin, then took a drink. "Yum, this is the best."

"I offered to teach you how to make the

caramel," Ellie said, beginning her usual lecture on frugality. "My version of a caramel bliss costs pennies compared to what Joe charges."

"Maybe so, but Joe's is less work. Besides, you know I don't have the cooking gene."

"Beside the fact that making flavored coffee really isn't cooking, that's just plain silly. Everyone has a cooking gene. They simply need to find it."

"I'd rather find the Bergdorf gene, or the Ralph Lauren gene. Kirna Zabete or Dernier Cri would be great, too."

"With all the money you spend on clothes, I'm amazed you can pay your mortgage," Ellie said, straight-faced.

"Hey, I'm in the 'making money' business. I have to look like I'm loaded so my clients will trust my advice on managing their cash." She unwrapped her bagel. "I'm doing okay, but the 401(k) is suffering these days. How about you?"

"I'm doing okay, too. I paid Mother the last cent I owed her in August."

"Well, good for you." Viv sipped her coffee, eyeing her friend carefully. "Maybe you shouldn't have donated all the money Gary left Rudy to the ASPCA and Best Friends."

"Those animal charities deserved every penny. Me, I'm fine. Even now, after paying an assistant, there's enough for the bills—and new clothes, if I want them."

"Then tag along with me this afternoon. I'm going to a couple of places for new duds. If you don't want to buy anything, you could give me a candid opinion and deliver me from some simpering salesgirl who tells me everything fits like a glove and I look like a million bucks."

"But you do look like a million bucks," Ellie said, grinning. "I hate you."

"Yeah, sure you do." Viv crossed her arms and leaned back in her chair. "So, tell me about last night."

Twenty minutes later, Ellie had filled her in on what she knew of Flora's interrogation. Then she added the part about Sam. "He seemed okay with losing his spot as lead detective, but I think he was putting on an act so I wouldn't worry."

"Those cops are crazy. Ryder is the most straight-up law officer I know."

Ellie downed the last of her coffee and unwrapped her bagel. "Not to spoil your assessment of Sam, but how many cops do you know?"

Viv huffed out a breath. "A few . . . maybe one or two." When Ellie raised a brow, she came clean. "Okay, just Detective Dreamy, but he's as honest as—as you are."

"Thanks for the compliment, but Sam has me beat by a mile. I'll give back extra change at the register, but he'll give back a nickel or a dime even if he's already on the sidewalk."

"Okay, so he's a model of manly virtue," said

Viv, chowing down on her bagel. "Did the cops say anything about that liver?"

"Plenty, but the bottom line is there's still no report from toxicology. No report means no murder weapon, and without a murder weapon there's no proof of a crime."

"Maybe there's a private lab they can go to. Too bad you don't have a sample. If you did, you could have it done yourself."

Ellie jumped to her feet. "But I do! I just forgot about it. I'll be right back."

Later that afternoon Ellie sat in front of her computer going through the Web sites of private labs available on the Internet. Overwhelmed, she drummed her fingers on the desktop. "I swear, there's so much information online, I could probably find the plans to make a home version of the bubonic plague."

"Maybe. I just can't imagine why you'd want to," answered Rudy from his place at her feet.

"I wouldn't, but some of this information might come in handy one day. Take laboratories, for instance. There are dozens that do private work. If I convince Sam to send that liver to one of them—"

"Do you really want Detective Dismal to know you're still trying to solve Arnie's murder?"

She heaved a sigh. "I guess not."

"Then tackle the job yourself. If you have a

sample of the bad stuff, the doofus dick doesn't have to know. When you find the killer, he'll forgive you. If he doesn't—drop him."

Ellie stretched to work out the kinks in her shoulders. She'd made a trip to the Gourmet Garage and Gristede's and fixed a decent lunch at home, but when she combined that with her lousy night her head hurt and her eyes watered. Now, after searching the Internet for labs, she was beat.

"I'm too tired to think about it. I'm going to take a nap."

When Rudy didn't answer, she glanced down and found him licking his privates at warp speed. "That is so disgusting. Please stop."

"Hey, licking the area where I used to have balls is about all I have to look forward to." He stood and nosed her knee. *"If we nap, we'll have a hard time falling asleep tonight. You might even have a second round of bad dreams."*

"I certainly couldn't handle another night like that. What do you suggest?"

"I say we pay a visit to Lulu and Mrs. Steinman, find out if the old girl's thought of anything else that might help with the case. Flora is sharp, even if it takes her a while to get up to speed. Besides, I thought you told me she asked you to stop by today."

"She did."

"Then let's get moving."

259

Rudy followed her to the kitchen, where Ellie checked the thermometer hanging in her window over the sink and noted it was a balmy forty-five degrees outside. "It's warmed up a little, but I still think it's too cold for you. How about wearing your new coat?"

He shook from head to tail, then stood on his hind legs and checked out the tabletop. *"As long as Lulu thinks I look good in it, why not?"*

"It's in the front closet," Ellie told him, heading for the foyer. She found the red-and-black wool coat and squatted. After draping the garment over his back, she fastened the straps under his belly and chin. "Hold still. You want to look your best, don't you?"

"Not for every Tom, Dick, and Harry on the street, I don't. Just for my girl."

Ellie stood and slipped on her down jacket, but left her hat and scarf on the shelf. After she clipped Rudy's lead to his collar, they took off for the street. The wind had quieted down and the late afternoon sun warmed the air. They passed the usual parade of pedestrians as they crossed Second Avenue, then Third, Lexington, Park, and Madison. On Fifth, they made a left and arrived at the Beaumont. Inside the lobby, Ellie thought she should announce herself. This was Saturday, not one of her regular days to walk Lulu. Mrs. Steinman might be napping or out somewhere.

Unfamiliar with the weekend doorman, she

introduced herself and asked him to buzz Flora's apartment. He did as she asked, got instructions, and nodded toward the elevator. "Mrs. Steinman says to go up. Said you know the way."

When they arrived on the correct floor, Ellie led Rudy toward the apartment, and the door opened before she rang the bell. "Come right in," said Nelda. "Ms. Flora's expecting you."

Ellie handed the housekeeper her coat and Rudy's. "Is she all right?"

Nelda shrugged. "As right as can be expected when you're past seventy and you spend half a night in jail."

"She wasn't 'in jail' exactly. Just there for questioning," Ellie reminded her.

"I know, but it still breaks my heart imagining that sweet old thing in such a place."

"Ellie? Is that you?" a voice called. Walking slowly, but with regal bearing, Flora arrived in the foyer from the direction of the kitchen. "Nelda, I've put the kettle on and popped a few of your delicious scones and two of those pecan tarts in the microwave. We'll have tea in the living room, if you don't mind."

Flora took Ellie's arm. "Lulu's around here somewhere. Let's look in my bedroom, shall we?"

A few minutes later, Lulu and Rudy were happily gnawing on chew treats while Ellie and Flora sat on the silk-covered sofa in the living room.

Dressed in a pale pink woolen caftan, Flora appeared frail and tired. Ellie patted her hand. "How are you doing? And tell me the truth, please."

Flora sighed. "As well as can be expected. I had a call this morning from that criminal attorney Mr. Leroy mentioned. He asked me a list of questions and told me if the police came to see me again, I wasn't to go anywhere with them. Just call him first, and we'd decide what to do."

"I think that's wise."

Nelda strode in carrying a tray and tea fixings, and Ellie decided to stay mum while the house-keeper did her thing. When Nelda finished pouring, she said, "It's time I went home, Ms. Flora. You going to be okay without me for the next day or so?"

"Of course I will. Peebles can drive you, if you like."

"No, thanks. It's just a short subway ride and the weather is on the decent side. I'll be here on Monday. Try not to stress yourself tomorrow." Nodding good-bye, Nelda left the room.

"For some reason, I thought your housekeeper was live-in help," said Ellie. "But it sounds like you're alone on Sundays."

"I am, and I manage all of Lulu's walks myself unless the weather is bad, in which case Peebles takes over. During the week, you see to my baby in the morning and afternoon, and Nelda gives her a final outing around nine, then goes home. On

Saturday, she usually does each walk, but I told her I could do the afternoon and evening ones today and she could leave early. During the week she mostly just tidies up, takes care of the laundry, and keeps me company. Some days we play canasta or watch game shows. Whatever strikes our fancy."

Ellie thought about Georgette and her faithful housekeeper, Corinna, who had almost the same schedule, though no dog was involved. It was difficult to imagine any woman agreeable to giving up her own life for that of someone who wasn't a relative. "Nelda is great. You're lucky you have her."

"That I am." Flora sipped her tea. "So . . . how did you sleep last night?"

"Me? Um . . . fine. What about you?"

Flora stared off into space. "Not well at all. I've been thinking . . ."

"Yes?"

"You've been so kind to me, almost like a granddaughter. I hate to ask this of you, but . . ."

"Yes?"

"Could you please figure out who killed Arnie? I'm afraid those detectives don't have a clue, and I know you've been successful in the past."

Ellie set her cup and saucer on the table. "You want me to find the person who murdered Mr. Harris?"

"I know it's a lot to ask, but I simply cannot believe he died of nothing, and I know you don't believe it either. If the police aren't having any luck narrowing things down, it's up to us, and I'm afraid there isn't much I can do, so . . ."

Ellie decided to tell Flora a bit about her predicament with the sometimes controlling detective, ending with, "I agree something has to be done, but Sam's already warned me to stay out of it."

Flora frowned. "Oh, well, then . . . I wouldn't want you to do anything that would get you in trouble with your young man."

"It's already too late for that. I got an idea last night and I'm sure he wouldn't approve. Would you like to hear it?"

When the older woman nodded, Ellie told her about the private lab theory and reminded her of the liver sample Arnie had given her for Rudy on that first day.

"We have nothing to lose by sending the sample out. I say we do it," Flora told her.

"Okay, then. I'll take care of it on Monday." The look of hope in Flora's eyes prompted Ellie to ask, "Do you have plans for dinner?"

"Just the meal Nelda left in the refrigerator."

"How do you feel about takeout?"

"If it's Chinese, I love it."

"I know a great place and they deliver." Ellie dug in her tote bag and pulled out a crumpled menu. "Take a look and we'll call in an order. My treat."

Chapter 15

Sam groaned at the sound of his chirping cell phone, then willed himself awake. Who the hell was calling at—he peered at the clock on his bedside table—seven a.m. on a Sunday? It was a hell of a way to start his first morning off in a week, especially since his latest case had him stumped by a mile and he was on Ellie's shit list.

At least, he assumed he was on the list of people she hoped would drop into the East River. And after he and Vince had been forced to question Flora Steinman, he didn't blame her.

Heaving a sigh, he reached out, lassoed the charging phone, and flipped it open. "Ryder."

"Sammy, it's me."

He slumped into the mattress, positive that whoever had invented caller ID had a mother just like Lydia Ryder. Besides Vince or the NYPD, who else would dare raise him at this ungodly hour? Lucky for him his sisters didn't take after Lydia in the nosy department. Susan and Sherry rode him hard about his lack of interaction with the family, but they were too busy living their own lives to give a continuous critique of his.

"Hey, Ma," he said after clearing his throat. "What do you need?"

Deafening silence. Then, "Do I always have to 'need' something if I want to talk with my only son?"

He swung his legs over the side of the bed and sat up. A voice in his head warned him to tread carefully. "Of course not. I just thought, it being a Sunday and all, you might want me to do something for you."

"What I want is company for dinner tonight. You've skipped the last three family gatherings in a row, and I miss you. Queens isn't that far away, you know."

"Ma, look—"

"And what's going on with you and that girl who walks dogs? The one you keep hidden in a closet." She huffed out a breath. "Are you still seeing her?"

"I don't hide her in a closet. We're busy people with a lot on our plates and—"

"So bring her to dinner tonight. Whenever I've asked to meet her—and it's been a dozen times at least—all I get is an excuse. I'm tired of being ignored."

"I haven't been ignoring you. I'm just not sure what Ellie's up to this weekend. She could be busy or . . . something." Like sticking pins in a brown-eyed voodoo doll wearing a NYPD detective's badge.

"You are still seeing her, right? Because if you want to tell me something private about your love life, you know I can handle it."

Private? Love life? Sam rolled his eyes. "Please, Ma, not the gay thing again."

"I'm in tune with the twenty-first century. I know there are men who like . . . men. If that's you, I'd rather you tell me now than I find out about it through the grapevine."

"I refuse to discuss this with you. I'm straight. Just too damned busy."

"Well, thank the Lord for that," she said, relief ringing in her tone. "I still don't like the fact that you're alone, Sammy. You're nearing forty, too old for a man to be by himself all the time."

"I was thirty-four on my last birthday, Ma."

"Time passes quickly. Before you know it those six years will be gone." She waited a beat before saying, "Please don't tell me you broke up with Ms. Engleman."

"No, no. But there's a lot going on in the department. I haven't been able to pay Ellie the attention she deserves or—"

"Ha! Just like with all the other women in your life. Didn't you learn your lesson with Carolanne?"

"I don't intend to put any woman through what I did to my ex-wife, even if I was only doing my job." In his heart, he knew Ellie would never pull a Carolanne and cheat on him. She was too loyal, too honest, too good a person. "Be patient. You'll meet her soon enough."

"If you won't bring her here tonight, you can bring her for dinner with your family on turkey day. Sherry and Tom, Susan and her current boyfriend, your aunt Isabelle and uncle Henry, Jack and Lorraine, even a few of your cousins will be here. We might even have a baby to enjoy."

Where the hell was Sherry's kid, anyway? He dreamed of the day when little Julie would arrive, because from the moment his niece took her first breath, Lydia would forget about him and channel all her energy into being the world's proudest grandmother. "I thought the happy couple was going to Tom's parents' house on Long Island."

"They are, for a one o'clock dinner, but they'll be here for the Ryder family meal at six."

He and Ellie hadn't spent one second discussing the upcoming holidays. Yes, he wanted to spend them with her, but she had a wealthy mother and a retired superior court judge for a stepfather, and she probably had the same obligations he did. Sharing the holidays with her ritzy family was the last place a working stiff belonged.

"I might be able to make it, but I can't speak for Ellie."

"You *might* be able to make it? What the heck does that mean? Are you on duty?" She took a deep breath. "Wait, that's a dumb question. You're always on duty."

"I'll either be off on Thanksgiving or Christmas, maybe New Year's Eve, but it's a toss-up. I have to work out the schedule with the department."

"Are you saying it's two weeks until turkey day and you have yet to pin down your time off?"

Okay, color him stupid, first for not taking care of it and second for letting Lydia know he'd dropped the ball. Again. "Cut me a break, Ma. We're up to our eyeballs in cases downtown. I'll take care of it."

"Today?" When he didn't give an immediate answer, she said, "Sammy, you're going to do it today."

"Okay, okay. Today. And I'll ask Ellie about turkey—I mean Thanksgiving."

"And you and Ms. Engleman will stop by for supper tonight?"

"Yeah, okay, fine." Whatever.

"Dinner will be on the table at six. Pork roast, smashed sweet potatoes, onion and apple gravy—"

"Sounds like a new menu. Are you still watching that Rachael Ray woman?"

"Of course I am. She's a smart one, with so many recipes. I know you love my stuffed pork chops, but I'm making a roast instead, which means it won't be ready in thirty minutes like Rachael's other dinners, but it doesn't matter. I'm sure it will taste—"

"Fine, Ma. Anything you cook is good. I'll see you at six." Sam hung up before he had to hear another word about the brilliant Ms. Ray, his mother's foray into new recipes, or his lack of attention to the holidays. He headed for the bathroom to shower. After a decent breakfast, he would call Ellie and invite her to meet Lydia Ryder without the rest of the family hanging around.

He shrugged. Maybe it would be better if Ellie was still angry with him about Mrs. Steinman. Then he could take his time getting back in her good graces, and by then the Arnie Harris investigation would be over. After that, dragging her to his mom's for Thanksgiving would be a breeze.

Ellie scanned the computer screen while drinking her Sunday-morning home version of a caramel bliss. Satisfied that this was a third reputable private laboratory, she hit the "contact us" prompt and wrote an e-mail asking for the particulars on how to send a sample of the item needing analysis. So far, each of the labs she'd found promised to carefully inspect whatever was sent and assured her that every request would be kept in confidence and the findings known only to the sender.

In the inquiries she'd just posted, she asked how the sample should be sent. On ice? Via registered mail? By private courier or by one of the regular delivery services? Though she'd already double-wrapped and sealed the treat she'd received from Arnie, she still wasn't sure if she should divide it into thirds and mail a section to each lab or mail every bit of it to the first lab that answered.

What if the liver shouldn't have been kept cold at all, but at room temperature? If that were the case, would the lab be able to name the chemical or poison on the treat, or would the test results come up negative? The goo had been sitting in her jacket pocket in a closet for a couple of days. Was it possible she'd already ruined the sample and rendered any tests it was given useless?

After hitting the send key, she breathed a sigh of relief. She'd never done this kind of thing before and had no idea of the proper channels to follow. She had more questions than answers and no clue as to where to go for help. If the independent laboratories couldn't do what she asked . . .

"I take it you did the deed?" said a voice near her feet.

Glancing down, she locked gazes with her yorkiepoo. "I asked each of the three labs willing to do an independent study how the sample should be sent. I expect I'll get an answer sometime tomorrow."

"What happens if you send a sample to each one and they all come back and tell you they didn't find a trace of anything suspicious?"

"I won't have the faintest idea what to do next. Maybe Sam can—"

"Yer dreamin' if you think Ryder will cut loose a chunk of liver the cops are holding, Triple E."

"But—"

Rudy stood on his hind legs and rested his paws on her thigh. *"He made it clear he doesn't want you involved—in any part of the investigation."*

"Okay, I see what you're saying." Ellie ran a hand over his head and scratched his ears. "We'll just have to think positive thoughts. Our liver will be good enough to produce results."

"Bigger question. What if it does?"

"You mean what if they tell me they *did* find poison on the treat?"

"Yeah. What if?"

"I'm not sure." Thinking out loud, she leaned back in her chair. "I'll still have to figure out who doctored the treats and switched the Baggies, and it will still be up to the police to arrest the guy, so I guess I'll be forced to tell Sam what I did anyway."

"Good luck with that one."

"The cops should be happy I took charge and came up with results they didn't, don't you think?"

"Hah! My guess is the demonic dick will be furious you disobeyed a direct order. And there's no way the cops will accept your results, when they're waitin' on their own sample to come

back. By the time they figure it out, the killer could be a million miles from here, or find a way to cover his tracks."

"But if I don't do something, I'll be letting Flora down. For some reason she felt confident I would be able to prove that Arnie was murdered and find his killer."

"Lulu wants the truth, too. She misses the old guy."

"Really? She told you that?"

"Not in so many words, but she did say she wished he was still around, for Flora's sake, of course."

"Ah, for Flora. Well, it's nice that she's thinking of someone else for a change."

"For a cosseted canine, she's not so bad."

"You're only saying that because you want Little Miss Pickypants for yourself."

"Maybe so, but just think how she's been treated her entire life. Flora acts like Lulu's more precious than oxygen, she wins big at all the fancy shows, and people are always telling her she's a cutie." He dropped to all fours and shook from head to tail. *"You can't blame her for being full of herself."*

"I understand that she's spoiled, but I don't like the way she treats you." Ellie reached down and held his muzzle in her hands. "You're my boy. There isn't another dog like you, and there never will be."

Rudy licked her fingers. *"Aw, I love it when you get all kissy face with me."*

"Just stay the way you are, no matter what that tease of a Havanese says, okay?" Before he could answer, there was a knock at the door. "Funny, I didn't hear the outside buzzer. Maybe it's Viv and Mr. T."

Arriving at the door with Rudy on her heels, Ellie peered through the peephole. After doing a double take, she glanced at her pal. "It's Sam," she whispered. "What should I do?"

The yorkiepoo gave a doggie shrug. *"Pretend we're not home and he'll go away."*

Pound, pound, pound. "Ellie, I know you're in there."

Still gazing at Rudy, she bit her lower lip. "He knows we're in here."

"Well, duh. No kidding," he gruffed. *"He's probably guessing. That's all."*

"I thought we worked things out last night," Sam said evenly. *Pound, pound, pound.* "Having people think you're wanted by the police is not a smart way to stay on good terms with the other tenants."

She peered through the peephole again and saw Sam propped against the opposite wall, his jaw clenched and his eyes narrowed, fingering a familiar-looking key. She gave Rudy another pleading look. "He's taken out that key I gave him a while back."

"I told you that was a dumb idea."

"It seemed so sweet for him to ask."

"He just wanted you at his whim, is all."

"He wanted to be able to reach me if I was in trouble."

"In your own apartment?"

"It made perfect sense at the time."

"Ellie, is someone in there with you? Who are you talking to?"

She rested her forehead on the door. "I'm talking to myself."

"Undo the sliding bolt, or I won't be responsible for what happens." *Pound, pound pound.* "Come on. Let me in."

Rudy sneezed.

Ellie dropped to her knees and told her boy, "If I don't answer, every person on this floor, maybe everyone in the building, will think I'm in trouble with the cops again."

"Suit yourself."

She stood up, unfastened the top slider and stepped back. Sam turned the first lock, then the next, and opened the door. "That's more like it. Can I come in?"

"How did you get in the building?"

He grinned. "An older couple let me in when I showed my badge. I told them I thought your buzzer was broken."

"But you didn't ring the buzzer."

"Maybe I should have a key for the outside door, too."

Ellie held back a gasp. "Was it the Feldmans?"

"Yeah, I think that was their name. I tried calling, by the way, but you didn't answer your cell."

"I've been working on—I've been busy. And thanks for letting the building busybodies know I'm involved with the police," she said in a sour tone.

"Since you didn't pick up, it's your fault I'm here." He stepped near. "Come on. I thought we parted friends last night."

"I'm still busy."

"Sure you are."

"This isn't a good time."

He inched closer and lowered his voice. "The reason I'm here has nothing to do with the MACC case. I came to issue an invitation."

Ellie closed the door and stared at her four-legged buddy. "He wants to invite me some-where."

"Unless it's on a luxury cruise to the Caribbean in the presidential stateroom, sans him, the answer would be no."

She ran her fingers through her curls.

Pound, pound, pound. "NYPD. Open up."

"I told you the man was a moron, but did you listen? Noo-oo." Rudy turned and trotted down the hall. *"You're on your own with this one."*

Ellie heaved a sigh. Sam was the last person she wanted to see right now, and he didn't want

276

to discuss Arnie's murder, which was the only thing on her mind. She loved picking his brain about cases, but she'd be in trouble if she said a word about the labs and confessed she'd had a sample of that liver treat all this time. And he wanted to extend an invitation. To where? For what?

Taking a calming breath, she straightened her shoulders. Then she opened the door, and caught Sam in the act of knocking again.

"Hey," he said, lowering his fist. "Can I come in?"

"I don't see how I can stop you."

He sauntered past and she closed the door. Before she could talk, she was in his arms with her back against the foyer wall.

"I wanted to do this last night, but I knew you were angry. It's been too long since we spent time together," he murmured, rubbing his nose under her ear. Then his lips skated over her jaw, her chin, her mouth, and every sensible word she planned to say flew out of her head.

Lifting her leg, she wrapped it around his hip and hooked her foot behind his knee. He raised her up, pushing his pelvis into hers, and she found him more than ready to go further. He was correct. It had been a while since they'd been this close, this intimate.

Sam pulled her away from the wall and began walking her down the hall. When she realized where they were headed, she tore her mouth away. "Wait. No."

He gazed into her eyes and smiled. "No?"

Ellie shook her head. "It's not that I don't want to—"

"Then why not?"

"It's—I'm—confused. There's too much on my mind to think straight." He stepped back and she exhaled. "I know you said you weren't here about the case, but it's all I can focus on."

Holding her hand, Sam pulled her into the living room, led her to the sofa, and took a seat beside her. "I can't discuss Harris's death with you, Ellie. You know that."

"You already said, so aside from—you know—" She touched his lips with her index finger. "What's the invitation?"

"Ah, well, that's a totally different story." He clasped his hands and rested his elbows on his knees. "I'll understand if you say no, because I realize this is asking a lot, but—"

She placed her palm on his forearm. "Just spit it out."

He cleared his throat, stared at the floor, and finally turned in her direction. "My mother wants to meet you."

Meet his mother? Ellie opened and closed her mouth. The request was not what she expected. "I—um—when?"

"Tonight. For dinner." When she didn't speak,

he continued. "I know it's short notice, and I'll be fine if you tell me you have other plans, like going out with Vivian or doing something with your mother."

She leaned back into the cushions. Other than discussing things that happened while on the job or during their formative years, this was the first time Sam had brought up meeting his mother. She knew Lydia Ryder was concerned about her son; with a kid in Sam's line of work what mother wouldn't be? She was also well aware of the way his mom pried into his personal life on a regular basis. Still, learning that Lydia Ryder wanted to have dinner with the woman her son was dating was . . .

"I'm not scheduled to see Georgette or the judge until one night this week, and I think Vivian has plans with Dr. Dave."

"Which means you're free."

"I am." Copying his pose, Ellie bent forward and rested her elbows on her knees. "So."

"So," Sam said at the same time.

"If you don't mind my asking, whose idea was this?"

He shrugged. "Ma's been pestering me to bring you around for a while, but something always came up before I could do it. She caught me at a weak moment this morning, half asleep and without a good reason to say no."

"Then I take it you're not keen on the idea.

You'd rather I had a prior engagement or something."

He twisted to face her. "Not because I don't want you to meet my mom. It's just that she's a nudge. Can't mind her own business. I can guarantee there will be questions you won't want to answer, and it could be uncomfortable."

"It sounds like the way things go with most mothers and their adult children."

He grinned, visibly relaxing. "Then you understand?"

"Sure I do. Georgette pretty much acts the same way with me, though she'd be insulted if she knew I told you that."

He clasped her hands as if they were a lifeline. "Okay, then. You'll come with me for dinner?"

"Sure. Fine. What time?"

Sam stood. "I'll pick you up about five fifteen."

She followed him to the door. If they spent some time together and she was able to cajole him into a good mood, maybe she could tell him about the liver in her freezer. "What do you have planned for the afternoon?"

"I'm going to the precinct to talk things over with the captain, and then I'll call Vince. The clock's running on the Harris case." He held up a finger. "But you didn't hear that from me."

So much for spending time together and cajoling. Crossing her arms, she said, "I'll be ready at five fifteen. See you then?"

"See you then." He gave her a quick kiss on the check. "Thanks."

The second Sam shut the door, Ellie's cell phone rang. Thinking it was Joy or the woman with the black Poodle she'd met the other morning, she raced to the kitchen. After one look at the caller ID, she closed her eyes and groaned. There was no use trying to escape, so she flipped the phone open.

"Hello."

"Ellen Elizabeth."

Georgette's tone did not bode well. "You've got me, Mom. Is something wrong?"

"I'll know that in a minute or two. Is there anything you'd like to tell me?"

Ellie swallowed. "Um . . . no."

"Then Renata Bowman must have been wrong. She has a dog, you know."

"Really. What kind?"

"Something big and obnoxious, but that's not the point of this call."

There could only be one point to the call, but Ellie wasn't going to be the one to bring it up. "Then why don't you tell me what is."

"Renata passed along some disturbing information. She said she saw you on television the other night, handling a dog at one of those competitions. I almost said that couldn't have been you, because my daughter would have let me know if she was going to appear on national television, but I held my tongue." Her mother blew out a gust of air. "Though it wouldn't be the first time you forgot to inform me about the things taking place in your life."

"Oh."

Georgette waited a beat, then said, "So it's true? You appeared on television with a group of dogs?"

Coming from her mother, it sounded as if she'd been a guest on *Jerry Springer*. "Not just any dogs, Mom. Champion canines. The best in their breed. And the dog I handled won her group competition."

"I know."

"How do you know if you didn't watch the show?"

"Because Renata seemed to think I was holding out on her, keeping my daughter's accomplishments a secret. I had to phone the television station and they gave me a number for the show's sponsors. When I called them and asked for a copy of the tape, I had to jump through hoops and pay a fortune to get it. It arrived today, by the way."

"Then you did see the competition?" Ellie asked, annoyed that her mother already knew the answer to her questions.

"I wanted to hear the truth from you first. Now that you've confirmed the news, Stanley and I will watch your performance when you come for dinner Thursday night. You can comment and tell us exactly what happened from your point of view."

Ellie stifled a curse. "Okay, fine. See you on Thursday."

Several hours later, Ellie gazed out the window as Sam's car entered the Queens Midtown Tunnel. The lanes were jammed and exhaust fumes filled the air, coloring it a murky gray.

"Damn. I was hoping to avoid all this," Sam muttered, his eyes on the traffic.

"Is it always this crowded?" she asked, settling back in the seat. " 'Cause if it is, I'd never want to commute by car."

"It's a pain in the ass about eight times out of ten," he admitted. "And one of the reasons I moved to Manhattan after my divorce."

"I guess that made your mom kind of sad, huh?"

"It made her crazy," he answered. A flotilla of brake lights flared in front of them and he stopped. After assessing the situation, he put the car in park and turned to her. "Then again, just about everything I do makes her crazy."

"It's your job, isn't it?" She figured that was the problem, because his occupation made her nuts, too. Even now, on his day off, Sam wore his gun, and if trouble arose in this traffic jam she knew he wouldn't hesitate to take charge and use it if the situation warranted. "Don't be angry with her because she cares. She loves you."

"I know she cares. But it would be better if she accepted the fact that I'm a grown-up, with a life of my own and a career I'm compelled to excel at. If I don't report in every day, she's on the horn, asking questions or making up stories about what happened to me."

"She thinks you're hurt or worse, I imagine."

"Sometimes." Traffic moved and he put the Chevy in gear.

"And she worries that you're in too deep."

He shot her a smug grin. "She wants all the details, but not as often as another woman in my life."

Ellie poked his shoulder. "I don't ask. You offer."

His expression turned innocent. "Who said you were the woman I was referring to?"

"You mean there's another girl out there who hangs on your every word?

"You? Hang on my every word? Since when?"

"Since I met you, you big dope."

Now out of the tunnel, Ellie smiled and inhaled a gulp of less suffocating air. Then she pulled down the visor and glanced in the mirror. She'd tamed her curls and applied a light coat of mascara, blush, and lip gloss. She'd dressed in her black wool blazer, matching slacks, and a soft pink sweater. If Lydia Ryder wanted to meet her, she had to take Ellie Engleman as she was: a practical woman who believed in comfort over fashion.

"You look great," Sam interjected, seeing her self-inspection. "Don't worry. Ma's going to like you."

"Did she like Carolanne?"

He shrugged. "At first—even though both sisters told me they didn't. After a while, Lydia grew wise to Carolanne's shenanigans and tried to get us to counseling, but Carolanne told her to mind her own business. That's when Ma gave up and accepted the divorce."

"And she's going to like me because . . ."

He grinned again. "Because you're intelligent and you care about other people."

"You told her that?"

"I didn't have to. Once I explained how much trouble you went through to find the white puff ball—Bobby—er—Buddy and how you risked your life to save your own dog, she decided you were good for me. Not that I approve of any of what you did, of course."

Ignoring his last comment, she said, "But they're dogs, not people."

"So what?"

"Not everyone who cares about people is an animal lover, Detective Ryder. You're a prime example."

He merged onto a road that ran parallel to the

Long Island Expressway. "I have no problem with animals. What I object to is a dog treating me as if I were something he'd be happy to eat for dinner."

"Rudy doesn't do that to you."

Sam took an exit and turned onto a side street. "No. He treats me like someone out to do you harm."

"I keep telling you, he's my protector." Ellie took a good look at the neighborhood of neat brick houses with small front lawns and on-street parking. "He keeps me safe."

"Whatever." After making a right, Sam pulled into the first parking space he found. "We have to walk a block or two, but the weather is good and this is probably as close as we're going to get to the house on a Sunday night."

He jumped out and opened Ellie's door. Standing on the sidewalk, she waited while he locked the car. "You know, I almost brought Rudy with me, but I was afraid you'd have a cow."

"I doubt it would have bothered Ma, but you might be better off talking about a soap opera, hair salons, the cost of groceries, or—or babies. My mother can't wait for Susan's kid to arrive. Women like babies, right? What could go wrong?"

Chapter 16

Sam considered the evening a Grade B experience. His mother and Ellie had made friendly conversation throughout the meal, Lydia hadn't said a single thing to embarrass him, and Ellie seemed relaxed. If he could just keep his mother from tossing his best girl a zinger every couple of minutes, he'd go home a happy man.

"It's so nice to meet a young woman who isn't afraid food will harm her figure," Lydia Ryder said, throwing out another almost-insult.

He suppressed a frown. On second thought, maybe he should have gone with his gut and simply refused the dinner invitation when it was first made so Ellie didn't have to suffer.

Lydia held a serving dish piled high with mashed sweet potatoes in Ellie's direction. "Please take another helping."

"No, thank you, Mrs. Ryder. Dinner was delicious, but I'm stuffed," Ellie answered, her cheeks sporting a blush.

"Please call me Lydia," his mom said for the tenth time. "And don't be shy. There's plenty more to eat, and I made a wonderful dessert."

Sam loved Ellie's curvy body, but he knew that sometimes, thanks to her mother and her ex, she hated it. "Ma, stop pushing the food. Dinner was great, but we're both full. Couldn't eat another bite."

"But you must have room for dessert. I made your favorite—apple pie with crumble topping." His mother dangled the promise of dessert as if Sam were a three-year-old. "You never say no to my apple pie."

Fed up in more ways than one, he was about to announce that he and Ellie were leaving when the doorbell rang and Lydia jumped to her feet.

"I wonder who that is?" She smiled at Ellie. "I'll be right back. Just think about that apple pie."

The minute Lydia disappeared, Ellie turned and gave him a grin. "Apple pie with crumble topping? And you never told me?"

He raised an eyebrow. Maybe his mother hadn't upset her. "Are you saying you would have made one for me?"

"I doubt I could match your mom in the gourmet baking department, but I do know how to shop. I could have bought a Mrs. Smith's or tried to find one at Gristede's on Third."

When Ellie stood and began clearing the table, he grabbed her wrist. "What are you doing?"

"Self-preservation. If I remove the dishes, your mom won't be able to force-feed us anymore. Besides, it's the polite thing to do, especially after she went to all the trouble of preparing such a mammoth supper."

"With Ma and food, there's no such thing as trouble. She believes a meal has to contain a thousand calories a serving or it isn't worth making. If you think this was something, just wait until you come for one of our family-night feasts."

Ellie stacked plates and added silverware to the pile. "Your mother is a great cook. It wouldn't hurt for you to give her a hand, you know."

He shook his head. "Are you nuts? Ma would smack me if I tried. And she's not going to be happy when she finds out that I let you do it, either, so just stay put."

Dishes in hand, Ellie headed for the kitchen. Sam tossed his napkin on the table and rose to chase her down. Then he cringed. The voices coming from the front room were familiar. Very familiar. He had two choices: warn Ellie of the descending horde or confront the mob and lay down a few ground rules. A raucous whoop made up his mind for him.

He arrived in the living room in three strides and found his sister Susan, her husband, Tom, and his baby sister, Sherry, laughing and chattering as they hung coats in the front closet. Before he spoke, his mother turned and faced him.

"Sammy, it's not nice to leave your friend alone in the dining room."

"Ellie isn't in the dining room," he replied, positive that his next words would get her moving. "She cleared the table and she's in the kitchen helping stow the dishes."

"Oh, no! She's company!" Lydia cried, scurrying away.

Sam took the opportunity to scowl at his sisters. "I think I already know the answer, but I have to ask: What are you two doing here?"

"Mom called and told us you were bringing the mysterious Ms. Engleman to dinner, so we thought to meet her ourselves," said Sherry, taking command. "You got a problem with that?"

He ground his back molars. "At lease you're honest about it." Crossing his arms, he glared at Tom. "But you have no excuse, bud. You know how Lydia can be, especially with these two bulldozers bringing up the—"

His brother-in-law shrugged as Susan spoke. "Hey, I resent that." She put one hand on her swollen belly, the other on her husband's elbow. "We let you eat dinner in peace, didn't we?"

Sam hadn't seen his pregnant sister in a couple of weeks. Had she swallowed a watermelon while on one of her bizarre eating binges? Or maybe a baby elephant? "I thought you'd be on my side in this. You know how Ma is. If you had one iota of care for my feelings—"

"Stop being such a baby," Sherry ordered, walking toward the dining room. "If you showed your face around here more often, we wouldn't have been so sneaky about meeting your girl."

"She's right. If you called and told us what was going on in your life or showed up here once in a while, we might have waited." Susan gazed at her husband, a triathlete masquerading as a lawyer. "Tell him how many times you had to listen to Mom rant about my pregnancy, or you replaced a lightbulb, or fixed the dishwasher. You even mowed the lawn a couple of times because Sam reneged on family night."

Tom, six feet tall with coal black hair and brilliant blue eyes, shrugged again. "Don't look at me, pal. I know better than to stand up to the unholy trinity. If you're smart you'll start doing as you're told."

Tom followed Sherry while Susan trailed behind. In the archway, she propped herself against the doorframe. "Come on, Sam. We don't bite, and we've been dying to meet Ellie. We'll be nice. I promise."

When she winced, Sam shot to her side. "You okay?"

She heaved a breath. "Sure, fine. But Julie's been holding an in utero step class all day long. I'm hoping dessert will calm her down so I can get a decent night's sleep."

Sam grabbed her arm and escorted her into the dining room, where he held out a chair. "Here, sit and take the load off." He scoped out the table and saw that coffee cups, fresh forks, and dessert plates were stacked in front of his mother's seat.

When he aimed for the kitchen, Sherry said,

"Stay here, big brother. Mom won't hurt your date; she'll just talk her to death."

The door swung open and Ellie entered, carrying a tray holding the apple pie, a tub of vanilla ice cream, a can of spray topping, and coffee fixings. Seeing the crowd, she colored pink from her collarbone to the roots of her hair.

"I'll take that," said Sam. He set the tray at his mother's place, then pulled out Ellie's chair. "Relax and I'll introduce you to these questionable characters. I should have prepared you for this surprise attack, but for some reason I thought my family had grown up a little."

Instead of cowering, Ellie smiled at the waiting crew and took a seat. "Hi, I'm Ellie. It's nice to meet you."

Sherry passed cups and saucers around the table as she spoke. "You mean Sam actually told you about us?"

"You must be Sherry," Ellie answered. "Sam said you had a smart mouth."

Sherry snickered. "Shows you what big brother knows. My mouth is brilliant."

Grinning, Ellie said, "I've heard a lot about all of you. Most of it nice, I might add."

"Funny, we've heard very little about you," said Susan. "I'm Susan, the middle child, and this is my husband, Tom."

Tom nodded. "Ellie, don't pay any attention to these two. They like to think they run the show, but Sam and I know better. Lydia is the four-star general of this clan."

Sam held his head in his hands. He'd been an idiot to think the evening would go smoothly. Just then his mother floated in, wearing a huge smile and toting a full coffee carafe.

"I made decaf. Wouldn't want to keep the little mother awake tonight." Sherry stood, commandeered the coffee, and walked around the table filling cups while Lydia continued. "So, Ellie, have you met everyone?"

"I did. You have a wonderful family."

"They're my pride and joy. I can't wait to be a grandmother." After cutting the first slice of pie, Lydia passed it to Ellie, her eyes brimming with tears. "If only their father were here to see—"

"Dad is here in spirit, Mom," Susan said, accepting the next piece. "I'm going to tell Julie all about him when she grows up."

Sam gave Ellie a sideways glance. She'd lost her dad when she was in her teens and had confided that she still missed him. This was not the time to dwell on such a sensitive topic. Accepting his pie, he deftly changed the subject. "So, Tom, been in any competitions lately?"

"Haven't entered a single one since the temperature hit freezing. I like competing when it's cool, not when it's downright frigid."

"In case you didn't know, Tom's a triathlete." Susan dropped a scoop of ice cream onto her pie. "And he's promised to cut his competitions back to one every two months until Julie and I can join him at the sites."

"Sam mentioned that he was a serious athlete, and I know you enjoy fitness training." Ellie refused the offer of ice cream or whipped topping. "Have you eased up since your pregnancy?"

"Some, especially this week. The baby hasn't been happy for the past couple of days."

"Julie will be here before we know it," Sherry said. "I can't believe I'm going to be an aunt."

Sam breathed a sigh of relief. This wasn't so bad. His sisters were treating Ellie more politely than they'd treated Carolanne at their first meeting. He clasped Ellie's hand under the table and gave it a squeeze.

Focusing on Sherry, Ellie squeezed back. "I understand you're going to graduate from NYU in the spring. That's my alma mater, too."

"No kidding? What was your major?"

"I earned a bachelor of fine arts. Which prepared me for absolutely nothing, I might add. How about you?"

"Business, with a minor in psychology. I figure that will help when I need to find out what makes the big boys tick."

"Ah, good idea."

"I hear you're a dog lover," said Tom.

"Walking them is how I earn a living. My boy, Rudy, is the best dog in the entire world."

"And he gets along with Sam?" asked Sherry. "That I'll have to see to believe."

"Her dog and I have an understanding . . . most of the time." Sam scooped up a forkful of pie. It was getting damn hard to keep the conversation centered on a neutral topic. Asking Ellie questions was fine, as long as she didn't take off on one of her canine tangents. "This pie is great, Ma."

"Thank you, dear. Cream, Ellie?"

"Yes, please." She accepted the pitcher and helped herself. "Anyone else?"

Smiling, Tom captured the creamer and poured a liberal serving into his wife's cup, then his own. "I had a great dog growing up. Susan and I have talked about getting one for Julie—when she's old enough to understand the responsibility, of course."

"That's very wise," Ellie told him. "Too many people are unprepared when they get a dog. They're excited when they bring it home, and the next thing you know, they're giving it to a shelter because they can't take care of it properly or it's too much to handle."

"Maybe you'd be willing to help us choose a good one when the time comes," said Susan. "If you and Sam are still—"

Sam did his best not to choke on his coffee. "Time to go. Ellie and I both have a big day ahead of us tomorrow."

"We do?"

"I have that special case and you have that . . . thing . . ."

"That thing?"

He pulled out Ellie's chair and clasped her elbow. "Yes, *that* thing."

She stood. "Uh, oh, yeah, right. *That* thing."

"Samuel Ryder, you can be such a child." His mother tsked. "Ellie can be a friend of this family even if the two of you aren't involved in a relationship."

"Ma—"

"Ease up, Mom," Susan chimed. "Sam's finally found a good one. Give him time to work it out." She rose to her feet and grinned in her brother's direction. "Say good night, and I'll see you to the door."

Sighing, Lydia stood, walked to Sam's side, and kissed his cheek. Then she took Ellie's hand. "Thank you for coming. Maybe next time you visit, it will be for one of our Thursday-night family dinners." She gazed pointedly at her son. "If Sammy can't make it, come by yourself."

He and Ellie followed Susan into the living room. Sam kept his lips zipped because he didn't want to upset his sister in her delicate condition. While he retrieved his leather jacket from the closet, Ellie and Susan did the girl thing, speaking in hushed tones about the meal, the visit, and the upcoming special event.

Hoping to speed things along, he opened the front door. The sooner he got Ellie out of here—

Without warning, Susan doubled over, her hands on her belly. "Oh—oh—no!"

He jumped back when water gushed from between her legs and puddled on the floor. Still hunched forward, Susan inhaled deeply and raised her eyes. "Call Tom, big brother. If the baby books are right, I'm going into labor."

Worn out and ready for bed, Ellie glanced at her watch. Midnight was two hours past her normal bedtime. No wonder she was so tired. After opening her apartment door, she heaved a sigh and rested her back against the foyer wall. The evening had been more than she'd bargained for in every way imaginable. Meeting Sam's mother and his extended family; following Susan, Tom, Lydia, and Sherry to the hospital; calming Lydia down. Heck, calming down the entire Ryder clan had been exhausting.

"It's about time you got home. I'm dancin' here." Rudy gave a yip and circled her feet. *"I need to go outside bad."*

"I'm sorry, but tonight's delay was unexpected. Not only did I meet Sam's mother, sisters, and brother-in-law, but I went to the Flushing Hospital Medical Center in Queens." She removed Rudy's leash from the doorknob and dropped to a squat. "I'll tell you about it while we walk."

"You were at a hospital? What happened? Did the demonic dick's mother give you food poisoning? It figures she'd be a crap-hat cook."

"Lydia Ryder is a wonderful cook. We were there because of Sam's sister Susan. She went into labor right before we left the house."

"Labor, as in babies? Sam's sister had a litter?"

Ellie grinned as they headed down the stairs. "I've already explained this to you a thousand times—humans don't have litters. They have one baby, maybe two, rarely more than that at a time."

"Hey, it's not my fault I judge everything in canine terms. That's how my brain works." Now outside, he raised his leg against the side of the porch. *"I am a dog, you know."*

She decided to cut their usual evening constitutional short and only go to the corner and back. From the sound of it, Rudy was sure to do his business quickly. "Don't be a smart-ass. It's your fault I forget, because you act almost human most of the time."

"What do you mean 'almost'? I thought I did a pretty good job with the real thing." He sniffed the porch three buildings down and gave another leg lift. *"Except for doing business outside—"*

"And eating every meal as if it was your last, circling before you lie down, growling at whatever doesn't suit you, oh, and let's not forget licking your privates."

"You would bring that up," he groused, muttering more human qualities he thought he possessed as they made their way to the corner. *"I watch television, keep up with the news and current events. I even try to pass gas and belch with a little finesse. What more can you ask for?"* After doing big business, he added, *"It's the way I'm made. I can't help it."*

Ellie scooped the poop into a Ziploc bag and tossed it in a trash can. "Okay, okay, you're more human than most people. Is that what you want to hear?"

"It doesn't hurt."

"Can we please change the subject? I certainly don't want this topic of conversation to be the last one on my mind before I fall asleep."

"Fine. I'll change the subject. Did the sister have a boy or a girl?"

"She's scheduled to have a girl, but Julie still hadn't arrived when Sam and I left the hospital. First babies sometimes take a while to be born."

Approaching their condo, Rudy continued his grilling. *"So did the dopey detective bring you home or send you off in a cab?"*

They climbed the outside stairs and Ellie unlocked the door. "Sam brought me home, but I'm not sure if he's going back to the hospital or his apartment."

"Nervous, was he?"

"Sam's always cool under pressure."

They took the next two flights in silence. When they arrived on the third-floor landing, Rudy said, *"So what's his family like? Do they hate dogs as much as he does?"*

"Sam does not hate dogs." She unlocked the door and led him inside. "He's just unsure of them."

"Yeah, right."

Ellie unclipped Rudy's leash and hung it where it belonged, then headed into the kitchen, pulled her cell phone from her tote bag, and viewed the message notice. She'd turned the phone off so no one would bother her while she was visiting Sam's mother, and it was too late to answer who-ever had called. After plugging the phone into the charger, she went down the hall with the yorkiepoo on her heels.

"Sam never had a dog growing up, so he doesn't see the need for one in a person's life," she continued. "The more he gets to know you, the better he'll like you."

"Uh, I hate to tell you this, Triple E, but the defective detective has been in our lives for going on eight months now. Then again, time flies when you're having fun. Not."

In the bedroom, she began to undress. "Sam isn't defective, he's merely . . . suspicious. It's a part of his profession."

"Jeez, Vivian is right. You are a Little Mary Sunshine."

"I can be a realist when I have to be. I just think

it's better to anticipate the good before the bad."

Rudy jumped on the bed. *"That's one of the reasons the despicable dick is wrong for you. He sees the evil side of everything."*

"I disagree. I think that's what makes us a good match. Opposites attract and all that." She slipped into her bathrobe. "I'll be back in a couple of minutes."

After performing her nightly ritual, Ellie returned to the bedroom, pulled down the bed-covers, turned off the nightstand lamp, and snuggled under the blanket. "Sam said he had a lot of stuff to do at headquarters tomorrow, but I could tell he was concerned about his sister."

"Concerned how?"

"He's the one who took command of the father-to-be. For some reason Tom didn't want to go into the delivery room until the last minute, so Lydia and Sherry went in with Susan while he and Sam paced side by side in the waiting area. If you ask me, the poor guy looked ready to upchuck, but Sam kept him focused."

"That Tom guy should take a cue from us male dogs. Once we do the deed, we leave the scene. None of that 'raising the pups' business for us. We know better."

"Humans are not like canines. They form a family unit, stick together, and share parenting. They also share their lives whenever possible. You know that."

"And get nothin' but trouble for it," Rudy noted, yawning. "Too much work and worry if you ask me."

"No one is asking you. And look at it this way, a family unit is a pack, something wolves and dogs form in the wild. With human beings, the pack leaders are the mom and dad, the pack members the children. And a pack sticks together."

"Okay, okay . . . a human family is a pack. Got it. Mind if I change the subject again?"

She ruffled his ears. "As if I could stop you."

"I just want to know one thing. Did you do something stupid, like telling Detective Demento what you planned to do with that treat Arnie gave you?"

Ellie shot him an eye roll. "I didn't say a word about it. I've had a lot on my mind, what with learning how to be a handler and all. He'll understand."

"Fat chance. He doesn't want you messing with the case in any way, remember?"

"And I've been obedient . . . sort of. I didn't pester him about the murder at all tonight. He was more concerned about my interaction with his mother, and I tried to put him at ease." She pulled Rudy into the crook of her arm. "Lydia is a very nice lady, by the way."

He gave her cheek a sloppy lick. "Does she like dogs?"

"She didn't say, but Tom does. He and Susan are planning to get one when the baby is old enough."

"You'll talk them into going to a shelter, right? Rescued canines are grateful someone is giving them a second chance, so they do their best to be good."

She scratched his favorite spot, the underside of his chin. "If they're like you, they're the best."

"Nothing will ever compare to the relief I felt when you walked into that rescue center. Those seven days in the big house were the worst seven days of my old life and my new one."

"I'm sorry you had to suffer, but I always had the impression you knew I'd be along soon. At least that's the way you acted."

"I knew once I got into your head things would be okay, but I was still anxious. The eats in that place were awful. Dry kibble that tasted like squirrel poop, one biscuit a day, no shared table food, and not a drop of ice cream to be found."

"I'm never happy when you talk me into sharing my food. I'm sure I shouldn't."

"Of course you should. It's a bonding thing, sorta like the baiting trick those handlers use with the show dogs."

"Maybe so, but it got Arnie killed." She hugged him tight. "I've been thinking . . ."

"Uh-oh, look out."

Ellie ignored the sarcasm. "No, really.

Consider this. Whoever killed Arnie put poison in the dog treat. Since there doesn't seem to be a motive for his killing, that means Lulu was the target. All I have to do is explain it to Sam, and he'll see the light."

"What light?"

"He'll realize he doesn't need a motive for the murder. It was an accident, like it was with Professor Albright. All he needs is the murder weapon to prove his case."

"Since he didn't seem to think Buddy's kidnapping was a big deal, why should he care if someone wanted to kill a canine?"

"He'll care because it resulted in the death of a human. All Sam has to do is ask himself who wanted to see Lulu dead. He'll get the message fast."

"I don't know, Triple E. He doesn't seem that smart to me."

"Sam is a brilliant detective, but he's been focused on a motive for murder. When we prove there was something on that liver that killed Arnie, he'll see that my Edward Nelson theory is right."

"I gotta meet that Nelson nimrod. Sounds to me like you need an impartial assessment of the guy."

"He lives in Lulu's building."

"Then find a reason to stop by his place so I can take a look around his apartment. You know

I can sniff out the stuff humans miss, including poison."

"The problem is, I don't have a reason to drop by. I don't even know what floor he's on, but I'm sure Flora or Lulu could tell me."

"So come up with something and ask Mrs. Steinman for his apartment number."

"Okay, first thing in the morning. Now go to sleep. It's late and I'm beat."

"Roger that. And no bad dreams. They creep me out."

"Me, too. But I don't think you have to worry. I'm too tired to dream."

"How about if I put you at ease with a joke?"

"Not another one of your goofy lawyer digs."

"Aw, come on. You love 'em."

Ellie snorted. "Okay, one joke."

"This is an easy one. How can you tell when a lawyer is lying?"

"I have no idea."

"His lips are moving." He gave a doggie chortle. *"Get it? His lips are moving."*

She rubbed her nose in his fur. "You are too much. Now say good night and close your eyes."

"Good night and close your eyes."

305

Chapter 17

The next morning Ellie began her day by giving Rudy a quick walk around the block. Arriving home, she started the coffeemaker and pulled her toaster from the cupboard under the sink. Then she unplugged her cell phone from the charger and read the message screen. One call from her mother, one from Viv, and three from Joy. She rolled her eyes to the ceiling. There was a better-than-average possibility that her assistant wanted to beg out of today's rounds. She might as well hear the bad news first.

"Ellie, it's Joy. Call me." Short and to the point.

Erasing Joy's first message, she moved on. "It's Joy. We have to talk. Call me as soon as you get this." Almost the same as the first message, though her assistant's voice held a note of desperation.

She braced for message three. "Hi, it's me again. I wanted to give you this news in a person-to-person conversation, but you must be away for the day and I don't think it can wait." Joy blew out a breath. "There's no way else to say it . . . I have to quit. My life is too complicated to explain. I'll call you if things change, but I don't see that happening anytime soon, so . . ." Another audible breath. "Well, it was nice working for you. I'll mail you the keys, and ask that you do the same with my final check. Thanks."

Ellie refrained from knocking her head against a kitchen cabinet and grimaced instead.

"You look like you do whenever you pick up Sampson's big business," said Rudy, sitting at Ellie's feet. He always got a charge out of it when she had to clean up the waste produced by the world's chunkiest Pug. *"Are you in the middle of another smelly load of doo-doo?"*

She dropped an English muffin in the toaster, poured a cup of coffee, added sweetener and cream, and took a sip. She and Rudy had been up since seven. Now that Joy had quit, it would be a tiring day. She'd have to take care of her customers in the farthest north building along with all her others, which gave her little time for chitchat.

"A mess, yes, but not of my doing." The toaster popped and she spread the muffin with a thick layer of peach jam. "Joy left a message telling me she—"

"Quit."

Ellie narrowed her eyes. "How did you know?"

Rudy's muzzle creased in a doggie grin. *"Easy. You've had about as much luck with assistants as I've had growing a new set of balls. It just figures."*

"That's gross." She took a bite of breakfast and

washed it down with more coffee. "Though you're right about one thing. I do have lousy luck as an employer."

"So we're gonna take care of the guys in the Cranston Arms ourselves again?"

"Looks like." She finished her muffin, took a last swallow of coffee, and headed for the bedroom with her boy close behind. "Do you think Twink will want to spend the day with us?"

"If I know him, he'll be thrilled. Anything to show off his crazy new coat." The yorkiepoo jumped on the bed while she pulled off her sweatshirt and tugged a wool sweater over her form-fitting thermal liner. *"If you ask me, he's gonna be nothing but a big fat embarrassment."*

"He hasn't come with us for a week, so he needs the exercise." She chose a pair of heavy socks from her dresser drawer and slipped them on, then slid her feet into lined half-boots. Standing, she talked as she made her way through the apartment. "Guess I'll have to hang another round of flyers at the Columbia library and the university bookstores announcing the job opening." She collected the extra pile of announcements from the tray next to her printer. "While I'm here I might as well check to see if any of those labs replied to my e-mail."

After logging on, she waited while the machine began downloading e-mail. She sent the spam to her junk mail folder, kept the few personal messages on hold, and continued down the list until she found what she was looking for.

"Now we're in business," she told Rudy. "Prototype Labs says they'll take the entire chunk of liver, but it has to be sent on ice. They list the name of a mail drop here in the city and say the site will package it correctly for me. They've even assigned me a case number so the delivery service will know what they want."

"Any word on how long it will take to get results?"

"According to them, they won't know until the preliminary testing is finished, but a full screening usually takes one to three weeks."

"That's too long," he groused. *"We need to know now."*

"I agree, but what else can we do? Waiting to hear from another lab could waste time we don't have." She tapped her pencil on the desk. "How about if we send the liver with a note telling them to skip the normal tests and go straight to the weird and unusual?"

"How much is this gonna cost us?"

"I have to include a two-hundred-dollar bank check in the package. If it costs more, they'll bill me."

"Yowza! That's a lotta Dingo bones."

"But it's worth it." After jotting down the address of the mail drop and her case number, she exited her machine, charged into the kitchen, and headed for her fridge. "Good thing I froze this. We'll finish our rounds and go to the bank, then we'll hit the mail site. They can take it from there."

She slipped the plastic-encased liver into a bag of ice and added it to her tote along with the flyers, lab info, and her phone. In the foyer, she put on her parka and dressed Rudy in his new plaid coat. "You ready?"

"As I'll ever be. Let's get moving."

"I think it'll work best if we do the run backwards," she said as she locked the door. "We can tack up the flyers first, then hit the Cranston and work our way south. If we hurry the packs along, we'll only be a couple of minutes late for each building. How does that sound to you?"

"Like a plan."

They stopped on the second floor and knocked on Viv's door. When she didn't answer, Ellie used her key and found Mr. T standing in the foyer with a leash dangling from his mouth and a brightly colored sweater, complete with a brilliant array of feathers circling the neck-line, draped over his head.

"T, you look . . . um . . . you're . . ."

"I'm somethin' else, ain't I? I can't wait to strut my stuff up and down Fifth Avenue."

Rudy dropped to his belly and rolled onto his back, snorting as if in the throes of a mental breakdown.

Fearful that she couldn't answer the terrier without bursting into giggles, Ellie ignored her boy's fit and peered down the hall. "Shower's running. I guess that means Vivian is getting ready for work."

"Don't talk to me about Vivie. The fool hasn't let me wear my new duds even once since I got 'em."

Holding back a grin, Ellie dropped to a squat. "We have a lot to do this morning, so let's get going."

Twink danced in excitement while she worked his feet into the front leggings of the sweater and rolled it over his head. Ellie couldn't blame Vivian for hating the coat. Her best friend's idea of class was tailored elegance and designer originals, not the trappings of a deranged pimp. She was surprised that the ostentatious coat wasn't already in the trash. "It'd been warmer than usual. Maybe she thought you'd be uncomfortable."

"Don't think I can be more obvious. I bring this snazzy outfit over and drop it at her feet before each trip outside, but she just keeps makin' a face and hangin' it on a kitchen chair." He sneezed. *"I wasn't goin' out this morning if you did the same."*

"Considering the selection of clothes in my own closet, I'm the last person to knock someone else's fashion sense. And unlike Vivian, I'm definitely behind on what's in or out in the world of haute couture." She reached through the feathers to snap the lead to his collar. "Just don't gripe if you get laughed at by the other dogs. I don't want any fighting."

"Let 'em laugh," Twink yipped. *"It'll just be a cover 'cause they're jealous."*

"Oh, brother." Rudy shook from head to tail. *"You are too much. No self-respecting canine would be caught dead in that clown outfit."*

"Enough," Ellie pronounced, leading them into the hall. "We have to catch a cab."

Nelda answered the door when Ellie and the boys arrived at the Beaumont, their last building of the morning. "How is Mrs. Steinman today?" she asked the housekeeper.

"Ms. Flora is in fine fettle. Said you treated her to a Chinese dinner the other night. Giggled like a schoolgirl when she told me, the dear." Nelda leaned forward and gave Ellie a hug. "I want to thank you for that."

"No thanks needed," Ellie assured her. "She's done a lot for me over the past eight months, and I want to show my gratitude."

"Well, you're certainly doing that. Miss Lulu is probably in the bedroom with her right now. Hang on and I'll fetch her for you."

"Nice lady," Rudy pronounced. *"Almost as good as Corinna."*

"That reminds me—we have a date for dinner with Mother and Stanley on Thursday, so I'm putting you on notice. Prepare to come along without whining."

"I like spending time with the judge and Corinna. It's the ex-terminator that raises my hackles. Why do I have to go?"

"Didn't I tell you? Georgette found out about the MACC and actually bought a copy of the show. She expects us to provide color commentary while we watch it this Thursday."

"Uh-boy."

"You can say that again. And don't try getting out of it, either. I need you there for moral support."

"Is Corinna cookin'?"

"I'm sure she is. Why? Do you want something special?"

He licked the drool from his lips as he stared up at her. *"Short ribs would be nice. Last time she made 'em, she gave us the bones to bring home."*

"That's right," T added. *"They were beef-o-licious."*

"Okay, I'll call and put in the order. Anything else?"

At that moment Nelda appeared, holding a ready-to-go Lulu in her arms. "Here's our girl," she said, setting the Havanese on the floor. "Her new sweater was in Ms. Flora's room, so I took the liberty of putting it on for you."

Ellie let Rudy, Mr. T, and Lulu say hello while she talked to the housekeeper. "Do you by any chance know Edward Nelson's apartment number?"

"It must be written down somewhere. I'll look for my address list while you're out. If I don't find it, we can ask Ms. Flora."

In the hall, Ellie smiled down at Lulu. "Any chance you know the Nelsons' apartment number off the top of your fuzzy head?"

"Of course I do." The Havanese sat on the tile and gave Mr. T a narrow-eyed stare. *"Let me guess. You're trying out for a revival of* Joseph and the Amazing Technicolor Dreamcoat. *"*

"You're just itchin' to swipe my designer duds, ain't ya, little girl?"

"And so it begins," grumped Rudy when Lulu continued to goad the Jack Russell.

Ellie collected Cheech and Chong, Bruiser, Ranger, and Boscoe and rode the elevator to street level while the ribald comments from this group echoed those of the other packs. Since T's snappy comebacks were still going strong, she allowed the verbal sparring to continue while they crossed Fifth Avenue and headed into the park. Then she checked her watch, saw that she was almost back on schedule, and ignored the quibbling while the canines investigated piles of dead leaves on the damp autumn ground.

After a few minutes of business and waste disposal, she sat on a bench and tried to focus on her afternoon as the dogs lay at her feet in the late-morning sun. If that liver treat was doctored, and Edward Nelson did it, the deed had probably taken place in the privacy of his home. Lucky for her Edward had said their apartment was being painted. She'd drop by this afternoon and finagle an invitation inside from the painters.

And if Mitzi and Edward were home, well, she'd think of something else—maybe more talk about Edward handling Lulu at the Garden. Either way, she was determined to get a peek at their apartment today.

Glancing down, she found Lulu gazing at her. *"You want the Nelsons' number or not?"*

"I definitely want it."

"14-C. It's a modest two-bedroom about a third the size of mine and Flora's."

"Then you've been inside?"

"Sure have. Edward and I sometimes practiced there before a competition. If you ask me, the place doesn't smell at all the way an exclusive Upper East Side condo should."

"What does it smell like?" asked Ellie.

Lulu sniffed. *"Nothing I can put my paw on. Just off somehow."* She tossed her head. *"Edward smells the same way sometimes. I think that's why he uses so much aftershave."*

Ellie stared into the bright blue sky, her mind mulling over the Havanese's comments. On the two or three occasions she'd met Edward, she'd never noticed an odd odor but she had caught the slight scent of cologne. It hadn't offended her, but she didn't have a canine's ultra-perceptive nose.

"Rudy, Twink, and I have an errand to run after I bring the pack home. I thought I'd pay Edward a visit later this afternoon."

"Good idea. You just might find a clue to Arnie's murder."

"Find a— Who said I was looking for clues?"

"Rudy, of course. And Flora did ask for your help. You wouldn't want to let an old lady down, would you?"

"You, Ms. Pickypants, are a royal pain in the butt." She frowned at Rudy, who'd been intent on the conversation. "Nice to know you've been spilling our secrets, pal."

"I have no secrets from my girl," he told her, nuzzling Lulu's ear. *"So, did you give her the Nelsons' apartment number? And tell her about the smell?"*

"Sure did." Lulu cocked her head. *"So what are you waiting for? Get it in gear and find Arnie's killer."*

Two hours later, Ellie and Rudy returned to their apartment. They'd taken a cab to the bank and the drop site, where she'd sent off the Baggie holding the iced liver treat. Then Twink had whined that he was cold and tired and every-thing else he could think of to be brought home. While there, Ellie ate lunch while she checked her e-mail. When she realized that neither of the other labs had answered her call for help, she was happy she'd sent Prototype the entire treat. Like she'd told Rudy, waiting for another test site to answer would waste time they didn't have, and this only proved her point.

"Time's a wastin', Triple E. We goin' on a hunt at the Beaumont or what?"

She powered off her computer and leaned back in her chair. "We'll go, but first we have to finish the afternoon runs." She looked out the window and wrinkled her nose. "This weather has been crazy. It was pleasantly cool this morn-ing, and now it looks like it's going to snow."

Rudy jumped on a living room chair and did his own outdoor check. *"Uh-oh. We never had to walk the guys in snow before. That's gonna be a bummer."*

"Tell me about it. Makes me think I should listen to Sam and hire help to do the actual walking while I sit home and run the business."

"You want to do that?"

"Not really. Interacting with the gang is the fun part of this job, plus it's my only form of exercise. If I didn't walk ten miles per day, I'd be as fat as Georgette thinks I am. You'd be a porky pooch, too, like Sampson."

"Not likely. You feed me primo kibble, and my business doesn't look a thing like that Pug's does when it comes out the other end. Or maybe his owner lets him graze in the dishwasher or troll the kitchen trash."

"Hmm. I should talk to Mrs. Lowenstein about his diet. Dogs who eat food with a lot of additives do seem to process a bigger load." Just then her phone rang. "Paws in Motion," Ellie answered when she didn't recognize the number on caller ID.

"Is this Ellie Engleman?" asked a woman.

"It is. Can I help you?"

"I hope so. You and I met last week at the Cranston Arms. You handed me a card."

"The woman with the black toy Poodle?"

"Right. I'm Gretchen Fielder and my dog is Rocco."

Great name for a canine, thought Ellie, and Rocco had seemed sweet, too. "How can I help you?"

"I was hoping we could meet and go over the things you do for your clients. I've settled in my sublet and I have a few days free before my schedule goes crazy, so . . ."

"Sure. I'm on my way to your building right now, as a matter of fact. Is this a good time?"

"It's fine. Apartment 4-A. Buzz me and I'll let you up."

Ellie disconnected the call, her mind in a whirl.

Had Ms. Fielder said 4-A, the number of Hilary Blankenship, her former assistant's apartment? The coincidence was too weird. She glanced at Rudy. "That was the owner of the black Poodle in Arlo's building. She wants to talk to me about a walking schedule. What do you think?"

"I say you give her the skinny on what we do. If she can afford us, we can take him on."

"I think so, too. You ready?"

He hopped off the chair. *"Only if we cab uptown. It gets dark early these days, and I don't wanna be out if it snows."*

"I don't blame you, but it's something we have to get used to with winter coming and all." They donned their coats, stepped into the hall, and continued the conversation until they hailed a taxi on Lexington.

When her phone rang during the cab ride, she thought it might be Ms. Fielder, but one look at the caller ID told her she was wrong.

"Sam, hi."

"Sorry I didn't call this morning, but I have news."

"About Susan and Julie? Is the baby all right?"

"Julie is doing great, and so is Susan. Tom's the one who needs a vacation."

"New-dad jitters?"

"Big time, but he's home for the next few days, so he'll calm down."

"How much did Julie weigh?"

"Uh . . . weigh?"

Ellie grinned. "I don't suppose you know how long she was? Or her hair color?"

"I'll find out this weekend, when Ma says I can visit. She'll be staying with them when Tom goes back to work."

"She must be thrilled."

"That's putting it mildly. So, where are you?"

"In a cab riding to the Cranston. I've lost Joy."

"Uh-huh."

"What's that supposed to mean?"

"Just uh-huh. Listen, I'm waiting for some info from Vince and the ME. If things pan out, I'll stop by tonight and we can talk. I'll bring dinner. How does that sound?"

"Um . . . okay. Just don't come too early. I have to run a few errands and . . . stuff." Like visit Edward Nelson and find something that would link him to Arnie Harris's death.

"No problem. See you later."

She dropped the phone in her bag and sighed.

Rudy put a paw on her knee. *"Detective Doofus is going to stop you from keeping that promise you made to Flora."*

"Not if I can help it. Besides, we might not have any luck today." The taxi pulled in front of the Cranston Arms and they got out. Inside, Ellie rang the bell for 4-A and was buzzed into the building. "We'll visit Rocco first, then get the others."

"What apartment number?"

"Didn't I tell you? 4-A."

They entered the elevator, where Rudy stood on his hind legs with his paws on her calf. *"4-A? You're joking, right?"*

"Nope." The door opened, and Ellie led him to Ms. Fielder's unit. "Spooky, huh?"

"I'll say. You think this pair is gonna be as out of it as Hilary Blankenship and Cuddles?"

"Cuddles wasn't 'out of it,' he was a puppy. And Hilary was going through a difficult divorce. Ms. Fielder sounded a lot more grounded, and you touched noses with Rocco and didn't complain, so I assume he checked out okay."

"I didn't notice anything out of the ordinary, but you never know."

"Okay, we're here. Be quiet, please. No interrupting."

She rang the bell and Ms. Fielder, a gray-haired woman wearing perfectly applied makeup, opened the door wide. "Come on in." Smiling, she held out her hand. "It's so good to meet you formally. And your dog."

"A pleasure to see you again, too." Ellie gazed at the Poodle standing at Ms. Fielder's Ferragamo-clad feet, his tail upright, his black eyes full of suspicion. "I see Rocco is ready for us, too."

"He's my protector, and please, call me

321

Gretchen. After all, if you're going to take care of my boy, we'll be friends. Come in and we can talk."

Ellie followed her, frowning when Rudy stuck his nose in the toy Poodle's butt. "Be nice," she whispered.

"We could touch noses, but this is the way dogs really check each other out."

"Uh-huh."

"Sorry, did you say something?" Gretchen asked as she took a seat on an enormous couch covered in red leather.

"Not exactly. I was just urging Rudy to mind his manners." Ellie chose a wing chair in matching leather and settled in. "Talking to my dog and my charges is a bad habit, or so I'm told, but I can't seem to stop doing it."

"So the reports I received from the other tenants are true. You do hold conversations with the dogs you walk." Gretchen's smile grew wide. "If you promise not to tell anyone, I'll let you in on a little secret."

Rudy circled the carpet and curled at Ellie's feet. *"She's probably going to tell you she talks to her toaster or maybe her can opener."*

"I never repeat a confidence," Ellie answered, poking the yorkiepoo with her toe. "Truly."

"I talk to Rocco, too. Tell him my hopes and dreams, ask his opinion on clothes, television programs, dinner choices." Gretchen's expression turned melancholy. "It's one of the reasons my husband and I divorced."

"Uh-boy. Here we go again."

After another gentle toe poke, Ellie said, "I'm sorry to hear that, but I know what you mean. Besides being a control freak, my husband wouldn't even consider letting me have a dog. It was at the top of my ten-reasons-to-get-a-divorce list."

"Then you understand some of what I've been through."

"I do, and don't worry—your past is safe with me."

"Thank you. Now, tell me a bit about the services you provide for your clients."

Ellie listed her fees for one and two walks per day, and explained that she didn't charge for feeding the dog or giving it medicine if she could do it on a regular stop. "I can also house-sit here or, if you prefer, keep Rocco at my place if you need to leave home for a week or less. And if you provide the food, the cost is about half of what you'd pay in one of the local boarding kennels."

"Do we sign a contract or something?"

"I've been meaning to draw one up, just haven't found the need or the time. But I am bonded and insured, and I collect my fee in advance. This is the middle of November, so I'd expect the next two weeks and the month of December now, then a check at the beginning of each month."

Gretchen rose to her feet. "I can't argue with that. Wait here while I get my checkbook and you figure out the amount."

She disappeared down the hall, but Rocco sat stoically on the sofa, staring.

"Hey, Rocco. I hope you're happy with the new arrangement. Rudy and I will walk you every morning with a couple of other dogs here in the building."

The Poodle raised its snout in the air.

"Great. Another empty fur coat," Rudy said.

"You don't know that for sure," Ellie chided. "Could be his knowing I can talk to him and he can answer back is a shock. Let's give him some time." She pulled her day planner from her tote and added up the days she was owed on her calendar. After totaling the amount, she wrote "Rocco Fielder" and his apartment number on her client page for the Cranston Arms.

Gretchen returned, checkbook in hand, and resumed her seat on the sofa. "How much, and do I make it out to you or to Paws in Motion?" she asked, holding her pen in the air.

Ellie gave her the amount. "And make it out to the business, please."

A moment later Gretchen stood and passed her a check for the full amount, along with a key to the apartment. "So you'll be here first thing in the morning. Correct?"

"The time varies between eight and nine,

depending on what I have planned for the day."

"I'll probably be gone by that time, so just use the key to let yourself in, same as you do for your other clients."

The woman escorted Ellie and Rudy to the door with the still mum Rocco following behind. In the foyer, Gretchen said, "I was thinking about the contract thing and I think I might be able to help."

"With your luck she'll ask for a job, just like Hilary did. Say no, Triple E," yipped Rudy. *"Just say no."*

"Oh, um, I'm fine. I really don't need any help," Ellie answered, just in case her boy was correct.

"Not with the actual walking of the dogs," Gretchen continued. "But with a contract. I'm an attorney, you see. I'd be happy to draw one up for free, as a thank-you for taking care of my little man."

Chapter 18

"Don't even think it," Ellie said as she and Rudy hurried down the hall.

"Hey, come on. You don't really expect me to pass up the perfect moment for a lawyer joke, do you?"

"There's no time to stop for one of your lame attorney jibes right now."

"So listen while we collect the gang."

Ellie led him into the elevator. "Okay, but this had better be good."

"They're all good, Triple E."

"In your opinion, maybe, but sometimes they're just too— On second thought, forget it for now. We have more important things to take care of." She tapped her toe, willing the elevator to move, which it finally did. In a show of defiance, Rudy shot her a raspberry and kept quiet, but she refused to give in to his silent treatment.

The moment they stopped on the twelfth floor, they aimed for the Lowensteins' apartment. Once there, Ellie knocked, even though she knew Mariette made a trip to a spa each afternoon for a massage. After using her key, she found the paunchy Pug sitting in the foyer with a pained expression in his eyes. "Hey, big boy, you ready to go?"

Sampson responded with a loud burp, then, *"I ate somethin' that didn't agree with me. The faster we get to the park, the better."*

"Uh-oh, look out," warned Rudy.

Ellie snapped on Sampson's lead and walked quickly to the elevator, where she punched the button for the fifteenth floor. "Cross your legs. We still have to get Freud and Lily."

"Ready for the joke yet?" Rudy asked, ignoring the moaning Pug. *"It's good, I promise."*

"I should have known better than to think

you'd give up," she muttered. "Okay, fine. Anything to get my mind off of what I might have to clean up from you-know-who." The elevator door opened and Ellie raced toward the Gordons' apartment.

"Ahem." Trotting behind her, the yorkiepoo cleared his throat. *"What's the difference between a leech and a lawyer?"*

"Ee-uww." Ellie flinched. "I can't imagine, but it must be gross." She knocked on the Gordons' door, figured Esther was still at her studio, and let herself in. "Hi, little man. We're in a hurry, so let's move it. Do you need your coat?"

Freud gave a full body shake. *"Nah, but thanks for asking."*

After she clipped on his leash, the French Bulldog stared at the Pug with suspicion. *"What's up with the big guy? Looks like he's got a cramp someplace important."*

"You don't wanna know," said Rudy.

On a normal day Ellie would have joined in the pack's byplay, but she was on a mission. She made tracks for the elevator and they rode to the last stop. The Wisemans had two teenagers who were involved in a ton of after-school activities. Sometimes they were home; most of the time they were not. When no one answered her knock, she went inside and hooked Lily to her lead. "Sorry, bitty girl, but we're in emergency mode. We have to get outside fast."

Back in the elevator, Ellie sent the car south while the dogs chatted. When she glanced down, Sampson's eyes were closed, his breathing labored. In the lobby, she scurried the pack out and into the dim afternoon light, where the Pug let out another loud burp, or was it a—

"For God's sake, put a sock in it," groused Rudy.

"Yeah, man, take it easy with the gas," shouted Freud.

"That goes ditto for me," Lily chimed.

Sensing that time was critical, Ellie jogged across the street and stopped in front of the park, where Sampson squatted immediately. While the other dogs began a leisurely search for the perfect dumping spot, the Pug passed a second volley of gas and grunted. After a moment, she pulled a bag from her tote and gazed at his questionable creation. "What in the heck is that?"

The dog stared up at her, his expression wounded. *"Guess it's whatever was bothering me."*

She squatted and made an inspection. "It's blue and . . . purple?"

"Can't tell. Color-blind, remember?"

Holding her breath, she scraped up the big business and sealed the bag. "That should have made you feel better," she said as she stood.

"I guess."

"Let's walk, gang," Ellie ordered, and led the

dogs into the interior of Central Park. Thirty minutes later, she had returned Lily and Freud to their homes and written their daily notes, but she'd saved Sampson and Mariette's place for last.

"What'cha writin'?" asked the Pug while she scribbled.

"I'm advising your mom to one"—she held up her index finger—"put you on a diet, and two, be more careful about leaving whatever it is you've been eating lying around. And to cut down on the size of your business, I'm also recommending she feed you a preservative-free kibble with no corn, wheat gluten, or fillers. I've even given her a couple of brand names."

"Just make sure it tastes good," Sampson grumped to Ellie's departing backside.

She and Rudy beat feet down the hall and rode the elevator to street level. "That took longer than I expected," she said, eyeing the large bank of clouds hanging like dirty cotton balls over the darkening city. "It's coming up on four and we have three more buildings to do. Let's get going."

"What about my joke?"

"Joke? Oh, the leech thing. Give me the opening line again."

"Okay, but pay attention. What's the difference between a lawyer and a leech?"

They crossed at the light on Eighty-sixth Street. "I have no idea."

"When you die, a leech has the decency to fall off before suckin' your last drop of blood." He snickered. *"Get it?"*

"I do, and I still say ee-uww." Ellie smiled. "But it is sort of funny."

"Did it cheer you up?"

"Strangely enough, yes. Let's finish so we can stop in the Nelsons' apartment and get home before it starts to snow."

Two hours later, Ellie and Rudy were through with their second runs in the unmanned building and the Davenport, and dropped off Lulu and the rest of the Beaumont dogs. At close to six o'clock, it was time to enter her target's lair. She had a couple of plans in the works. She was crafty. She would get into that apartment whatever way she could.

On the elevator ride, she and Rudy discussed strategy. "If we're lucky, the painters will still be there and it will be easier to get inside. But if the Nelsons are home, I'm going to be extra nice no matter which one answers the door. Either way, I want you to promise you'll can the wisecracks."

"You're going to kiss ass?"

"It's a possibility, though it's not something I want to do, believe me."

"I don't like the idea of you sucking up. I didn't much care for either Nelson when I met them."

"You met them? When was that?"

"The night of the party. You went to the police station with Flora and the dopey dick, and left me with Vivian. That Ditzi woman—"

"Her name is Mitzi."

"Whatever. She hung out with Viv until her husband went loopy with the champagne. I can't put my finger on the reason why, but she gave me the willies."

"Please explain to me how you can be such a good judge of character about everyone you meet, and so off the mark when it comes to Sam."

"I got him pegged. You just don't wanna to listen."

The elevator stopped and Ellie got back on track. "Okay, we're here. Forget about Sam and concentrate. Remember, not a sound," she ordered as they slipped into the hall. "Just keep your eyes open and your nose to the ground, and let me do the talking."

"Oh-oh. Looks like we're in luck. Those painter people are still on the job," Rudy told her, gazing straight ahead. *"Time to play it cool and do some fancy talkin'."*

Ellie sucked in a breath as she watched the parade. Men wearing spattered coveralls were carrying ladders, buckets, and all manner of supplies out of the Nelsons' apartment. Rudy sneezed and she wrinkled her nose to fend off the smell. Squaring her shoulders, she let two workmen pass, then she edged around the door, into the foyer, and pressed on into the living room.

Well-used gray drop cloths covered a pile of what had to be furniture pushed to the center of the room. A cold breeze blew in from barely open windows, making her shiver. Poison was sometimes kept in a kitchen pantry. If she could sneak in there and do a quick scan—

"Comin' through," said an older gentleman carrying a clipboard. He passed them, then backed up a step. "You aren't Mrs. Nelson."

"Uh, no, I'm not," said Ellie, crossing her fingers. She'd be caught red-handed if the real Mitzi walked in, and then what? "I'm a—a— friend."

"They expecting you?" the man continued.

"I'm here to—uh—check out the paint job. I was thinking of hiring someone to spruce up my apartment, and the Nelsons said I could stop by and take a look when you were through."

The man pulled a card from his pocket and passed it over. "Here you go. I can give you a couple of references in the building, too. Name's Hurley, and I own the company."

"I'll keep that in mind," said Ellie, dropping the card in her tote bag. "Do you know when Mr. or Mrs. Nelson is supposed to return?"

Hurley glanced at his watch. "Sometime in the next fifteen minutes. You can wait, but I got to supervise my guys. I'll be back in a few."

"Take him up on the offer," Rudy said, straining at the leash. *"I'm gettin' a vibe here."*

"I think I will. Thanks." When he left, she glared at her boy. So much for his promise to be quiet. Then she noticed he was sniffing the air with gusto. "What are you doing?"

He dragged her forward, his nose twitching. *"This paint stench is bad, but there's a whiff of something else . . . something I recognize in the background. Turn me loose."*

Ellie inched forward into a small rear foyer with three doors, two of which were ajar. "I don't think we should go any farther. This might be their bedroom."

"I don't care if it's their private taxidermy lab. There's somethin' hinky in that room."

He continued pulling, his toenails scraping a throw rug until it bunched under his paws. "Stop, you dolt. You're going to scratch the floor."

"Then let me go! Let me go!"

Ellie looked over her shoulder. There was no sign of Hurley or any of the workmen. Just then, Rudy gave a jerk, the leash slipped through her fingers, and the yorkiepoo disappeared into a room dead ahead.

After another scan of the living area, she tiptoed behind him, squinting in the darkness. Running a hand against the wall to her left, she flipped a light switch and found Rudy standing on his hind legs with his front paws braced against a stand that held a large aquarium. She rushed over and took a look inside.

"What's in there? What do you see?"

She swallowed as she assessed the glass tank's interior. "I'm not sure, but it looks like some kind of habitat for a lizard or turtle." It was then she remembered what Vivian had told her. "Or a frog?"

Rudy yipped. *"So that's what I'm pickin' up. It's swamp stink, kinda like how the lake in the center of the park smells when it's really hot."*

She narrowed her gaze and studied the tiny reptile. Or was it an amphibian? "Then you've smelled this stuff before?"

"It doesn't smell exactly like the lake, but close enough. And yes, I recognize the scent."

The few creatures she spied hiding amid the plants spaced around the interior of the aquarium caused her mind to race. There was something odd . . . different . . . unusual about these frogs. The dim lighting might have an eerie effect on their skin tone, but was it enough to turn these creatures from froggy green to a brilliant golden yellow?

Stooping down, she squinted through the glass and counted a total of four tiny hoppers. She stood, reached into her tote, and started to dig. "Hang on while I take their picture."

Ellie chose the photo setting on her cell phone, aimed it into the tank, and pushed the button. Then she glanced around the room and realized they weren't in a bedroom but some kind of holding area. There were several other tanks with more brightly colored frogs and smaller glass cases that reminded her of the ant farm she'd played with as a child.

"This place is giving me the creeps. Let's get moving." She dropped the phone in her bag, picked up Rudy's leash, and gave it a tug, but he planted all four paws on the floor. "This is no time to be stubborn, fella." When he continued to ignore her, she ended up dragging him from the room as if he were a canine statue.

"Wait! Give me another minute. I got a bead on that smell."

"We don't have another minute," she whispered. "I hear voices."

She skittered into the living room with Rudy lagging behind just in time to see Mitzi in the foyer talking to Hurley. Heat suffused her chest and inched up her neck. Taking a calming breath, she willed away the red that she was certain covered her face. Then she sidled into the center of the room and began examining the paint job as if she were a city inspector.

"Well, hello." Mitzi was at her side a second later. "Ellie, is it? What are you doing here?"

"I stopped by to talk with Edward. The—um—door was open and workmen were leaving the place, and my dog pulled his leash free and raced inside, so I had to come in to get him."

Mitzi made an attempt at raising one sculpted eyebrow and gazed at Rudy, who gave her a doggie grin. "Your dog pulled his leash free?"

"Right. I came here to speak with Edward."

"You came to converse with Edward?"

Converse? "I was hoping we could continue the talk we had at Mrs. Steinman's party."

"The talk you had at Mrs. Steinman's?"

Ordering herself to stay mum about the echoes, Ellie smiled instead. "Yes, didn't he tell you?"

Mitzi crossed her arms. "I didn't realize you and Edward knew each other that well."

"We don't. I mean, we didn't until the MACC. I thought maybe I could help him and Flora get back together again."

"And that's what you were discussing at Flora's party? Your willingness to aid Edward in getting his handler's job back? That's very . . . interesting."

This time both eyebrows moved, or at least Ellie thought they did. It was hard to tell, given all the chemicals Mitzi had injected in her forehead. "Is your husband expected home anytime soon?"

The woman continued her stone-faced perusal. "I'm not sure when he'll be in. Does he have your number?"

After reaching into her tote bag, Ellie passed Mitzi a business card. "Give him this and tell him he can phone me anytime. I really do want to

. . . converse with him." Turning, she and Rudy aimed for the exit, with Mitzi's footsteps tapping behind them. "It was nice seeing you again," Ellie called as they walked out the front door.

"*Act natural. Don't race like your tail's on fire or that broad will know you were up to somethin',*" Rudy muttered as they marched down the hall.

Ellie forced her rubbery knees to lock and her feet to move. Her boy was right. If she hesitated or showed weakness in any way, Mitzi would guess she'd been lying.

"*Just keep breathin' in and out, nice and easy, Triple E, and head straight for the elevator. That's it. Eyes front and don't look back. Now press the button.*"

The elevator door opened and they stepped inside. Propping her back against the wall, she looked up and found Mitzi watching. She gave a casual wave as the door slid shut, then slumped forward and huffed out a breath. "Good Lord, what a disaster. Don't ever let me do anything that stupid again. Please, I beg of you."

"*You did fine. She's just got a suspicious nature. And is her face for real?*"

"Her face is a billboard for her business," Ellie quoted, remembering what Vivian had said about Mitzi's profession. "She's a walking ad for facial reconstruction and the chemical peels her company specializes in."

"Next time, let me try tellin' her one of my lawyer jokes. I wanna see her face crack like an egg when she smiles."

"We'll discuss Mitzi later. Right now I want to get home and make a dent in some Häagen-Dazs Caramel Cone."

"Don't you wanna hear how I recognized that stink?"

The elevator door opened and Ellie raced into the foyer. Nodding to the evening doorman, a guy a lot less friendly or talkative than Natter, she charged onto the sidewalk. "I certainly do."

"The scent matched what I smelled on that liver treat you said Arnie gave you."

She stopped short and squatted to face him. "Are you saying the odor coming from that terrarium and what you smelled on the liver treat were the same?"

"Duh, yeah." He gave her face a sloppy lick. *"What do you think of that?"*

"I think you may be onto something." Because of their golden coloring and tiny size, the frogs were definitely unusual. And certainly not your typical house pet, which matched the description Mitzi had given her the first time they'd met. She recalled Viv's comment about Mitzi and frogs and Edward's earlier profession when Viv told her what had happened after Flora's party. Now that Rudy had linked the frogs to that liver . . .

"Stop starin' into space and make tracks," the yorkiepoo ordered. *"You have to get home and study up on those frogs."*

Ellie arrived at her apartment wet, cold, and hungry. After hanging up Rudy's damp sweater and her jacket, she mixed her boy a tasty supper, using his usual dry kibble and favorite canned food. Then she pulled out the Caramel Cone. She had work to do before Sam arrived, and she'd never get it done without fuel, especially if she intended to do some serious research.

She sat at the table and dug into her ice cream as she phoned Sam. When she got his voice mail, she left a message saying he should take his time because she was running behind. She didn't know how she was going to tell him about the barely legal manner in which she'd entered Mitzi's apartment. But that wasn't nearly as important as explaining about the frogs she'd found in that tank. She had a picture of the hoppers for evidence, but no matter what she said, or how she phrased her confession, he would accuse her of deliberately disobeying his direct order to stay out of the investigation.

After tossing the empty ice cream container in the trash, she went to her desk and booted up her computer. While the machine did its thing, she walked to the window and stared out at the courtyard. Fat snowflakes swirled, dancing in the light from the streetlamps and drifting down to form pockets of white in the courtyard below. Thanks to the weather, there was little chance the Nelsons would be going anywhere tonight. Maybe, if she gave Sam the same story she'd told Mitzi about wanting to talk to Edward, and then explained to him about the frogs, he wouldn't pitch a fit or . . .

"Let me guess. It's snowing," Rudy said, breaking into her thoughts.

"Yes, but it doesn't appear to be a serious storm." She heaved a sigh. "I love when it snows. The city always looks so fresh and new once it's over." When Rudy didn't answer, she had to ask. "You remember snow, don't you?"

He shivered. *"How could I forget something that made me feel like I'd been hangin' in a meat locker?"*

"But you have a coat now. I'll even buy you winter boots if you want."

"No, thanks. I'd rather have worms."

She tsked. "What's with you? You've been disagreeable and cranky ever since we got home."

"What I've been is waiting patiently for you to do some big-time investigating." He sneezed. *"Get the lead out and start finding what we need to have that Nelson guy arrested."*

She moved from the window to her desk and said, "I'm worried about what Sam will say."

"You're worried about Detective Doofus?

That's plain stupid. Who cares what he thinks? If he's not smart enough to figure this case out, he deserves to be upstaged by us."

Ellie shrugged. "It's not just that. Sam's a by-the-book kind of guy, and when I explain what we found he's going to want to know how we did it. Our entry into the Nelsons' apartment wasn't exactly legal, so he won't be able to use what we tell him, even if we find something incriminating on the Internet. He's going to need a search warrant to get into their place, and I don't think our on-site info or his gut feeling will get him one."

"What about that photo? If he brings it to a judge, won't that be reason enough? Especially if you have info on those stinky frogs."

She wanted to kick herself for not being as smart as her dog. Could Rudy be right? "Possibly, but I'm not sure—"

"You could always call Judge Frye. He'd give you the skinny on how to get a search warrant."

"I'd rather keep Stanley out of it. Mother will have a hissy fit if she knows I'm involved in another murder, and she'll disown me if I pull the judge into it."

"So tell Stanley to keep it a secret, or make up a reason why you need to know."

"I hate lying—"

"You just need more practice at it, is all. Now how 'bout we concentrate on gettin' said evidence and worry about what to do with it later?"

341

"All right, fine. I'm sitting. See?" She pulled out her desk chair and plopped her bottom down. "Now I'm linking to Google . . . and I'm typing in 'frogs' . . ." She sighed. "Great. Eighty bazillion hits. I'll never wade through them all."

"Not just frogs. Try 'poison frogs,' or 'yellow frogs,' or maybe 'smelly, disgusting frogs.' "

"Okay, okay." She tried "poison frogs." Half a second later the top entry on the screen read: "Do you mean Poison Dart Frogs in Captivity?" When she clicked onto the question, she received the mother lode for information sites —a list of more than 364,000. If she didn't narrow the search, she'd be here all night.

"Good grief. I had no idea there'd be so many." She hit the first one, but the frog pictured in the article was a brilliant blue, almost the color Sampson's business had been that afternoon.

"What do you see? What are they tellin' you?"

"Hang on a second." She walked to her kitchen table and pulled the cell phone from her tote bag. Back at her desk, she called up the photo she'd taken at the Nelsons', then typed "golden poison dart frog" on the search line. Crossing her fingers, she clicked on the first one and the picture of a frog identical to the one on her cell phone shot into view.

"I'll be damned," she muttered. *"Phyllobates terribilis."*

"Phyllis? Who's Phyllis and why's she so terrible?"

"Not Phyllis, silly," Ellie corrected. "*Phyllobates.* And not terrible, but *terribilis.* It's the Latin name for this genus of frog. And here's what it says in the first paragraph: 'As a warning to predators of their extreme toxicity, Poison Dart Frogs are spectacularly colored. The poison comes via eating insects, ants in particular, which have, in turn, eaten certain plants containing the toxins. Depending on their diet, captive specimens may not be poisonous like their wild counterparts.'"

She leaned back in her chair. "That must be why Edward keeps ants in the smaller tank. They're the kind with a property that turns the frogs in the aquariums toxic."

"Wow, maybe we could sic one of those Phyllis the terrible frogs on Eugene. He'd stay far away if he knew we could drop him like a rock."

At the mention of Ellie's disagreeable competitor in the dog walking world, she frowned. "This is no joking matter."

"Who's jokin'? Eugene deserves to be poisoned. He's a creep and he hates canines, even though walking us is his bread and butter."

"Listen, there's more. It was written by some guy named Gerald Durrell back in 1955."

"Let me see. Let me see."

Ellie moved her chair away from the desk and Rudy jumped into her lap. After pulling closer, she read the next paragraph out loud, which explained more about the frogs and ended with " 'The yellow Golden Poison Dart Frog photographed above'—see it looks just like this picture of the frog in Edward's tank—'is reputedly the deadliest creature in the world, with enough poison in it to kill ten humans.' "

The yorkiepoo pointed his muzzle at the monitor. *"Look at that banana-peel skin and those beady black eyes. And what's with the three toes stickin' off each leg like claws?"*

"There are hundreds of different types of frogs, just like there are hundreds of different national-ities of people and breeds of dog. Humans don't all look the same, so why should frogs?"

"Yeah, yeah, whatever you say. So how does a person get hold of this poison, say, to put it on a liver treat?"

Ellie grasped his middle and set him on the floor. "I don't know, but I'm going to find out. Let me read—"

A knock on the door interrupted her. "Oh, golly. That's probably Sam. I bet he didn't get my message asking him to take his time." She stood. "If he bothered the Feldmans again, I swear I'm going to take back my key."

"Maybe it's Vivie and Mr. T, wantin' to see what we been up to."

"I hope so. You stay here while I let them in. Viv might know a clever way for us to use this stuff to trap Edward."

She hurried down the hall and peeked through the peephole. Then she inhaled sharply. The visitor was a surprise, but she had to open the door. She needed all the information she could get on those frogs.

Chapter 19

"Detective Ryder, it's Emily Bridges. I received a report on the man who died at the dog show from the NIH in Atlanta," said the ME. "After looking it over, I realized you should have the information ASAP."

Obviously, word had yet to reach her that he was now second in command on the case. But Vince was home with his family, and he was still at the office, so why not?

"Since when have we been using the lab at the National Institutes of Health?" Sam asked the medical examiner. "I thought our facility in Albany was top of the line."

"Top of the line for normal tests, yes, but the victim's sudden drop in blood pressure and the description of the way he died got me thinking, so I asked the big guns to run some tests that were more along the lines of unusual. I also asked them to make it priority one."

Thank God for Dr. Bridges. The woman was tenacious as well as brilliant. "I assume what they found is going to give me the real reason Harris died?"

"I'm ninety-nine percent positive it's the cause of death, but I'm running another set of tests just to be sure. Now that I know what we're looking for, I hope to pinpoint the toxin in the man's remains."

Sam sat upright. "The toxin? Then it was poison?"

"Not just any poison. Let me explain and you'll see what I'm talking about. Oh, and I just faxed you the complete report. You might want to pick it up so you can follow along."

Sam walked to the fax machine to retrieve the pages spitting into the collection tray. Fifteen minutes later, the ME wrapped up her mind-numbing and technical explanation and waited for his reply.

"So the victim was killed by a poison exuded by one of the half-dozen or so species of dart frogs that inhabit a very few countries in South America," Sam echoed, still trying to come to grips with the report.

"Correct."

Drumming his pencil on the blotter, he formed a question he hoped showed some semblance of intelligence. "Isn't the importing of certain deadly species illegal in the States?"

"Many are, but this type of frog and its poison have been approved for medical research, so those studying the creatures are able to come in contact with the substance. Since the frogs exude

346

the poison only if they continue their diet of a certain type of beetle or ant, they would have to be cared for by someone fairly well educated in entomology and herpetology."

"Entomology? You mean bugs?"

"Bugs *and* amphibians, because they'd also have to know that if the frogs are fed a 'normal' diet they revert to a non-poisonous state and become a regular amphibian. Therefore, most people in the U.S. who own them do so for their beauty and uniqueness alone."

He stared at the image on the top sheet—a speckled frog sitting on a rock. "Could you explain to me what about this frog might make it beautiful?"

"Sorry, I thought you'd get the message when you read their common names. Are you near a computer?"

"I am." He frowned at his cantankerous machine.

"Good. Call up Google, type in 'Poison Dart Frogs,' and click on the first site listed. Then you'll see exactly what I mean."

Sam did as she instructed. Moving from site to site, he saw that the ME was right. The frogs that were in black and white on the faxed pages showed up on his monitor in amazing colors. He wasn't sure he'd call them beautiful, but they were striking. The odd look probably gave whoever owned them more party conversation than they could handle.

He gazed at the frog sitting on a rock, its color on the computer screen now a brilliant sapphire blue. "It says the color variations are deliberate, a tactic called aposematic coloration."

"That's correct. I'm fairly certain I sent you everything there is on dart frogs in general. Unless we learn the exact genus we're dealing with, we may never know more." She cleared her throat. "Find out who owns this type of frog and also has the capability to obtain those specific bugs, Detective, and you'll have your killer."

Dr. Bridges promised to get in touch with him when the latest toxicology results arrived, and they ended the conversation. Thanks to the ME's information, Sam's brain was imploding. The details in the report were much more complex than the ordinary layman could absorb, but at least now, with the info in hand, he could go over the facts and try to figure out who might be the most likely candidate for Arnie's killer.

He flipped through the fax pages again, thinking about the amphibian business. According to these reports, there were several likely types of poison dart frogs that one might find in the States. More than one hundred toxins had been identified from the skin secretions of members of the *Dendrobates* and *Phyllobates,* but only frogs of the genus *Phyllobates* produced the super-deadly batrachotoxin.

Sam read that the batrachotoxin was used to

kill the frogs' prey or their enemies when the need arose. It was so deadly that a drop the weight of two grains of table salt was enough to kill a normal-size human, either by ingestion or by contact with the skin. And there was no known antidote or cure.

The toxic compounds had been studied for years here in the U.S. in the hope they could take the place of more-addictive drugs in the use of pain relief. Unfortunately, there'd been no success to date, and the research had been dropped, but a number of the frogs were still being raised in home environments for their brilliant coloring and party-talk attraction.

Bottom line, Arnie Harris had ingested a liver treat laced with the poison, which had caused his blood pressure to drop instantly. Most likely, he was dead before he hit the show ring floor.

Sam ran a hand through his hair. Now what? He was damned if he knew how to proceed. Yes, the animals were uniquely colored, but finding one would require a visit to every suspect's home, and he still might not be able to locate the frog if it was kept somewhere else. He couldn't imagine anyone carting a frog on an airplane, but they might have extracted the poison, put it in a regular medicine container, and packed the container in their luggage.

His first thought was to take another look at the two suspects who lived in the area, and worry about the two people who had flown in tomorrow. That dropped the J boys, as Ellie liked to call them, to the bottom of the list, and left the Apgar woman, who had come by car from Connecticut, and Edward Nelson, who lived here in the city. With snow in the forecast, he doubted either of them would be going anywhere tonight.

It was near six thirty, and he was due at Ellie's soon, but he had to delve into the background information on Nelson and Apgar that Vince had gathered before he had taken the lead on this investigation. If Sam found anything that would convince the ADA to go for an emergency warrant, he'd call Vince and they would head to the suspect's home to run the search.

He chose Edward Nelson's file first because the man was local, which would make obtaining a warrant easier. He'd have to jump through State of Connecticut hoops to get one for the Apgar woman. After skimming the current data on Nelson, he read further, learning about the man's family history and education.

What he found turned his gut inside out. Ellie had told him at least a dozen times that Nelson was her first choice as Arnie's killer, but he hadn't found anything to link the man to the death until now. Vince had probably labeled the information as unimportant and not called it to his attention, while Sam's girl had been right all along.

He dialed Phillip Mortensen, the ADA on this case and a guy he knew was fair and fast-acting, and gave a sigh of relief when he found the attorney in his office. After explaining the situation, he got a positive response.

It was time to call Vince.

"Mrs. Nelson. What brings you out in the middle of a snowstorm?" Ellie asked, after swallowing her surprise.

Wearing an expensive fur coat that Ellie guessed had cost enough to support a small nation, Mitzi gazed at her in the same stone-faced manner as in their previous encounter. "We need to talk. May I come in?"

"I smell trouble, Triple E. Shut the door and lock it tight," Rudy warned.

When she glanced down, his body was rigid and his hair stood on end. Never a good sign. "I was . . . um . . . we were just about to go to bed. Can't it wait until morning?"

"Bed? But it's early. At least allow me to come in and warm up before I leave." With that, Mitzi swept through the door and headed down the hall with Rudy on her heels.

Surprised by Mitzi's direct and borderline-rude actions, Ellie followed them into the living room. When she arrived, the woman was already perched on a chair, her coat wrapped tightly around her and her handbag—was that the

Jimmy Choo snakeskin shopper that retailed for three thousand dollars?—on the coffee table in front of her. She made a mental note to describe the bag to Vivian, who would know the designer details for certain, but she was positive of one thing: the skin-sculpting and -rejuvenation business was booming.

"Could you do something about your dog?" Mitzi asked, pulling Ellie out of her fashion daydream.

She tsked at her yorkiepoo, who was glaring at Mitzi as if he were a gunslinger at high noon. "Rudy, enough," she chided. Then, with her good manners firmly in place, she smiled. "Can I offer you a drink? Soda or a cup of tea—"

"Get out and run to Vivie's place. Call the cops. I'll hold her off here," her boy ordered. Growling low in his throat, he took a step closer to Mitzi. *"Do it now."*

The woman drew back in the chair, her expression one of disdain. "Is he always this . . . this unfriendly?"

Rudy gave another growl. *"I'll show you unfriendly, you Mount Rushmore clone."*

Ellie bit her lip to keep from grinning. "Sorry. Let me get him under control. Come on, big man," she said, tugging on his collar. "We'll take our nightly trip around the block in a few minutes. Until then, you're on a time-out."

When he continued to growl, she picked him

up and he wriggled in her arms. *"Let me go! I smell frog stink, I tell ya, and that means trouble."*

Carting him out, she talked as she walked. "Please calm down. I'll get rid of her and come to get you soon." When they arrived in the bedroom she kicked the door closed and dropped him on the bed. "What the heck is wrong with you?" she muttered. "Of course you smell frog. The woman shares an apartment with the things. It's natural you'd catch their scent on her—or maybe it's on her coat."

"But I'm tryin' to tell you, it's more than a scent. It's a full-blown smell, like one of them frogs is right there with her." He jumped off the bed. *"Lemme back in that room and I'll show you the smart way to run an investigation."*

"You're acting completely over the top," Ellie told him, inching toward the door. "We parted on good terms this afternoon, so she's just here for a chat."

"In the middle of a snowstorm?"

When Rudy put it that way . . . "Okay, maybe not. Stay put and I'll get rid of her. I'll rescue you as soon as she leaves."

"No! Hey, wait! Let me out of here!"

When she closed the door, Rudy's shouts turned to frantic barks and she rolled her eyes. The Feldmans lived directly above her. The way her luck had been going lately, they'd be knocking at her door to lodge a complaint. They might even involve the police.

Straightening her shoulders, she returned to the living room and saw that her guest had removed her coat. Great. Now she'd never get rid of the woman. "I could phone for a cab. That way you wouldn't have to stand on Lexington in the snow. I imagine hailing a taxi will be a bear right now. I'd be happy to make you a cup of tea while you wait."

"It's kind of you to offer, but only if you'll join me."

Mitzi appeared to smile, but Ellie couldn't be sure. "I'll be right back." She winced at the sound of Rudy's continued barking and headed for the kitchen, where she filled a china teapot with water and placed it in the microwave. While it was heating, she set cups, saucers, and an assortment of tea bags on a tray.

"I'll just be another minute," she shouted. "Shall I call that cab for you?"

"Take your time," Mitzi replied, sounding almost jovial. "I have their phone number programmed in my cell."

When the nuker dinged, Ellie retrieved the hot pot, added it to the tray, and carried everything into the living room. Mitzi snapped her phone closed, and Ellie set the tray down, then offered the woman her choice of tea. Mitzi selected a calming chamomile.

"Good idea," she said, choosing the same. Cocking her head, she realized that Mitzi still wore her gloves, but she lost focus of that odd fact when Rudy's barks turned to yowls. "I'm sorry my dog is acting so crazy. He's usually good with strangers."

Mitzi didn't comment, but she did stir her tea with a vengeance. Then she reached for her handbag and dug inside. "I usually carry sweetener, but it looks like I'm out. Could I trouble you for some?"

"Oh, gosh, of course. I have regular sugar or the artificial kind. Which do you prefer?"

"Anything is fine—and take your time." Mentally kicking herself for being so forgetful, Ellie stood. "Hang on a second. I'll be right back." She found sugar in the kitchen and brought it out, along with the pink and blue packets. "Here you are." She placed them on the table. Rudy howled again and she sighed. "I am *so* going to scold that dog when you leave." After stirring her tea, she squeezed out the bag and dropped it on the tray. "Did the cab company say how long they would take?"

Mitzi leaned back and took a dainty sip of her drink. "They told me it might be a while. You know how difficult drivers can be when it snows in this city."

Ellie nodded in agreement, though she hated acting like Mitzi's good buddy. It was clear Rudy didn't trust the woman, and neither did she, but being rude just wasn't in her makeup. Besides, what if Mitzi had come to reveal something important about her husband? "What is it you wanted to discuss?" she asked, keeping her tone polite. "Did you get a chance to tell Edward I stopped by?"

Mitzi blew on her tea, then took another sip. "I just wanted to ask you a few questions. This tea is delicious, by the way. You should try yours."

"Questions? But you could have called me for that. Is this something about Edward? Where is he, by the way?"

"He's at home, rearranging the furniture and putting the apartment to rights. He told me to thank you for the visit, but said he didn't need your help with Flora. He'll take care of things himself, if not tonight, then later on."

Ellie jumped when she heard a series of bangs coming from the direction of her bedroom. Seconds later, the racket reverberated through the hall again . . . and again. She pursed her lips. "Do you mind if I bring Rudy out? He's acting crazy and I'm afraid my upstairs neighbors will call the cops if he keeps it up."

Mitzi's expression grew solemn. "Enjoy your tea first. He's not making that much noise."

"Oh, but he is, and from the sound of it he plans to keep it up until I set him free. I'll be back in a second." She rushed to the bedroom and threw open the door.

Panting, Rudy glared at her. *"It's about time you got here."*

"You are insane. You could have been hurt, throwing yourself against the door like that. I'll bring you into the living room, but only if you promise to behave."

"Yeah, yeah, sure. Whatever you say."

She gathered him in her arms and they headed out, then they turned the corner into the living room. "Sorry. I'm back and—" Ellie stopped short and gasped.

Mitzi held a gun, and it was pointed in their direction. "Sit down, you goose, and drink that tea."

"I told you she was here to cause trouble—"

She clasped Rudy's muzzle and walked to the sofa. Planting her bottom on the cushion, she drew in a breath. "I'm . . . I'm not sure I understand."

"Of course you don't," Mitzi said with more emotion than Ellie had heard in their previous conversations. "I doubt you have any idea what I've gone through to keep my business afloat. Facial sculpting and rejuvenation is an extremely competitive field. It's dog-eat-dog out there, if you'll pardon the pun, and I can't allow anyone to ruin what I've created."

"Mrs. Nelson, are you sure you're talking to the right person? Because I promise you I have no desire to start a business like yours. I wouldn't even know how to begin."

"Perhaps. Then again, one never can tell. Once I realized you'd learned about Edward's pets, it didn't seem that impossible."

"Edward's pets? Oh, you mean—" Ellie wasn't about to say the word. Let the nutcase lady be the first to bring up the frogs and their poison. "What *do* you mean?"

"You know exactly what I'm talking about. Edward can't seem to control his mouth when he drinks, and I know you and that Vivian person are friends. After Edward told me about the talk he had with you, I thought about the questions Vivian asked me and put two and two together."

"I don't know what you're talking about," Ellie lied. She wasn't about to implicate Viv in this mess.

"Oh, really. Well, the next time you decide to have a snoop session in someone's home, I suggest you turn off the lights when you leave the room you've just inspected." She reached into her purse, pulled out a cylinder, and began attaching it to the barrel of the gun. "We're wasting time. Let's just get on with it, shall we?"

Ellie glanced at the clock over her fireplace mantel. Sam should have brought their dinner an hour ago. Where the heck was he?

Mitzi finished reworking the gun and raised her chin. "Please stop stalling and drink your tea. If you don't, I'll be forced to use this and someone may hear it go off even with the silencer." She threw Rudy a look. "Too bad you brought that mutt out here. His barking would have helped muffle the sound of the shot."

Rudy pulled his chin from Ellie's chest and twisted in her arms. Sniffing the air, he leaned toward the coffee table. *"It's frog poison, Triple E. It's in your tea."* He wriggled to get free. *"Lemme at her. I know I can bite her before she fires that cannon."*

Holding him tight to her breast, Ellie finally got the message. How could she have been so dense? And why hadn't she listened to Rudy? Of course Mitzi wanted her to take a swallow of the tea. She'd added some of the same poison that had killed Arnie. "Mrs. Nelson, please, think about what you're doing. You didn't exchange the doctored liver treats with those Arnie Harris had in his pocket, your husband did, so you're only an accessory. But if you force me to drink this, you're the one who'll be accused of murder."

Mitzi's stony expression stayed in place. "Edward? Don't make me laugh. Unless it has something to do with dogs, the man doesn't have an inventive bone in his body. I'm the one in charge of our relationship, and he switched the bags on my orders. He couldn't stop whining about the way Flora had taken her dog away from him, so I ordered him to just get rid of the little bitch." She shrugged. "He wanted to kill

Flora Steinman, but I convinced him that losing the dog she loved would be a much more fitting punishment for her."

"Lemme go! Lemme go, I tell ya! This babe is toast!"

Ellie again grabbed her boy's muzzle. Sam was sure to arrive any minute now. He knew she was waiting for him. When she didn't answer the buzzer, he'd find a way into the building and use his key to let himself into her apartment. She just had to keep Mitzi talking.

"I can assure you it will be quite painless," the woman continued. "Just one small swallow and everything will be over in less than a minute." She pointed the gun at the table. "Now, drink up, or I'll be forced to use this on you and your dog."

Sam paced as an officer snapped the cuffs on a disgruntled Edward Nelson's wrists and led him out of the apartment. Forensics and CSU were here, still pondering what to do with the "evidence" in the back room, especially after Sam had told them about the possible dangers in merely handling the frogs. He doubted anyone in the Crime Scene Unit had ever had to collect half a dozen terrariums filled with ants and poisonous croakers before, never mind figure out how to bag and transport them in this weather.

When he and Vince asked Nelson about the

care and feeding of the frogs, the man had acted completely blasé. What did he care if the evidence deteriorated until it became unusable?

Sam had no idea if bringing the frogs and ants, whose natural habitat was a South American jungle, out into the cold would neutralize the poison or kill the critters, but he and Vince didn't want to risk it. They'd decided to finish up and have an officer guard the evidence until someone could talk to a herpetologist and a bug man, but who knew how long that would take.

Vince came out of the back room and strode in his direction. "Christ. Just when you think you've seen it all in this business, something happens to prove you wrong. I still don't believe what we have as a murder weapon."

"Tell me about it," Sam agreed. "Which of our boys is willing to babysit the back room?"

"Nortak said his wife is out of town, so he'll stay. He's also aware that there's an APB out on Mitzi Nelson, and he's ready to take her into custody if she returns home."

"For a minute there, I thought our man would rat out his wife, but he didn't," said Sam. "It's going to be tough figuring out which of them to pin this on. I figured the mister switched the bags, but the frogs were here and the wife had to know about them. Maybe we'll turn up something at her spa."

"Did the ADA say when we'd have the search warrant for her business?"

"Best guess, sometime tomorrow morning. It'll be interesting to see what we find there." Just then Sam's cell phone rang. "Ryder."

"This is a courtesy call, Detective," said George Burns, the sergeant on desk duty. "We just received a disturbance call. Someone's complaining about noise in the apartment below them. Thought you might like to know about it."

"Are you out to lunch? Fugazzo and I are securing a crime scene and apprehending a murderer."

"I know, I know, but I think you'll be glad I phoned you on this one. The racket's coming from your girlfriend's apartment. Neighbors say her dog's been barking for the last twenty minutes. Claims that's very unusual. Seems Ms. Engleman is a model tenant. Her dog, too."

Sam broke out in a cold sweat. Ellie would never let her dog bark for that long, unless she wasn't home. And she had to be home because it was snowing to beat the band outside and she was waiting for him to bring dinner. "I'm on it." He snapped his phone closed, then asked Vince, "Can you take care of the wrap-up here?"

"Sure. What's up?"

"Something's happening at Ellie's place. I'll let you know what as soon as I can."

Chapter 20

Ellie's downstairs buzzer rang and Mitzi shot upright in her chair. "Are you expecting anyone?"

"Ah, no. Not that I recall." That had to be Sam. Now what?

"Then ignore it and they'll go away." Standing, her captor paced to a window and stood sideways, staring out at the front of the building. "It's probably a mistake. I don't see anyone going down the stoop."

"She's distracted. Lemme down."

"Absolutely not," Ellie whispered, nuzzling Rudy's ear. "At this range she won't miss."

"I'm fast. I'll strike like a snake."

"I said no. Now be quiet so I can concen—"

"It figures you'd be one of those idiotic canine fanatics who talks to their dog," said Mitzi, returning to her chair.

"I'm not a fanatic, but I do use Rudy as a sounding board." Ellie racked her brain for a question that might divert Mitzi's attention. "And why are you so against dogs? They're a main part of your husband's profession. Surely you knew that about him when you got married."

The woman pursed her lips. "When I met Edward he was already teaching, so I thought his dealing with canines had been a phase and it was over. Once I realized I was wrong it was too late."

Well, thought Ellie, that answers absolutely nothing about the reason the woman doesn't like dogs. Maybe if she pushed on to the matter at hand . . .

"What are the frogs for? I mean, if you consider them pets, why keep them in poison mode?"

"Ah, so you know about that, do you?"

"I took a picture of the yellow one, then did some research on the Internet after I arrived home."

"When I told Edward that I'd found you in the apartment, he said you'd figure it out. He thinks you're some kind of female Columbo, stupid dog and all, playing dumb but on top of things on the sly. Says you already solved a couple of murders all by your lonesome."

Ellie almost grinned at the compliment, then realized who'd given it. "I wasn't totally alone, but yes, I did get to the bottom of Professor Albright's death, and a friend's, too."

"I'll show her who's stupid," Rudy griped. *"Just give me two seconds and I'll take her down."*

"I'm still waiting for the frog explanation," she prodded. *Come on, Sam. Buzz Vivian or the Feldmans and get yourself up here.* "Unless you're afraid to tell me."

364

"Afraid?" Mitzi nodded toward the gun and gave a grating laugh. "Did you forget who has the upper hand?"

"You're in charge, but I'd still like to hear your logic," said Ellie. "Why feed the frogs a diet that keeps them poisonous—unless you're killing people on a daily basis?"

"The frogs started out as research, a proposed secret weapon for my skin-enhancement procedures. We've been working on a process to get rid of the pain during and after surgery. You'd be surprised how many of our clients want heavy-duty drug prescriptions for weeks afterward."

"People aren't idiots. They have to realize there will be discomfort anytime someone slices them up with a scalpel." Ellie goaded the woman on intentionally.

"The wealthy have higher expectations and demand more. I have several excellent physicians on staff, but we refuse to overprescribe. We don't want the law sticking its nose in our business."

Ellie gave a mental head shake. How could Mitzi and Edward calmly kill someone and imagine that the law would stay out of their so-called business? "And you didn't think anyone would wonder about Arnie's death? The police have the liver treat out for analysis and toxicology testing right now." *And so do I.* "Eventually they'll put two and two together and figure it out."

"The venom is only detectable if the lab knows what type of poison to look for. Since this type is unique, my guess is they'll come up empty on all counts." She again aimed the gun toward Ellie. "Now drink that tea, or I'll shoot."

Ellie heard the almost silent opening of her apartment door while Mitzi talked. It had to be Sam. Thank heavens he had suspected something when she didn't answer the buzzer.

"You're the only person who has an inkling of what we've done, but that's going to be over soon. When they find you, it will look like sudden adult death syndrome, even after an autopsy. Boo-hoo-hoo, another youngster cut down in the prime of life for no apparent reason."

"Don't listen to her. Nothin's gonna happen to you, because I won't let it."

"Shh," Ellie said, hoping to soothe her boy and calm herself in the process. Rudy was right. She was not going to buy in to this crazy woman's predictions. "But why keep the frogs in your apartment?" she asked, trying to stay on topic. "From what I've read, they're dangerous if their venom merely touches the skin."

"The frogs started out as Edward's hobby. When he explained the scientific community's thoughts on what could be done with the venom, I encouraged him to find a way to get me some for use in my lab. He still has friends in South

America, where he studied for a year, so he wrote to them and they sent him the ants."

"Ryder's in the hall, Triple E. I can smell him."

"But why not keep them in your own laboratory?" she asked, trying to give Sam time to formulate a plan.

"Again, Edward's idea. The frogs need a certain climate in which to thrive, and he felt it was easier to monitor them at home. You probably didn't notice, but that room has two humidifiers and a space heater, just so the creatures have the proper temperature and atmosphere."

"How about if I take her down now and let the dopey dick do the cleanup work?"

She gave Rudy a squeeze. "But Edward's not a scientist or a pharmacist. Who does the actual research and testing?"

Mitzi shrugged. "I don't believe that's any of your concern." She waved the gun. "Now this is my last warning. Drink up. That tea is cold by now, but so be it. You still won't be able to taste a—"

"NYPD, Mrs. Nelson. Drop the gun and put your hands in the air." Sam's voice rang out loud and clear.

The moment he spoke, Ellie read the fear in Mitzi's eyes and sensed that the woman wasn't about to do as ordered. When Rudy jumped free of her arms, she dropped to the floor. Then, from under the coffee table, she watched as her boy pounced on Mitzi's lap just as her gun went off.

Mitzi screamed and dropped the pistol when he attacked, then yowled when Rudy buried his teeth in her gun arm. And he hung on, even as she stood and tried to shake him off.

Sam rose from his spot behind the couch and raced around to kick Mitzi's gun away. Now on the floor, Rudy stood like a bird dog pointing at his quarry, his hackles raised as he growled.

"Don't touch that tea, Ellie," Sam told her, reaching for his handcuffs. He snapped them on Mitzi and waved his Glock toward the chair.

Cradling her bloodied arm and sobbing, Mitzi did as ordered. "I demand a physician, and I want my lawyer." She snarled at Rudy pretty much the way he was snarling at her. "Stay away from me, you hound from hell."

"Sam, thank God you came," Ellie said, rising to her knees. Walking to Rudy, she gathered him up, returned to the sofa, and nestled her nose in his neck. "You could have been killed, big man. I told you to stay put."

Sam holstered his gun. "I called for backup. A couple of teams should be here soon. In the meantime, I'm going to read Mrs. Nelson her rights."

He began the spiel, and Ellie turned her head when she heard footsteps in the hallway.

"Ellie, are you okay?" asked Vivian, peeking around the doorframe.

She nodded, grinning. "Since you're here I guess it was you who let Sam in the building when I didn't answer the buzzer." Rudy jumped down and went back to standing guard over a still-sobbing Mitzi. Ellie stood and shuffled to her best friend's side. "I owe you one."

"Great. I'll add it to the list," Vivian said, hugging Ellie tight.

A siren sounded in the distance, its wail growing louder by the second. Sam must have heard it, too, because he faced them and said, "How about the two of you go downstairs and direct the posse up here? Tell them everything is under control and they won't need their weapons."

Vivian opened her mouth, but Ellie gave her a one-eighty twirl and pushed her down the hall. Now was not the time to ask Sam anything. "Please do like he says, and stay out of the way. I have an exhausting night ahead of me and I don't want to argue."

Much to her surprise, the apartment was cleared a short time later. CSU had found and removed Mitzi's bullet embedded in the top of the sofa, a mere two feet to the left of where Ellie had been sitting. Forensics had taken pictures and fingerprints, collected the teacup and its contents, and bagged whatever else it deemed necessary. Mitzi had been carted out under a police escort, demanding that she be taken to the doctors at her skin-rejuvenation factory, not the ones manning the emergency room at Beth Israel, because she didn't want those "heathens" touching her.

Sam hadn't pressed Mitzi for answers about Arnie's murder, but Ellie had listened carefully while he spoke to someone on the phone and told them they could cancel the APB he'd put out on Mitzi a couple of hours earlier. She also gleaned from his conversation with another officer that Vince had left the Nelson apartment after setting up an overnight guard for the dart frogs.

She sat and stared at the shredded bullet hole now gracing her couch. The fabric was a stain-proof polished cotton with a beautiful floral design in varying shades of yellow, orange, and green on a cream background. It was comfortable and warm, with the homey appeal she loved instead of the stark and formal feel that her dickhead of an ex had insisted upon. Maybe she could hire a furniture company to come in and repair it. If not, she'd offer it to a charity and shop for a new one.

Sam walked into the room and took a seat next to her, wrapping her in his arms. "You okay?"

She grimaced as tears started to well. "Sort of. Actually I'm more upset about my sofa than I am about what almost happened to me. Do you think I can sue Mitzi for a replacement?"

"That's doubtful," he said with a smile in his voice. "She and that husband of hers are going away for a long while. By the time they pay their attorney fees, I don't think they'll have much left of their cash." He opened his arms and she fell into them. "Only you could care about a sofa at a time like this."

"Are you sure they won't go free?" she asked, sniffing away a tear.

"Not a chance. Vince and I caught Nelson with Arnie's murder weapon, toxic ants included, we have the ME's report explaining how it was done, and Mrs. Nelson came here with a gun, intent on forcing you to drink a cup of poison. Even if the Nelsons make some kind of deal, I don't see how Edward can get out of being tried for killing Arnie Harris and the Mrs. for attempting to murder you."

Ellie snuggled into his chest and stifled a sob. "I still can't believe someone would kill a defenseless canine just because they wanted to get even for being fired from a job. You do realize the intended victim wasn't Arnie but Lulu, don't you?"

"Yeah, I got that impression, though I doubt the DA will believe it when they give their statements. Which is a good thing, because

371

there's no jail time for trying to kill a dog, but a human, well, that's another story."

"Mrs. Steinman will be happy to hear we got to the truth. I can't wait to tell her."

"You do that, but don't give her the details. No talking to reporters, either. We don't want to jinx things before we go to court."

"I'll be careful." Almost back in control, she sat up and glanced around the room. "Have you seen Rudy?"

Sam heaved a sigh. "I've been a little busy, babe."

"I know you have. It's just that I owe him my life. If he hadn't gone on the attack and grabbed Mitzi's arm, that shot might not have gone wide."

"My guess is she would have missed anyhow. She wasn't exactly playing with a full deck, and she certainly wasn't trained in handling a firearm."

"So you aren't going to give my boy any credit for wrapping up this case?" She poked him in the ribs. "What's the matter? Too proud to share the spotlight with a dog?"

He put his hands on his knees and stood. "I'll think about it. Meanwhile, get a good night's sleep. You'll be spending a couple of hours at the station tomorrow afternoon."

Ellie followed him down the hall. At the door, he cupped her jaw in his palm. "Give me a few days to set things straight, then you and I will go out on the town."

"Or we could stay in and I'll cook. I'm even willing to invite your sisters and Lydia."

Sam's mouth quirked up at the corners. "Don't even think about it."

"I'd be happy to make your favorite meal plus an apple pie with crumble topping for dessert."

He brushed her lips gently, then pulled away. "I don't care what we eat for dinner, just as long as you and I are the only guests. And forget the apple pie. I have a more creative idea for dessert."

"You can always put in your order, but I'm not promising you'll get what you want."

He grinned. "We'll see about that." Then he gave her a quick kiss and walked out the door with his typical "lock up" orders.

Ellie threw the dead bolts and headed down the hall. It was time to find her boy.

In bed next to Rudy, she heaved a huge sigh. She reached out to scratch his ears and pulled him to her side. She figured he'd slipped out of the living room as soon as the cops arrived, because she hadn't seen him since.

"You okay, pal?"

"I been better."

"I'm sure. Did you tear any teeth loose when you attacked Madam Stone Face?"

"Nah, but Dr. Dave should prob'ly gimme a tetanus shot. That woman tasted like rancid frog."

"Maybe so, but I don't think dogs can come down with anything from biting a human. You didn't catch anything when you took a chunk out of Thompson Veridot, remember."

"That woman is poison, through and through. I'm lucky to be alive. You, too."

"I agree, but I still think I should punish you for outright disobedience. Going after Mitzi while she held that gun was a very foolish move."

"So says you. If I hadn't, you might be dead right now." He licked her jaw. *"Detective Demento, too. If you ask me, I deserve a reward."*

"Hmm. Let me think on that." She pulled up the covers. "Right now we have to get to sleep. Since I don't have an assistant, I'm on tap for walking the gang in the morning. Then I have to go to police headquarters and answer a slew of questions, plus sign a statement."

"Make sure you tell 'em to add dog-o-cide to their list of crimes. That should tack on an extra twenty years to their sentence."

"Sam doubts the ADA will believe that Lulu was their original target, which is good. They wouldn't get any time for attempted murder of a canine, but they'll get a huge hit for killing

Arnie. And Mitzi will take the fall for trying to poison me, plus the shooting."

"It figures no one would care about us dogs."

"Ah, but I care." She ruffled his ears. "And as your reward, you, my friend, can stay in and laze the day away tomorrow. No trekking through the snow and freezing your paws off."

"With a Dingo bone?"

"I think that can be arranged."

"You know, I'm gettin' real tired of rescuing you. Think maybe next time you find a body or get involved in a crime you could just walk away?"

"Now you're starting to sound like Sam. I don't go looking for trouble, you knucklehead. Trouble just seems to—"

"Find you. Yeah, yeah, yeah, I've heard it all before."

He yawned, and a few moments later his snores rattled her ears. Ellie breathed a sigh of relief. Everything her little pal had said held a ring of truth. He was the one who'd surprised Mitzi, and latching on to the woman's arm had caused her to drop the gun. If that hadn't happened, she might have fired again, and a second shot could have hit Sam.

She also owed him and his superior sense of smell for having the smarts to sneak into the Nelsons' back room and find those frogs. She doubted she'd have had the courage to do so if she'd been alone.

All in all, her boy was her hero . . . again. Too bad Sam didn't agree, because her life would be perfect if Rudy and the man she cared about got along. But she wasn't ready to give up. There was plenty of time to get them in tune with one another—maybe not in the same key, but in harmony.

She would just have to be patient and wait them out.

Epilogue

"Detective Ryder," said Ellie's mother. "Please have another helping of apple pie. Corinna so loves it when our guests enjoy her food."

"I don't know about Sam, Georgette," Flora chimed, "but I'd be happy to have another serving of that lemon meringue pie. I can't thank Corinna enough for her cooking expertise, especially the trouble she went to in making Lulu a special meal."

"Yeah, Mom, Corinna outdid herself," added Ellie, grinning. "Rudy cleaned his plate, too."

Sam hid a smirk behind his napkin. He'd eaten fancy soup loaded with sherry, a salad barely big enough to fill a cavity, and mouse-sized birds with bits of white paper on their legs, plus a lot of other dishes that had names he'd only heard of. It had all tasted okay, but it was hardly what he'd call a Thanksgiving dinner.

He could tell from Georgette's pinched expression that she was holding her tongue, and he was fairly certain he knew the reason why. Ellie had made her mother jump through hoops to have her only child spend the holiday at her penthouse. He hadn't been involved in the many rounds of discussion and bartering, but Ellie had told him of the final result.

Best of all, her stepfather the judge had backed her on every request. If Georgette wanted her daughter to share the afternoon with her, the woman had to accept Ellie's dog, and Flora and her dog, too. And she had to let the animals eat in the dining room with the humans, no snide comments or rude questions allowed.

So what had Ellie given up? She hadn't come right out and said so, but he imagined it had something to do with his being there at the table, too.

Flora had put away her second helping of pie before Judge Frye said, "Flora, I find your life as the owner of a purebred canine fascinating. Please tell us again how many championships your Havanese has won."

Flora began her third—or was it her fourth?— listing of Lulu's greatest triumphs while Georgette settled back in her chair wearing an expression of absolute boredom. When the

Fryes' housekeeper stood to clear the table, Ellie's mother looked as relieved as Sam felt about the meal coming to a close. "I'll help Corinna, Mother," Ellie said, before turning to him and saying, "You can entertain my mom."

Sam didn't want to keep the haughty woman company. Hell, he didn't even want to be here in her four-, maybe five-million-dollar penthouse. But there wasn't a thing he could do about it. After all, Ellie had promised to spend the evening at his mother's, and Lydia was just as much of a trial as Georgette, only in a very different way.

"Tell me, Detective Ryder," Georgette began when her daughter left the room.

"Please call me Sam," he reminded her again. "I'm off duty, which means I'm here as a civilian."

"But it's so difficult to ignore your impressive position and list of accomplishments," she continued. "Ellie sings your praises whenever we talk."

Doubtful, thought Sam. If he believed his girl, and he had no reason not to, Ellie kept her personal life to herself where her mother was concerned. She hated the prying and manipulation of an interfering parent as much as he did.

"And what has she been telling you?" he asked, just to make conversation. Besides, it might be fun to yank the ex-terminator's chain.

Georgette's pinched expression returned full force. "Why, lots of things. That you're the—the best detective in the city. That you can solve cases no one else will touch. That you—"

"Tell me, has she mentioned her own ability to sniff out the bad guys?" he asked, aware of how much she disapproved of her daughter's involvement with the criminal element.

The woman blanched. "I believe she's mentioned it a few times, but Ellie has assured me she's finished sticking her nose—I mean, being drawn into situations over which she has no control."

"Yeah, I don't like it, either," he confided, especially since it was the one thing they probably agreed on. "In fact, I made her take a self-defense course so she could handle herself when I wasn't around."

"Self-defense?" Georgette's eyes opened wide. "You mean karate or kung fu or another one of those physically demanding sports?"

"Not a sport, Mrs. Frye. A real honest-to-God course in self-protection. She learned how to punch, stomp, and gouge with the best of them." He swallowed his laughter as he pushed ahead. "She might even take up kickboxing—professionally."

"Professional kickboxing?" Georgette swallowed. "In front of an audience?"

Ellie came back and stood next to the judge

before Sam answered. "So, what have you all been talking about while I've been gone?"

"You, of course," Judge Frye answered. "Sam told your mother you were thinking of taking up professional kickboxing."

Ellie held off giving an eye roll and tossed Sam a look that promised he would suffer later. "Oh, really? Sam said that? He is such a kidder." Then she gave a ladylike smile. "But I haven't told you the big news. He's thinking of running for mayor."

Sam almost choked on his coffee. Georgette clapped like a child who'd just opened a favorite present, while the judge and Flora raised their glasses in a toast.

"Here, here! We'll drink to that," said Stanley.

"Now, Ellie," Sam said, telegraphing a warning. "You know I haven't made a final decision yet."

Ellie walked around the table and stood behind him. "I certainly hope you make up your mind before we get to your mother's, because I'm going to tell them all about your plan to run the second we're in the door."

He pushed back his chair and stood. "Speaking of my mother's, I think it's time we headed out. It could take an hour to get to Queens if traffic is bad."

Fifteen minutes later, Rudy, Ellie, and Sam waved good-bye to Flora and Lulu, who'd left in

380

their limo, and walked toward the parking garage she'd convinced Sam to use for the afternoon. Fading sunlight was the only remnant of a beautiful crisp day, and she knew he was right about the time.

When he took her hand and tucked it in his elbow, she smiled. "Professional kickboxing?"

"That's no worse than telling them I was running for mayor."

"Okay, so it was tit for tat." They stopped to let Rudy water a stanchion. "Just tell me you'll behave at your mom's house. No tall tales or talk about my latest crime-solving spree."

"I'll behave. I just can't promise that my relatives will." They arrived at the garage and he walked to the booth, where he handed his ticket to the attendant and waited while he totaled the charges.

Rudy looked up at her and she grinned. "All set for an evening of making new friends?"

"Not me. I plan to find a corner and take a nap."

"That might be fine, too, but I'm going to ask you the same thing I asked Sam. Please behave."

"I was good at the ex-terminator's, wasn't I?"

"Only because you were trying to impress Lulu."

"Maybe so, but I'll give it my best shot tonight."

"Good. That's all I can ask for."

Sam returned to her side. "That's right. Get it out of your system now, because I have no idea how my family will act if they hear you holding a conversation with your dog."

Ellie poked his arm. "I told you I wouldn't carry on a full-blown conversation, but I do want your family to accept me, and my dog, for who we are."

"And what might that be?"

"Yeah, Triple E. What might that be?"

"A single unit," she said with a smile. "Love me, love my dog, and all that. Think you can handle it, Detective?"

Sam heaved a sigh. "I guess I'm going to have to."

"Aw, that's sweet. Isn't that sweet, Rudy?" she asked, smiling down at her boy.

"I'd rather jump off a speeding subway," he griped. *"But I get the feeling we're gonna be stuck with the doofus dick for a while, so I'll manage."*

The Chevy arrived and Ellie slid into the passenger seat while Sam tossed Rudy in the back and made his way around the car. "So you're willing to give Sam the benefit of the doubt and let me date him in peace?"

"Yeah, sure. Fine. Whatever." He curled into a ball and yawned. *"Just don't expect me to like it."*

Ellie breathed a sigh of relief. Sometimes, when the planets were aligned and the world was in tune, good things did happen to good people and their dogs. It was all she'd ever asked for, and now it looked as if her wish was coming true.

Center Point Publishing
600 Brooks Road ● PO Box 1
Thorndike ME 04986-0001 USA

(207) 568-3717

US & Canada:
1 800 929-9108
www.centerpointlargeprint.com